First published in **1984**
by **Faber and Faber Limited**
3 Queen Square London WC1N 3AU

© Jon Savage, 1984

British Library Cataloguing in Publication Data
Savage, Jon
The Kinks.
1. Kinks
I. Title
784.5′0092′2 ML421.K5

ISBN 0-571-13379-7

ISBN 0-571-13407-6 Pbk

Printed in Great Britain by
Butler & Tanner Ltd, Frome, Somerset
All Rights Reserved

Designed by **Neville Brody**
and **Valerie Hawthorn**

Typeset by **The Printed Word**

PICTURE CREDITS
 Picture Research by **Roxanne Streeter**

COURTESY OF MICK AVORY: 22,42,52-53 ● **ANDRE CSILLAG/PHOTO
FEATURES/CHRIS WALTER**: 54,63,73,103 ● **THE DAILY MIRROR**: 42,48 ●
COURTESY OF DAVE DAVIES AND HIS MUM: 4,7,8-9,10,12,13,14,16,28,49,70,
98-99,152,160 ● **ERICA ECHENBERG**: 132-133,138 ● **FAB MAGAZINE**: 55 ● **BILL
GRAHAM/FILLMORE WEST**: 117 ● **KEYSTONE PRESS AGENCY**: 29,33 ●
COURTESY OF KONK STUDIOS: 131 (John McKenzie), 135,140-141,143,146-147,149
(Sam Emerson), 151,157 (Robert Ellis), 161,162-163,169,170 ● **LFI (LONDON
FEATURES INTERNATIONAL)**: 59,76-77,78,85,91,94-95,144,154 (Paul Cox), 156
(Michael Putland), 166 ● **MIKE LEALE**: 88-89,92-93 ● **LINDA McCARTNEY/MPL**:
86 ● **NEW MUSICAL EXPRESS**: 6,67 ● **GUY PEELLAERT**: 82 (illustration from
''ROCK DREAMS'' by Pan Books) ● **PICTORIAL PRESS**: 27,56,64,74,84,105 ●
BARRY PLUMMER: 137 ● **POP PIC LIBRARY**: 50 ● **PYE RECORDS/PRT
(PRECISION RECORDS & TAPES LTD.)**: 23,58,72,81,100 ● **RCA RECORDS**: 122 ●
REX FEATURES: 6,18,24-25,26 (Bruce Fleming), 34-35,36,90,150 (Richard Young) ●
REX FEATURES/DEZO HOFFMANN: 37,39,41,47,66-67,83,112-113 ● **ROLLING
STONE**: 130 ● **SYNDICATION INTERNATIONAL**: 20,30-31,62,69,123 ● **WARNER
BROTHERS RECORDS**: 114 ● **BARRIE WENTZELL**: 106-107,120-121,128 ● **VAL
WILMER**: 44-45,60 ● **CHARLYN ZLOTNIK**: 148 ●

CONTENTS

LIFE-LINES of THE KINKS

	MICK	RAY	PETE	DAVE
Real name:	Michael Charles Avory	Raymond Douglas Davies	Peter Quaife	David Russell Gordon Davies
Birthdate:	February 15, 1944	June 21, 1944	December 31, 1943	February 3, 1947
Birthplace:	Hampton Court	London	Tavistock, Devon	Muswell Hill
Personal points:	5ft. 11in.; 11st. 11lb.; greeny-brown eyes, dark brown hair	5ft. 11½in.; 11st. 6lb.; green-grey eyes, dark brown hair	5ft. 10½in.; 10s. 4lb.; hazel eyes (red when angry!) and black hair	5ft. 10in.; 10st.; green eyes; dark brown hair
Parents' names:	Charles and Marjorie	Mum and Dad !	Stan and Joan	Mum and Dad !
Brothers and sisters:	Two brothers	Five sisters and a brother	David and Anne	Five sisters and a brother
Instruments played:	Drums	Guitar, harmonica and piano	Bass, guitar and bongos	Guitar, piano and banjo
Where educated:	Molesey—Weybridge	Hornsey Art School and Croydon Art School	Coldfall and William Grimshaw, Borstal !	William Grimshaw, Hornsey
Musical education:	Tuition in Ashford	Mike Picker	Studied under Rachmaninoff III !	
Age entered show business:	13	11		11
First public appearance:	Molesey Carnival, 1957	A pub	William Grimshaw	A pub
Biggest break:	Joining the Kinks	———	Meeting Arthur Howes and learning guitar	Meeting agent Arthur Howes
Biggest disappointment:	When I left the Stones (although I was only with them three weeks)	———	———	That our second record " You Still Want Me " didn't make it
Compositions:	———	" You Really Got Me," "It's All Right," ' I've Got That Feelin'," etc.	———	" One Fine Day " and others unrecordable !
Biggest influence:	Tutor	Big Bill Broonzy, Lonnie Donegan	Me	———
Former occupations:	Draughtsman, carpenter, sheet metal worker	Art student	Commercial artist	School
Hobbies:	Swimming, practising	Films, art form in general, sport and athletics	Art girls—Nicola !, flying, swimming and eating and sleeping !	Horse riding and athletics
Favourite singers:	Inez Foxx, Peggy Lee, Anita O'Day, Elvis	Varies with my moods	Barbra Streisand	Anita O'Day, Big Bill Broonzy,
Favourite actors/actresses:	Steve McQueen, Burt Lancaster, Kirk Douglas	Varies — Alan Badel, Finney—most people in show-biz	My manager !	Hugh Griffiths, Sophia Loren
Favourite Food:	Mostly anything		Curry, cheese and onion crisps and baked beans	Chinese and Indian
Favourite drink:	Bitter, milk	Newcastle brown, wines	Water, sterilised milk	Scotch and ginger
Favourite clothes:	Smart, well-styled suits	Casual	My own !	Casual
Favourite bands/instrumentalists:	Shorty Rogers and his Giants, Dave Brubeck and Shelley Manne	Glenn Miller, Chet Atkins, Sonny Terry and Brownie McGhee	The Patrick O'Shatgh-nessy big Irish top six sextet from India !	Tal Farlow, Broonzy and Cyril Davies
Favourite composers:	John Lewis	Chuck Berry		Bach, Gershwin, Berry and Ray Davies
Miscellaneous likes:	———	Truthful people, kinky birds, laughing inwardly, and Jack Benny	Most everything	Kinky girls, girls that drink beer, money, clothes and riding
Miscellaneous dislikes:	Red' tape, losing too much sleep and self-appointed critics	Liars and snobs	Most everything	Travelling by van, conceit, worrying
Best friend:	Money (in my pocket)	Me	Me	Me
Most thrilling experience:	Flying	Meeting my best friend for the first time !	Flying	Flying
Tastes in music:	Varies with my mood	Varies with my mood	Lousy !	Adore church organ music
Pets:	———	Dog	One pigeon—Kinky Klarence !	A dog and the pigeon
Personal ambition:	To go to the U.S. to learn the art of drumming thoroughly and meet most of the jazz giants	To be exceedingly successful and highly esteemed among my friends	See what comes	To roam country estates and be a lord of the manor
Professional ambition:	For the group to be recognised in its own right	To be ahead all the time and to make audiences like us	As personal	To be a success in America and Britain

COMMON TO ALL:

TV debut: " Ready, Steady, Go ! "
Radio debut: " Housewives' Choice "
Current hit and latest release: "You Really Got Me "
Present disc label: Pye
Recording manager: Shel Talmy
Personal manager: Larry Page
Musical director: Themselves
Origin of stage name: Took the name from the clothes we used to wear
Favourite colour: Kink pink

● New Musical Express, 11 September 1964

MUSWELL HILLBILLIES

Bomb devastation, the immense upheavals of the war years, the movements of people since then in search of work...had set up in Britain a vast social mixing trough. Great gaps had been, and were being, torn in the fabric of the old working-class England.

Harry Hopkins, *The New Look:*
A Social History of the Forties and Fifties in Britain (1964)

They'll move me up to Muswell Hill tomorrow,
Photographs and souvenirs are all I've got,
They're gonna try and make me change my way of living,
But they'll never make me something that I'm not.

Kinks, *'Muswell Hillbilly' (1971)*

● **Dave Davies, Ray Davies and friend Jackie,** c. 1952

Ray and Dave Davies were born, within three years of each other, into a large working-class family which had moved, after the Second World War, out of inner London to the borders of Muswell Hill and Highgate, suburbs lying to the north of the city. They were the babies of the family, numbers seven and eight respectively: before them were six sisters, whose ages ranged over twenty-five years. The oldest was Rose; then came Rene – who died in 1957 from heart disease – and then Dorothy, Joyce and Peg. The youngest sister, and the only one near the two brothers in age, was Gwen: otherwise they might as well have been from different generations.

Furthermore, the Davies family was part of a much wider network. Dave Davies: 'It was a very close-knit family, very big. My mum and dad, Annie and Frederick, used to live in the Islington/King's Cross area, where most of my family came from. My Gran lived there until she died. There were twenty-one children in my mother's family, and she was one of the first to try to break away from it. Muswell Hill was only five miles up the road, but it was a big move for them in those days.

'I always remember as a kid that it seemed like there were hundreds of people in the house. On a Saturday night they'd go up the pub and there'd be loads of kids and loads of people and it always felt as though there was a lot of singing and parties going on. Our mum used to sing when she'd had a few drinks, and my dad used to dance. We didn't have a TV – probably because we couldn't afford it – but it was the sort of environment where people used to make their own entertainment. The memories that I have are good memories of a close knit family.'

But it was because of the very size and closeness of that family that the brothers grew up apart. The age range within the family was important. Dave Davies: 'It's hard for me to remember what my and Ray's relationship was like when we were kids but I don't feel that it was very close. From about the age of six to about eleven, I didn't feel as though we were even brothers because I was closer to my nephew, Bob, who was about a year older than I was. Bob's mother was our sister Rene. Ray lived for a while in Highgate with sister Rose, her husband Arthur and their son Terry, who was a year younger than Ray.'

Ray Davies: 'Dave liked the close-knit set-up, but I always tried to get away from it. Terry was like my brother. I was closer to him than I was to Dave because we grew up as brothers. But they eventually went to Australia. I remember the day they left. I waved goodbye and I couldn't realize they were going. We had gone to Redcar to do a gig. After the shows I went on the beach and cried and shouted. They were gone.'

However close they might or might not have been at the time, both brothers were imbued from an early age with the musical sense that ran through the family. Ray Davies: 'My dad taught me about music. He used to tap dance. He loved Jack Buchanan, Fred Astaire, Gene Kelly and Max Miller, and he'd seen Al Bowlly sing at the local pub. My sisters always played their current favourites, just like kids read *Smash Hits* today. They were much older than me, but I was still old enough to hear all these songs. I could impersonate Perry Como and Frank Sinatra'.

Dave Davies: 'My sisters all played piano and my old man played the banjo, so there was always music around. My sisters' influence was very important: Dolly used to play Hank Williams and Slim Whitman records, and the younger ones used to play the Teddy Bears, Perry Como and the Crew Cuts – whatever was popular at the time.

'Ray got his first guitar on his thirteenth birthday; that was the night my sister Rene died. She showed him a few scales, then went out to the Lyceum to have a good time. She died later that evening, from a hole in the heart.

'Ray picked up how to play the guitar from our brother-in-law, Mike Picker, who was Peg's husband.'

By the time the brothers were both in their teens, this common interest in music brought them back into what appears like a more orthodox fraternal relationship. With the encouragement of the Davies family, they began to play guitar, first separately and then together. Dave Davies: 'I got my first guitar when I was eleven, and that's when I started to learn how to play properly – before that, I used to mess around on Ray's Spanish guitar. Mine was a Harmony Meteor: it cost about £40 then, and my mum put a £7 deposit down and paid the rest off monthly. When I started, Ray and I would play with Mike Picker, or we would go to his flat to exchange ideas and play records. Mike had a tape recorder which was the first one I'd ever seen; Ray and I did some recording in the front room – some little demos. I remember an instrumental of an old standard which we did with two guitars – it was called "South".

'I think that the first guy that influenced us was Big Bill Broonzy; he was the first blues guitarist we picked up on. We used to try to copy what he played. And I remember we used to play in a pub called the Clissold Arms, which was right opposite where we used to live in Fortis Green. We had to ask permission because we were too

● Rose Davies, Annie Davies, Frederick Davies, Jackie, Dave Davies, c 1951

● **Ray Davies with Terry on his left, Dave Davies with Bob on his left**, c. 1953

young to go into a pub – I was about twelve then. The publican was a mate of my dad's, and he let us play in the lounge that they had at the back of the pub, which was never used. Ray and I would play just instrumental things. Ray would do all the melody and I would do the rhythm; he would play lead guitar, picking, just like Chet Atkins. That must have been our first public engagement; we didn't have a name.'

By this time, Ray Davies had entered the local secondary modern school, William Grimshaw, in Muswell Hill; Dave followed him three years later. Neither brother liked school at all, as Ray Davies was to make clear nearly twenty years later with the *Schoolboys in Disgrace* LP: 'It was designed to turn people into factory fodder. I spent most of my school days skipping lessons. At one time my truancy was so bad I was sent to a psychiatrist. I was the first boy in the family after six girls, and I had everything I ever wanted. There wasn't anything significantly wrong with me. I was simply confused, trying to be individual but not knowing how to do it.'

Dave Davies: 'I had a friend called George Harris. We'd been really good buddies since I was eleven and we learned to play guitar together. His father was dead and his mum had to go out to work, so there was nobody at home during the day. He used to live round the corner, so I'd fake getting up and going to school, walk up the road and go down his turning. We'd sit around his house all day smoking and listening to blues records, any that we could get hold of. I'd come home at half-past four as if I'd been at school.

'On your end-of-term report they used to write notes. My last report said something ridiculous like "60 days' absenteeism". I remember I crossed out the "0" so that it read "6". All this time my parents thought I was going to school.'

Yet it was while Ray and Dave Davies were at William Grimshaw that the nucleus of the future Kinks came together. Dave Davies: 'Pete Quaife was in Ray's year; I can't remember how it started, but the three of us used to play together. Pete played guitar (we didn't use a bass then), a Futurama, which was really the thing to have. We used to jam in his front room or our front room, and then we formed a band with a drummer who lived round the corner from the school, who was also in Ray and Pete's year, called John Start.

'We used to do concerts at school, and we'd play anywhere locally. That was really where we got a taste of playing in front of people, that sort of excitement from an audience. We'd back beauty contests, playing instrumentals in the background. Whoever got the gig would be the band leader. It would be the PQQ – the Pete Quaife Quartet – if he managed to get the gig together, but I remember the first name we had at school was the RDQ – the Ray Davies Quartet.'

'We used to play all sorts of things. Buddy Holly songs, the Ventures, some blues songs. There was a guy at school – he was called Johnny Burnette, funnily enough – who said, "You must come round. I've got a collection of records by a guy called Chuck Berry." Everybody else was talking about the kind of slop that was being played then, that flimsy kind of pop which none of us liked: that's why we were listening to guitar instrumentals. He played me "Sweet Little Sixteen" and lent me three or four records out of this really obscure collection that he had. Then we started to dig out records like that which were much more to do with what we wanted to play.'

The year 1962 saw some changes in the academic status of the two brothers. In the early summer Dave Davies was expelled from William Grimshaw. 'The reason why they decided to terminate my school life was that I got caught on Hampstead Heath with a girl. I always remember that. At Kenwood they used to have really high grass and everybody would take their girls there, but the day I went there they cut the grass. I couldn't believe it. I got caught. I felt like a terrible criminal. My headmaster, Mr Loades, expelled me from the school. But that feeling of leaving school was of total liberation: the only other time I felt like that was when I got fired from my first job a few months later. Such a feeling of freedom, after all that pressure.'

'After getting sacked I had three weeks in bed, having a wonderful time, until my mum got me out of bed and said, "You've got to do something!" Then I had to start going down the labour exchange, the usual thing. I went to see a variety of jobs and I ended up at Selmers Music. They had a warehouse at the back of Shaftesbury Avenue, just off Cambridge Circus. I worked in there repairing musical instruments. Derek Griffiths, who now works as a comedian and musician on TV, was the other sweeper-upper and general dogsbody, and we used to rehearse in our lunch break – he played clarinet and I played guitar. We used to have the band going as well. I'd be doing gigs at night and getting about two to three hours' sleep – and then I'd fall asleep at work. In the end they just threw me out. That didn't matter because by then I was earning enough from gigs to get by.'

Meanwhile Ray Davies received some smart career advice from William Grimshaw: 'The art teacher suggested that I went to art college because he knew I liked music and I liked running. He said cynically: "Oh, you can play all the music you want at art school, and you've got lots of time off to go running." In other words he was saying, "Look, I know you really want to play music, so do it in art school time."'

During that year the brothers' musical obsessions, which had developed in the comparative isolation of north London, started to connect with what was going on in the world outside. If Dave Davies's own instincts were already leading him in the right direction, then Ray Davies was entering an anti-system of education – art school – that had informed virtually every post-war musical undercurrent. At that time the undercurrent was about to become a tidal wave.

The most readily available music in post-war England was big-band music and swing: American music, expensively produced and presented, a hangover from the war years. Yet around the country, particularly in ports like Liverpool and Tilbury, people were listening to traditional jazz 78s that sailors had brought back from America. Because of their close proximity to these ports, the art schools – like Liverpool and Camberwell in London – became the breeding-ground for the first post-war musical deviation, the jazz revival, spearheaded by bands like Chris Barber's or the Humphrey Lyttleton Band.

By 1955-6 this revival had achieved a certain popularity but was still the preserve of a predominantly middle-class, bohemian audience. The attention of the emergent mass 'teenage' market – then almost exclusively working-class – was directed mainly towards American rock 'n' roll stars like Bill Haley and Elvis Presley. Both audiences looked down on one another: pop fans thought that trad jazz was a horrible, unstylish noise, whereas jazz buffs considered that rock 'n' roll was trashy shop-girl stuff, on a par with candy floss or a day trip to the seaside.

Yet it was out of the jazz revival that the first decent indigenous British pop music of the 1950s emerged. In February 1956 Lonnie Donegan, a featured singer with the Chris Barber Jazz Band, had a massive hit with an old Leadbelly song, 'Rock Island Line', and became a pop sensation for the next few years. Hits like 'Jack of Diamonds', 'Grand Coolie Dam' and 'Cumberland Gap' may have been rocked-up versions of old Leadbelly and Woody Guthrie songs, but they were actually quite good: Donegan's nasal twang and ratty appearance gave these underdog songs an authenticity which translated well into the context of British pop, at that time itself very much a poor second-best to the flood of rock 'n' roll coming from America.

Not only did Donegan's versions of blues songs work as pop, but they helped to raise the whole post-war jazz revival – hitherto a purist affair – above ground. Apart from popularizing skiffle, they paved the way for hits by the Chris Barber Jazz band itself, like 'Petite Fleur' in February 1959. 'Trad jazz' became the dominant sound in British pop for a couple of years (1959-61), with hits from Kenny Ball, Terry Lightfoot and Acker Bilk, whose maudlin 'Stranger on the Shore' stayed in the chart for a whole year and killed the thing stone-dead. By this time the art schools had moved on to something else.

The whole jazz revival scene, and the art school involvement with it, had been based (as all subsequent pop undergrounds have been) on the idea of 'authenticity', and as soon as 'trad jazz' became pop, the groups and the audience turned to a different kind of music. Late in 1958 Chris Barber, while still in the thick of 'trad', had taken the innovative step of including a rhythm and blues segment – featuring Alexis Korner on guitar and Cyril Davies on harmonica – in his more mainstream show; he was also responsible for bringing over to Britain the genuine article: American bluesmen like John Lee Hooker, Otis Spann and Muddy Waters. Between them Barber, Korner and Davies helped to create a new underground at the beginning of the 1960s. But even this still had a purist base: the electric blues was played by ex-jazzers, thoroughly soaked in that idea of authenticity. Rock 'n' roll was definitely out.

Ray Davies remembers an incident from the time: 'A

● **Chuck Berry, c. 1961**

film called *Jazz on a Summer's Day* influenced me a lot. I saw Chuck Berry playing with all those jazzers. He was wonderful. He was doing ''Sweet Little Sixteen''. The Louis Armstrong band was backing him up, and they were just looking at one another behind his back. You could see they were taking the piss out of him. But he was there, and he was better than any of them. They knew it, and it was kind of a change happening.'

The generation which followed the jazzers was not too worried about authenticity; the result of what had been a hard struggle for the previous musical generation came naturally to them. They wanted something different: a mixture of the electric blues and rock 'n' roll, a music that could express an attitude ('It's MY life!') that was to become an integral part of the youth culture that spread throughout the Western world from the mid-1960s.

The first group to feature such an attitude was the Rolling Stones, who were playing the hip London circuit at exactly the time that Ray Davies went to Hornsey Art School in the autumn of 1962. 'I didn't walk through the doors and get asked to join a trad band or anything. I had to wait for it. But if I hadn't been at art school, I wouldn't have seen Alexis play the college around Christmas 1962. I went up to him afterwards and asked if he could get me some gigs. He gave me his number and I called him the next day. He suggested that I go down to speak to Giorgio Gomelsky (then the Rolling Stones manager, and

general R&B entrepreneur) at a place called the Piccadilly Club, which was in Great Windmill Street. I went down there one night, and there was this band playing, a blues band. A guy called Hamilton King ran the band with another guy called Dave Hunt. Giorgio suggested that I sat in for a couple of nights playing guitar to see if it worked out. It did, and they liked me, and took me on. That would have been in January 1963. I played with them for a while.

'But the night I went to see Giorgio, the Stones were doing the fill-in spot. Hamilton King and Dave Hunt had come out for a drink and were discussing them. I said, ''I'd like to see the group.'' I thought they were wonderful because the band I was joining were older musicians and had come from jazz. I looked at the Stones and thought, ''These are more what I want to be like.'' I wanted to play R&B because I thought it would be updating people like Muddy Waters and Chuck Berry, Howlin' Wolf and all those people, taking it away from purist blues and adding rhythm to it. Rhythm and blues. And I felt that the Rolling Stones were more what I was going to this club for. But Hamilton King said, ''Oh they're a skiffle group. Come and have a drink.'' But they were very exciting.

'The only person who stood out for me, really stood out, was Brian Jones. They were wearing the same pink shirts that I had, pink, tab-collared. I was cooler, I think – I was wearing a really good leather jacket.'

But neither the attitude nor the music was the exclusive preserve of art school bohemians. This notion of cultural freedom was also extending to sharp working-class lads like Dave Davies. 'That feeling of freedom was going on in different ways with all sorts of people. I was out of school for a year virtually and I used to lie about. In Muswell Hill there was a coffee bar called the El Toro. Ray and I played there. We'd hang out there with kids of our own age and just talk about the things that kids talk about.' Dave also went to the Piccadilly Club: 'That was when I first heard the Stones do "Reelin' and Rockin'"; it was great.'

Although developing along different lines, the two brothers' interests were beginning to run parallel. As would be apparent later in the 1960s, Dave was the extrovert brother, gathering the raw material during his excursions that Ray Davies would later transform in his work: 'I heard people like Muddy Waters through college but Dave was the one that bought the records. Chuck Berry had had a few hits, so he was a first introduction. He was on Pye International, and through that catalogue you got Bo Diddley records and a few Little Walter and Slim Harpo records. So it was probably a combination of those records being hits and seeing people like Alexis play and the Stones, who went to great lengths to explain the origins of their material at that time. "Well," they used to say, "Here's a Muddy Waters song." So I would go to record stores like the old Dobells and try to get records or at least listen to the records in the booths without buying them.'

Barry Fantoni was an established illustrator but was also playing the saxophone by night. He first met Ray Davies that spring in Soho: 'That was in a club called the Kaleidoscope, which was in Gerrard Street; it's now a Chinese takeaway. I think a pianist must have said to me, "Why don't you come along to a rehearsal of a band? If you want to play rhythm and blues as opposed to playing jazz, there are some rather good musicians." And it was a good band: Ray was playing guitar and I think his brother was there and a drummer who later became quite successful, Hamilton King. We rehearsed all afternoon. Ray and I sang the vocal line on "Money" and we were singing across the mike. I remember very vividly he was singing "That's What I Want!" and I thought he stood a very good chance of getting it because he actually looked the part and could play the part.'

While Ray Davies was playing with Hamilton King, his brother was keeping the group going in Muswell Hill. Dave Davies: 'We had lots of different names. We called ourselves the Bo-Weevils, which was taken from the B side of an Eddie Cochran record. Then we were called the Ravens. I think there was a film out at the time with Vincent Price, which was called *The Raven*. We still had John Start at the time. We would do some gigs, but we would hang out mainly; I remember Ray doing more gigs than me.'

Ray Davies: 'At that point I was mixing it up, playing with the blues band and playing with Pete, John and Dave in youth clubs. I remember playing one youth club in Muswell Hill: we did the Friday nights and Rod Stewart

● **Dave Davies with the Harmony Meteor, February 1964**

and the Moonrakers did the Saturdays. The Moonrakers were admired because they had fantastic echo chambers – they had Watkins Copycats – and were they envied. Also Rod did the greatest Elvis Presley impersonation in north London.'

By that summer the Hamilton King band had dissolved into thin air. It was at this time that Ray Davies left Hornsey Art School. It had been a tenuous relationship. Ray: 'I would do these gigs and then knock off early and come in for exams and things. That four-tier diploma at Hornsey – fine art, painting, art history, sculpture – was my last attempt at being a serious artist. I remember this girl saying to me, "I don't get it. You don't come to any lectures, you miss a lot, but you get it together on the exams."

'I remember really enjoying the lectures I did go to. I was pretty good at painting but not too good at sculpture or anything graphic. Anything commercial I just turned against. I had a friend at the time called Paul O'Dell. We started a film society and we went to the head of the college and asked if we could help start a film section in the school. He told us to piss off, go to another college. It happened at the end of term and I applied to the Central School and couldn't get in there because it was too late; so I was going to Croydon to fill in the gap, as that was the only college I could get into, their theatre department.'

But art school was not to hold Ray Davies for much longer. Other interests were becoming paramount. Barry Fantoni had gone to Croydon as an art teacher under the 'block' system then in operation in English art schools, whereby a teacher would take classes for one solid week a month and take the other three weeks off. Fantoni remembers: 'Ray would bring his guitar to the school and would play the mouth organ; he'd entertain people in the canteen very unself-consciously and everyone recognized his skills. There weren't many people who played well. There were a lot who imitated, but no one who was actually inventive with it or authentic. That was a quality that I would recognize again in his work: it had his own authorship on it.'

Ray Davies was to remain only three months at Croydon, as events were about to overtake him and his brother. For the fifteen months or so that he was at art school he had been exposed to, and had participated in, the mixture of music (electric blues and rock 'n' roll) that, through the Rolling Stones, was already becoming the next pop sensation. And if the musical barriers appeared to be crumbling, then so did the social: the coalescence of the middle and working-class audiences for pop was to form an entirely new mass phenomenon, catalysed by the Beatles in the autumn of 1963.

It was then that Ray Davies decided to throw in his lot with the Ravens.

Dave: 'The fact that Ray lived with Rose in Highgate was good, really, because it meant that we had very different influences even though we were nearly the same age. We weren't stuck together like Siamese twins in the same house. In a way, it seems as though I was in a different class structure from Ray. I got involved with music through kids wanting to go and dance to music,

● Calling card, summer 1963

whereas I think Ray got involved in music through the artistic side of it, because it was an art form. We had very different ideas about things.'

The relationship between the two brothers was now closer that it had ever been, a fact that was later to bring not a few strains along the way. For although Dave might have provided the attitude and the suss, it was Ray who would provide the drive that was to propel the Ravens where they wanted to go.

MONEY-GO-ROUND

The 'pop explosion' of 1963 – 4 in fact marked the last consummatory wave of all that youthful and social upheaval which had begun back in the jazz clubs and art schools and among the South London Teddy Boys of the late Forties. Once again, the majority of the popsingers came from the same cities and seaports and the same primarily lower-middle-class origins as the playwrights and novelists and pop artists – but now members of the upper-middle and even upper classes were mixed amongst them, with the same smart or casual Cardin and Carnaby Street clothes, the same long hair and Beatle fringes, everything but the same accent…

*Christopher Booker, **The Neophiliacs**, 1969*

I think Pete and Dave realized it was a good thing to do.

Ray Davies in conversation, 1984

In the autumn of 1963 the Ravens picked up a couple of managers, Robert Wace and Grenville Collins – two upper-middle-class boys on the razz. Grenville worked on the London Stock Exchange as a dealer; Robert, who had been to Marlborough College, was working in his father's block-making business. He found it dull: 'I was nurturing this ambition when I was about twenty-one, in 1963, to have a go at being a singer. I thought it would be rather fun, and the idea seemed to me to be exciting.'

After hanging about Denmark Street – then the centre of the English music business – Wace met a drummer, Mickey Willis, who told him about the young group in Muswell Hill. Wace: 'I can remember seeing the three of them playing on a Sunday morning with all their relations sitting round. All three players were plugged into one little Wharfedale speaker and one little amplifier. Dave didn't play like other people: he stood side on and he bobbed up and down like a kangaroo. We got to know them better and we came to an arrangement with them whereby they could do their spot and I'd do mine, and Willis got sort of incorporated as a drummer. They started playing a few deb dances, a few other gigs.'

Robert Wace and the Bo-Weevils/Ravens went out on the road. Dave Davies: 'I remember one night we played at the Grocer's Hall with some party and Robert was singing "Raaaaave On" in his upper-class accent and jigging about. It was all right because we were getting paid £60 for it. If you played in a club, you got £20. Then Robert picked the microphone up and knocked his front tooth out. "Grenville! Grenville!" he shouted. So then Ray started singing "Rave On" because Ray and I used to sing together, and that was probably Ray's first public performance as a singer.'

Wace's career as a crooner didn't last long. Dave Davies: 'We played in the East End, in a club, and they thought he was dreadful and threw things at him,

cabbages, tomatoes, carrots.'

Whatever the absurdity of the situation, at least it got the Ravens out of Muswell Hill. For Dave Davies, still only sixteen, the experience was quite an eye-opener – he discovered a completely different world: 'I think it was the first time I ever went to Chelsea. I never even knew what Chelsea was. It was strange. Those Georgian houses – you'd be playing in one room with people ha-ha-ha-ing in the other. It was the first time I had champagne as well.'

Dave was already running wild: 'Pete and I used to have clothes competitions to see who could buy the most fashionable thing, or the silliest. I used to wear thigh-length boots. I even used to carry a sword with me, which they stopped me doing because I nearly stabbed someone in the neck one night at a party. I got into an argument with Mike D'Abo one night – he was with a snooty group called the Band of Angels – and got my sword out and clipped his neck. God, I could have ended up killing him!

'But generally the people were OK. I resented some of it because I always thought we were treated like a kind of novelty, almost like "Don't they speak quaintly?" And *we* always thought *they* spoke funny. But we started to do more gigs. We did a lot of clubs in Manchester – I think Mr Smith's was one. And that's when it started as far as I was concerned. We were playing in a club with real groupies and real kids, kids that I could relate to.'

Robert Wace: 'The upshot of it was that by November or December we had got to know them quite well, and we could see that Ray was very ambitious. Ray said, "I'd like to give this music business a go. Will you manage us?" I seem to recall we said we would give it a year. That's all my father would allow me to give it actually.'

So Robert Wace and Grenville Collins became the Ravens' managers. The influence of Wace and Collins – both their personalities and the world they represented – was to make itself felt once Ray Davies had got into his stride as a song writer. It is in the cadences and subject matter of 'Well Respected Man', 'Sunny Afternoon' and the 1966 LP *Face to Face* – whose 'Party Line' opens with Grenville Collins's quizzical 'Who's that speaking?' – that the pair's influence can finally be traced, long after the Ravens, three working-class layabouts from Muswell Hill, had played in the houses of the rich and privileged.

If the partnership, still not a legal arrangement, worked both creatively and socially, both parties were still faced with one central problem: nobody knew anything about the music business. At this stage the success of the Beatles and the cult of youth had made little impression on the music industry, which was still a tight little clique run from Denmark Street, vaguely

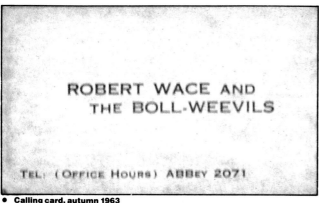

● Calling card, autumn 1963

disreputable. There wasn't quite enough money in the business to make it the multi-million-pound marketing exercise it is today: by comparison it now seems to have been a shoddy, fly-by-night affair, just emerging from its beginnings at the seedier end of showbiz. Wace and Collins were too young to get anything done – youth was not to become acceptable in the music industry until a couple of years later – but they needed access to the means of production, and fast.

Larry Page was young also, but by comparison with Wace and Collins, he was a music industry veteran, the UK manager of a company called Denmark Productions, which was owned by music publisher Eddie Kassner. He was approached late in 1963: 'Grenville Collins and Robert Wace didn't have a bloody clue about what they were doing and wanted somebody who knew the business. I gather they had walked up and down Denmark Street trying to get somebody to see their group. I agreed to see them in a little pub. I liked what I heard. They told me there wasn't a singer in the group, but that they were thinking of getting one. The drummer they weren't too sure about. I suggested that they didn't need a singer anyway because, having heard what they were running through, I thought that if Ray was to sing stock notes, that would be the answer. The thing that interested me was the excitement that they created, although none of the music was actually their own at that stage – basically it was all old blues numbers.'

By this point, the Ravens had done what other groups in their situation did and still do: they had made a demo tape and some acetates. During November and December they recorded five songs at Regent Sound: two R&B staples, Slim Harpo's 'Got Love if You Want It' and the Coasters' 'I'm a Hog for You, Baby'; one Ray Davies original, 'It's All Right', and two Dave Davies originals, 'One Fine Day' and 'I Believed You'. An acetate of 'I Believed You'/'I'm a Hog for You, Baby' still exists. It is very much a product of its time. Both tracks have an authentically inept yet enthusiastic garage style: 'I'm a Hog for You' is under-produced and rushed, with some farmyard grunts from Pete and Dave behind Ray's already distinctive vocal, while 'I Believed You' is an energetic love song in the then mandatory Merseybeat mode – trebly guitar fills, pert drum rolls and all. But the Ravens were still some way from finding their own style.

The tapes had little impact. The Ravens were turned down straightaway by two important companies out of the Big Four, Philips and Decca. The sessions had some positive results, however: Larry Page managed to place Dave's 'One Fine Day' with one Shel Naylor, who recorded the song for Decca early in 1964, and the tape came to the attention of an American freelance producer, Shel Talmy.

When Wace and Collins had been knocking on doors up and down the length of Denmark Street, one of the companies they'd been to was Mills Music, where Talmy worked. Born in Chicago in 1937, Talmy had decided to come to England to produce records: 'At that time England was following the American-style recordings.

'I must admit that I snowballed myself in by telling all

sorts of lies. Everybody here expected Americans to be brash and loud, and so that's just what I was. I walked into Decca and said, "Here I am", and reeled off a list of hits I'd made. Which of course I hadn't!'

Talmy hustled himself into producing a record for the Bachelors, 'Charmaine', which was a Top Ten hit in February 1963. After that, he could afford to dictate his own terms. By the time he heard the Ravens tape, he had a producer's contract with Pye Records: 'Robert Wace walked in with the demo and I liked what I heard. I brought it in at Pye, where I had a producer's deal, and they became interested.'

Things were moving fast for the Ravens, but before they signed the deal with Pye various matters had to be sorted out. The first was their name. They needed something rather more eyecatching. At the time there was a new Saturday night craze on ITV:

A black and violent thriller series, *The Avengers*, starring a bowler-hatted old Etonian actor, Patrick MacNee, and Miss Honor Blackman as a pair of mysterious secret agents. The show aroused particular excitement through Miss Blackman's 'kinky' black leather costumes. And indeed the London-centred craze for 'kinky' black boots, 'kinky' black raincoats, and 'kinky' black leather or plastic garments of all kinds raged throughout that autumn.

Christopher Booker, The Neophiliacs

There was another reason for the word's vogue. In the late 1950s the word 'kink' – which had originally been associated with the curls in ropes and, by the mid-nineteenth century, had come to mean 'crotchety', 'contrary' – had become a popular word by which to describe any full-blown sexual perversion: something that you might hint at, or even snigger about, but not spell out in public. The problem was that it was exactly those kinds of activity that were being practised, and spelt out in public, by senior members of the British Establishment. In summer 1963 the trial of osteopath Stephen Ward linked a Cabinet Minister, John Profumo, a Soviet attaché and two call-girls, Christine Keeler and Mandy Rice-Davies, in the sensation of the year (some would say the decade). Suddenly all the things that had gone on behind closed doors and had been spoken about in whispers were being paraded through the press in an orgy of speculation: two-way mirrors, men in leather masks, all manner of mutations out of Pandora's box. The British public lapped it up. A Mandy Rice-Davies memoir from the period, catches the flavour perfectly: 'Neither Christine or I took off our clothes but as I stood there I noticed that several of the men and women present had weals across their backs and buttocks. Others had shocking bruises.... It was all too "kinky" for us and we dodged into the dining room....' Even at that stage, for the general public the idea was new enough to warrant inverted commas.

Like any other group in a hurry, the Ravens needed a gimmick, some edge to get them attention. Here it was:

'Kinkiness' – something newsy, naughty but just on the borderline of acceptability. In adopting the 'Kinks' as their name at that time, they were participating in a time-honoured pop ritual – fame through outrage. It was one that was particularly in vogue on the R&B circuit, after the success of the Rolling Stones.

Like so much else about this period of the Kinks' story, quite who gave them the name is a matter for speculation and disagreement. Robert Wace: 'I had a friend who was an old Etonian ne'er-do-well. He thought the group was rather fun. If my memory is correct, he came up with the name just as an idea, as a good way of getting publicity, I suppose. When we went to them with the name, they were horrified, absolutely horrified. They said, "We're not going to be called kinky!" But when we told Larry Page that they were not going to be called the Ravens any more but were going to be known as the Kinks, he said, "Fantastic! Great!" '

Dave Davies: 'I think the name came from the fact that Pete and I always used to wear what they called "kinky leather". And the name stuck: I never thought it would really.'

Larry Page: 'I gave them the name the Kinks, which everybody thought was totally outrageous. I had photographs of them taken with whips and all the rest of it, which is what I wanted because I knew the only way they were going to achieve anything was by being brought to the public eye.'

Ray Davies does not think Page was quite as emphatic at the time but does believe that it was Page who came up with the name: 'Larry thought we were a really untogether mob and that we looked terrible. He said, "The way you look, and the clothes you wear, you ought to be called the Kinks." He said it as a joke, but that often happens to me: I take in everything people say and then I bring it back and use it in evidence later. So we thought, "Why not?" I've never liked the name. I'm still not mad about it. There's a clip of Brian Matthew on *Thank Your Lucky Stars* saying, "I have even heard of a group called the Kinks. That's unbelievable". It caused quite a stir.'

The next thing that happened was that the Kinks were discovered by perhaps the leading tour promoter in the country. Arthur Howes had put the Beatles on a Helen Shapiro tour in January 1963, just before the release of their first number one record, 'Please Please Me'. When they became the biggest act in England Howes's status rose considerably, and his patronage was a major boost to any young group. His discovery of the Kinks was the consequence of another of Robert Wace's strokes: 'Through somebody I knew on the *Daily Express* I got the group a date playing at the Lotus House on New Year's Eve, 1963. The Lotus House was a very big Chinese restaurant in the Edgware Road that showbizzy people like Frankie Vaughan used to go to. The group had already done a date somewhere else that night, and the idea was that they'd go and play at the Lotus House till dawn.

'Anyway Arthur Howes, the Beatles' promoter, was at this party. He thought that the group was fantastic and said to me, "You must call me tomorrow; I want to sign

● Patrick MacNee and Honor Blackman, the original Avengers, 1963

this group for live shows"."

Ray Davies now thinks that Howes's interest finally helped to cement the deal with Pye Records: 'Arthur was very taken with us. He put us on a tour that was to start in March 1964, so we had to have a record out, and I think the tour helped us get a record deal.'

There was one more matter to be sorted out: the Kinks' volatile management arrangements were made legally binding in January 1964. There were already four parties involved: Robert Wace and Grenville Collins as one half of the managerial team, Larry Page as the other half, Arthur Howes as tour promoter and Shel Talmy as producer. It was a complicated marriage of convenience, and one that was already feeling the strain. Even at this early stage there were too many cooks stirring the broth: Howes was ganging up with Wace and Collins against Page, and Page himself, according to Wace, was manoeuvring with Eddie Kassner, owner of Denmark Productions. Ray Davies now admits that there was no love lost between Larry Page and Boscobel Productions, the company formed by Wace and Collins after (Page now alleges) he had shown interest in the group.

It was at this point that Wace, Collins and the Kinks formalized this devil's brew and planted a time bomb in the whole fragile set-up. Ray Davies: 'They had the right, according to the Boscobel contract with us, to assign any rights they had. They assigned part of their 40 per cent to Denmark Productions, Larry Page's company, so it worked out at 10 per cent for the agent, 20 per cent for Boscobel and 10 per cent for Denmark. Denmark Productions – I didn't know this until much later – was co-owned by the Kassner Corporation, and, as it turned out the deal (I could be wrong) was that anything Denmark assigned had to be published automatically with Kassner. According to the Boscobel agreement with the Kinks, as individuals we had no say in the publishing; they could give the publishing to whoever. But when I signed it, I wasn't particularly thinking I would be a song writer.'

Robert Wace: 'At the time Ray was knocked out that anybody even wanted to publish his songs; it wasn't until later he accused us of doing all these bad things, and said, "Why did you give them those rights?" I write it off as a mistake, but we made it.'

The Kinks signed with Pye Records on 23 January 1964. Ray Davies had left Croydon Art College a month before that: 'I wanted to try being a musician. I didn't really write songs then. I just messed around. I never considered that I would ever write or sing; I just wanted to play. Pete and Dave were much more into the swing of things, the Beatles and all that. There was a really good documentary on the Beatles, just after they'd had "She Loves You" and "Please Please Me", and they were on their first sell-out tour. Watching the end of that documentary, I thought, "Well, I can do that".'

THE SEARCH FOR THE SOUND OF '64

● **Spring 1964**

The Kinks? You might call it Spring Fever, but a zany case of Pogo madness is what we'd call it! Help!!!
Fabulous, April 1964

The only thing we may have had problems with was the packaging. The commodity itself never changed.
Brian Somerville, Kinks' PRO, in conversation, 1984

In 1964 pop groups did not have the control over their publicity and marketing that they have now. The Kinks were entering an industry that could not think in the long term and saw long-haired beat groups as good only for a few quick hits and nothing more. The deal that Boscobel Productions signed on behalf of the Kinks – all three of whom were still under age at the time – was then the standard Pye contract, which might now seem ludicrously restrictive but was acceptable at the time – particularly to a hungry group chasing its first break.

Robert Wace: 'It was 2 per cent and 1 per cent on 85 per cent of sales for one year, plus four one-year options, a standard recording agreement. What Pye didn't do was to recoup the recording costs from artists' royalties, which they do now. They now pay the artists higher royalties, but they recoup the recording costs.'

The company to which the Kinks had signed was in the second rank of the Big Four companies that had the British music industry tied up in the 1950s: EMI, Decca, Philips and Pye. The label's chairman throughout the 1960s and 1970s, Louis Benjamin, remembers that period: 'There were really only two companies, EMI and Decca, with Philips as a powerful copy but, in those days, somewhat disorganized, a poor third. And Pye Records was virtually bankrupt. If Lonnie Donegan had a hit, we all got paid.' But Pye Records moved in fast at the beginning of Merseybeat. Alan Freeman was the company's A&R man at the time: 'When the Beatles broke really big and the Liverpool thing came into perspective, I said to my assistant, "For God's sake go to Liverpool and get us a group." And he came back with the Searchers.'

By 1964 Pye Records' investment was paying off. The Searchers were in the middle of a string of big hits: the week that the Kinks signed their deal 'Needles and Pins' was on its way to being their second number 1. But by then any astute music business ear could note that the Merseybeat boom was already waning: in London, thanks to groups like the Rolling Stones, R&B was the coming thing. But at that stage the record companies had problems with how to market it. They'd just about got used to Merseybeat and the mohair suits and endless grins that glossed over any rough Scouse exuberance. Already Merseybeat stars like Billy J. Kramer, Gerry and the Pacemakers and even the Beatles were being groomed for a conventional showbiz career – *Sunday Night at the London Palladium* and so on.

These shaggy-haired R&B groups were something quite different. The Rolling Stones, thanks to Andrew Loog Oldham, were only just beginning to articulate their politics of outrage, but even Oldham had colluded with Decca in putting the Rolling Stones into Carnabetian houndstooth jackets to promote their first single, the Mersey-sounding 'Come On'. However it is hard to blame the record companies: it is only with hindsight that the art school, R&B generation of the Rolling Stones, the Kinks and the Animals appear as different creatures. At the time they were just 'beat' groups, and that still meant Merseybeat. The story of the Kinks' first six months with Pye is the story of the various attempts made by the record company to market their new property in the way they saw fit, and of the attempts of the group, particularly Ray Davies, to resist this process and to do things their own way. This was a new phenomenon, and the Kinks, like the Rolling Stones, bore the brunt of the change.

The week that the Kinks were signed, they were whisked into Pye Studios. Four songs were recorded: 'I Took My Baby Home', 'You Still Want Me', 'You Do Something to Me' and a version of Little Richard's 'Long Tall Sally'. Although Ray Davies had written three of the four songs, it was decided to release 'Long Tall Sally' as the A side early in February. Ray Davies: 'They didn't like any of my songs. The Beatles were doing "Long Tall Sally" in their act, and Larry suggested that we cover it. We did "Good Golly Miss Molly" and a few Little Richard songs live, but we never did that one until they suggested it. We had to go and record it and put one of my songs on the B side. It was all done in one session on a Friday night; we did four tracks in six hours. It was the first time I had really heard my voice. I came up the steps of the studio and Dave was there and he said, "You know you've got a really commercial voice." We hadn't really thought about it before.

'They all came down: a guy called Terry McGrath, Arthur Howes, Page. It had to be the real thing because it was costing *money*, and they all told me how to sing, and told me how to improve my diction. So it was interesting.'

The four tracks recorded at this session were released as the first two Kinks singles: 'Long Tall Sally'/'I Took My Baby Home' on 4 February 1964 and 'You Still Want Me'/ 'You Do Something to Me' on 14 April. All are in the Merseybeat style and, apart from some reasonable vocals and playing, all are pretty derivative. 'I Took My Baby Home' has some notions about gender roles that would not have seemed out of place in the Kinks' later repertoire ('She had some piledriver kisses/They nearly knocked me out/They knocked me over/She had a hug like a vice/She squeezes once or twice/and I'm ooooooover'), but Davies was not allowed, or able, to exploit these potentially exotic ambiguities. Shel Talmy managed to squeeze out a reasonable drum and bass sound – one thing that most Merseybeat records, with their accent on rhythm guitar, harmonica and vocal harmonies, did not specialize in – but the Kinks still lacked the confidence and the ability to create their own style. It would be very easy to see these four tracks as an example of cynical record-company manipulation, and to an extent, of course, the Kinks were being manipulated, but at the same time they did not have the wherewithal to come up with anything significant of their own. They were to learn fast.

Before the hype started the Kinks had one more

● **The High-Lites – Mick Avory on drums, c. 1961**

matter to resolve: the question of a drummer. They hadn't had a settled one since John Start had left the previous summer. Wace and Collins put an ad in the *Melody Maker*, and Mick Avory answered: 'I had to meet them at the Camden Head in Islington for an audition, and they were playing all the stuff that I wanted to play – rhythm and blues type songs that were going around at the time. Chuck Berry stuff. Immediately I liked it, and luckily they liked me sufficiently to take me on. The first night there were just the managers, Robert and Grenville, and then two nights after that Arthur Howes came along with Larry Page. We ran through a few numbers to get their approval. Then one of the first things we did was a gig in Oxford, the town hall. And from there we went on one of those package tours with Dave Clark. That was an eye-opener. I didn't know really what to expect because I was absolutely new and green to the business.'

Unlike the other three, Avory was from East Molesey, a dormitory suburb of London some twenty miles south-west of the capital. After leaving school he had had a variety of jobs as a carpenter and a joiner and had ended up on a building site. 'But I decided when I was about eighteen or nineteen that drumming was what I wanted to do; after four or five years' work you think, "I'm fed up with this. I don't want this as a career".' Avory had played drums ever since he'd been in the Molesey Sea Scouts and had continued to drum for various local groups. In the summer of 1962 he had nearly joined the

Rolling Stones, just a few months before the Davies brothers were on the same circuit: 'A guy who used to get me gigs with his son phoned up and said, "Contact this person called Mick Jagger" – who I'd never heard of – "because he's got a band and they want to do a gig." I phoned up. Mick answered and said they were rehearsing at the Bricklayer's Arms in Soho. I went after work one evening and ran through a few numbers. Brian Jones, who was called Elmo at the time, was there, and Ian Stewart. I can't remember Keith Richard.

'It was their intention that I should join the band and become pro, but I was only doing one-off dates. So I said I wasn't thinking of turning professional.'

For Mick the Kinks audition was nearly his last shot. He had missed the boat once, and he was determined not to do so again. As for the Kinks, they were relieved to have found, at last, a drummer of their own age who wanted to play the same kind of music. They were now, finally, set to crack the big time.

From the outset the Kinks were hyped shamelessly. In the week that 'Long Tall Sally' was released there was a suitably garish front-page ad in the *New Musical Express,* then *the* pop paper, and Arthur Howes arranged for an instant appearance on *the* pop show, Rediffusion's *Ready Steady Go!* with a crowd of rented Kinks fans on the pavement outside. There was also a stream of articles in the teen press of the time, magazines like *Top Boys, Fabulous, Big Beat* and *Boyfriend*, plugging the Kinks as sartorial trendsetters. Then there was the nationwide tour, with the Dave Clark Five and the Hollies headlining, which was due to begin in March. Robert Wace: 'I think everybody lobbed in a bit of money.' But this investment was not without its immediate problems, due partly to everybody's lack of judgement about how to promote the group and partly to the intransigence of the members of the group themselves. The first publicity pictures took the Kinks' name rather too literally and presented them as full-blown sexual perverts. Ray Davies: 'We had whips, leather boots and everything, and they were banned totally. We were desperate to find something different, so we had some really expensive suits with all this leather stuff made by John Stevens. They were dreadful, but everybody who saw them being made thought they were the most far-out-looking things. Except Larry Page who said, "Oh, they'll be OK when they're finished."'

Robert Wace: 'They came up with some clothes themselves which were actually not very good: they were sludge-green jackets and trousers in a tweedy type of material, with leather trimmings and a little hat. The clothes didn't suit them, except Dave: he could wear anything and look good in it.'

After this hiccup the Kinks were quickly presented not as deviants but as young trendsetters with a slightly risqué name: 'Four Mods Set to Make their Mark,' declared a *Pop Beat* headline over a remarkably ludicrous photo of the four Kinks in their suits, glaring Nelson-like at the camera. 'Heard of the new colour? It's KINKY GREEN,' decided *Fabulous*, while posing the question: 'When the Kinks are thinking, do they call it KINKING?' Even by the standards of the day, this was all remarkably unconvincing. Furthermore, the Kinks themselves did not help. In their first major pop interview they were deliberately perverse. Ray was obviously determined to play up any sexual ambiguities: Were Dave and Ray related? the brothers were asked. 'Yeah. We're sisters,' said Ray.

Despite the image-building the Kinks come across as a distinctly motley crew in those early shots. Pete Quaife took it all in his stride, content to pose like something from the *Outfitter*, the magazine for which he had worked after leaving school. Dave excited controversy with what has to be the longest hair ever. 'Pete and I started to have hair about collar-length, with a French kind of bouffant, with a little parting. But I let it grow out and it just fell like that.' Mick, on the other hand, had a distinct hair problem: 'It was an accident. Everyone was having a Beatles cut, but the guy who was doing my hair didn't know what a Beatles cut was. So he overdid it with the scissors and couldn't get it right, and it came out more like a crew cut – which was the opposite to what the others had.'

Ray just looks excruciated: 'Larry Page said, "Listen, cock, you got a chance to go on *Ready Steady Go!* but you've got to do something about the teeth." He sent me to a dentist, who was going to cut them and put in a big plug. In fact, they did a test, and I did *Ready Steady Go!* with the gap between these two front teeth filled. Somewhere there are pictures of me smiling like a real person.

LONG TALL SALLY
Words and Music by ENOTRIS JOHNSON

Recorded by The KINKS on PYE 7N15611

2/6   SOUTHERN
MUSIC PUBLISHING CO. LTD.
8 Denmark Street, London W.C.2.

● 'I really enjoyed that photo session': whips and leather, January 1964

Then I had to go for the real job, and the dentist got the drill, just got it to my teeth, and I said, "I can't go through with this. Forget it." So I walked out.

'It made us less visible because I got a real complex about it for a few months. When we took photographs of the band I'd purse my lips.'

Eventually, sometime during May, the Kinks settled on an image with which everyone concerned was happy. As usual, there is some dispute about who thought of it. Robert Wace: 'Grenville and I certainly went with them to Montague Berman to order them, but I can't remember exactly whose idea it was. I do seem to recall, though, a conversation in which Grenville and I said "They're not really of this century. They're sort of Dickensian characters and that's the way we should go.'" Ray Davies: 'On the Dave Clark tour we were given Dickensian names: Mick was called Bill Sykes, Dave was the Artful Dodger and I was Filch. We had no image and the leather thing wasn't working out. We went to Monty Berman's and said, "Help! Help!" I think we saw a jacket there, and he said he would make some for us. They may have been a joke, but when we walked on stage in them everybody stopped and said, "These are great."'

The hunting jackets were to become the trade mark of the Kinks during the first phase of their success, but at the time they were also a useful antidote to excessive kinkiness.

While all this fine tuning was going on, the Kinks were on the Dave Clark Five tour. Ray Davies: 'The first gig we did was at the Coventry Theatre. They thought we had no stage act. Richard Green reviewed it for the *New Musical Express* and said that the band that was on second should go on first, that the only thing they had going for them was that the drummer could play maracas with one hand and snare with the other, and that they'd got quite a good song called "You Really Got Me". So the general feeling after the reviews and the fact that "Long Tall Sally" had dropped out at number 42, was that we weren't cutting it. The next date was at De Montfort Hall, Leicester, and I remember a telegram coming through. Arthur said, "Put the Kinks on first." That was considered to be a *real* put-down, a real demotion, but somehow we were stupid enough not to worry about it.

'We weren't making it. And then one day when I was washing my hair in a sink in the toilets at the Bedford Granada a guy walked in and said in an American Liverpudlian accent, "Excuse me, are the Kinks here?" and I said, "Oh, I'm in the Kinks." He said, "My name's Hal Carter. I've been sent to give you an act." That was his opening line.

'Hal, being Billy Fury's road manager and some sort of supremo in the lighting and stage act world, watched our show and watched us rehearse. He started getting us to cut all the blues numbers and to put in more conventional songs. I remember one day Graham Nash – the Hollies had taken us under their wing a little bit – shouted at Hal, "Don't let these guys do that. They're not like that. Let them do the things they want to do."'

● **'We've got a big family':** rented Kinks fans, Ready Steady Go **studios, February 1964**

● The 'sludge-green' suits, February 1964

'We were in this bed-and-breakfast place in Bridlington – all the other groups would stay in the Central Hotel but not us. We didn't have telephones in the room, but I got word that Hal wanted to see me. I went to his room, where he was sitting up in bed in polka-dot pyjamas and a hat. He said, "I understand that you're a song writer." And I said, "Yeah, well, I've written a few." He said, "Well, I think I'll write a song with you. I'll show you how to do it." The Mojos had just had a big hit, "Everything's Alright", and he said, "You know, if you play your cards right, we could write a song for the Mojos." He had this idea for a song called "Come on Baby, Got My Rabbit's Foot Working", because a mojo is a lucky charm.

'Hal had this feeling: "You've got to be personal, *personal* in a song. It's gotta be direct! That's why they don't like your songs." So I said, "I'll think about it," and went back to bed. I remember that when we went for the final recorded version of "You Really Got Me" I would sing, "Yeah, you really got me going/You got me so I don't know what I'm doing." And Hal said, "Make it personal, say 'girl'." You see, I wanted it androgynous because I was kind of bashful, but going through all that bit about "making it personal" in a way contributed.'

At this point the Kinks' second single, 'You Still Want Me'/'You Do Something to Me', was released. Without the heavy promotional push that had graced 'Long Tall Sally' – no *Ready Steady Go!* appearances this time! – it died, spectacularly. When the Dave Clark tour ended in May the Kinks were in the wilderness. Robert Wace: 'I was a bit worried, I must admit. I think the thing that worried me was that Ray had, in those days, a rather unusual voice, and it seemed to be difficult to record commercially. When you take on something like that, you can only work on instinct, particularly if you haven't got any experience. All you can do is back a hunch.'

It was make-or-break time for the Kinks. They went to Pye Studios to record their third single. Ray Davies: 'I'd made a demo tape at Regent Sound with four or five songs on it. The one song that nobody had any time for was "You Really Got Me". It was at the end of a roll of tape. Larry used to hear the other songs and turn the tape off as soon as the opening chord came.' At the time it was a common practice for groups to test out their material on audiences when playing live. 'You Really Got Me' had gone down well on the Dave Clark tour, and the Kinks had learned a great deal from being thrown in at the deep end. Ray Davies: 'The first version of "You Really Got Me" was awful. I sound terrible. I'd just come off a tour and my throat was bad. It was slow and awful and everybody thought it was wonderful. I insisted on not letting it go out. I felt really strongly about it, particularly as they had not let us record it before. I felt it had to be the way I wanted it, and I stormed out and felt very uppity and threatened. I went to see Page and Robert, and I said, "I'm not gonna promote that record if you put it out. I'd rather give up than let it go out." I was prepared to do that, and then I think Larry Page told me that they'd let us do another version.'

Twenty years later the subject still sends Robert Wace into a fury: 'They recorded "You Really Got Me" with

● 5 June 1964

Shel Talmy, and test pressings were made, and then – this is what makes me really, really angry – Ray comes to me and says that he really hates the record and that it's not the way he saw it at all and it's got to be redone. Pye Records said we could redo it provided I paid for it out of my own pocket. I think it cost about £85, which was a lot of money in 1964. I don't get anything out of that record now, and it absolutely infuriates me.'

Davies got his way. The group went into the IBC Studios in Portland Place and re-recorded the song in July 1964. It was released on 3 August. Ray remembers walking down Denmark Street with Shel Talmy that week: 'Shel said, "You'd better get used to walking down the street and not having people recognize you, because this is probably the last time you'll ever be able to do this." And I said that I didn't know what he was talking about; I was just interested in going out and having a good time that night. It was strange. I just *knew* I was winning – I was a total winner then – and I was in for a good few months because I thought I was better than anyone else and I was really on the case. I knew everything that was going on.'

TOP OF THE POPS

According to one theory, punk rock goes all the way back to Richie Valens's 'La Bamba'. Just consider Valens's three-chord mariachi squawk-up in the light of 'Louie Louie' by the Kingsmen, then consider 'Louie Louie' in the light of 'You Really Got Me' by the Kinks, then consider 'You Really Got Me' in the light of 'No Fun' by the Stooges, then 'No Fun' in the light of 'Blitzkrieg Bop' by the Ramones, and finally note that 'Blitzkrieg Bop' sounds a lot like 'La Bamba'. There: twenty years of rock 'n' roll history in three chords, played more primitively each time they are recycled.

Lester Bangs, 'Protopunk: the Garage Bands'
The Rolling Stone History of Rock 'n' Roll, (1976)

'You Really Got Me' was the ultimate sort of blues riff. I didn't know I was doing it.

Ray Davies in conversation, 1984

● **Pete Quaife, Mick Avory and Centre Point, early 1965**

Twenty years later 'You Really Got Me' still sounds extraordinary, both for what it is, and for what it represents. With it the Kinks exploded out of Muswell Hill, out of their inchoate Mersey/R&B beginnings, out of their tacky showbiz packaging, to take over the world. 'You Really Got Me' now appears to be not so much an act of will – which, of course, it was – but much more as part of a trio of records that defined an attitude to and through popular music that summer when the world's markets, softened up by the Beatles, were at their most receptive. Along with 'It's All Over Now' by the Rolling Stones and 'House of the Rising Sun' by the Animals, 'You Really Got Me' helped to create an entirely indigenous form of white, mass, urban music: after hearing it, you felt as though your world had changed.

What these R&B groups did was to take the coded sexual and social assertiveness of black R&B and to invest it with a white neuroticism and a superhuman drive, replacing the often subtle rhythms of the originals with monolithic blocks of sound – rather like the office towers that were sprouting up all over London at exactly that time. And what Shel Talmy and the Kinks did with this particular record, and with the follow-up, which re-defined the mixture even further, was to concoct the perfect medium for expressing the adolescent white aggression that has been at the heart of white popular music throughout its own adolescence and its prolonged, artificially retarded middle age.

'You Really Got Me' is not just about chatting up a girl. All of Ray Davies's multiple resentments, social, sexual and philosophical, boiled over at white heat under the

● Rotten Row, summer 1964. The Kinks did ride the horses

pressure that was being exerted on the Kinks – by their record company, by a music industry which appeared to regard them as transient jokes and by their own expectations. This occurred just when the Kinks had found their own voice: what Ray felt and sang, Dave Davies played and Shel Talmy produced. Davies was to articulate that same feeling two years later with greater directness in 'I'm Not Like Everybody Else'.

It is the received view that 'You Really Got Me' is a mutation of the Kingsmen's leering 'Louie Louie' but, according to Ray Davies, that is not the case: 'I didn't really think about the Kinks when I wrote it – I just wanted to write a jazzy song – sort of Mose Allison. Because the Blue Flames was a jazzy outfit I had this fantasy of writing songs for Georgie Fame when he was on the circuit and the band I was in, Hamilton King's, supported them at the Flamingo.

'And I was pissed off with the record company always insisting that ours should be a Merseybeat sound. I wanted us to have something different, something respectable, something that a purist could like. I wrote it very quickly: there's just four lines. I thought it was anti all the sweet-sugar songs – "Sweets for My Sweet" and "She Loves You" – which I was rebelling against, maybe because I couldn't write them.

'I remember seeing a programme called *Monitor* on BBC television one Sunday. A French group was playing water on glasses, and because of the tuning on the glasses they had to jump key. I thought it would be nice to make what I thought was a big jump, though it's only a tone, from G to A. And that's what attracted a lot of people. I remember one guy who was a session musician, quite a good keyboard player, said I'd really locked into something without really knowing. It's still a twelve-bar but I've changed the key. Someone else pointed out that it's like a Gregorian chant.

'It's a crude kind of song: it became part of our stage shows and eventually, because of audience reaction, it helped to make up the minds of the powers that were at Pye. I thought recently: how could I possibly write those lyrics? So simple. I wish I could do it now.'

If Ray Davies had hit upon the song, and the phrasing instinctively, his brother hit upon the perfect sound in the same way. Dave describes what he wanted out of his Epiphone: 'A distorted sound. After many failures I found the way to produce it. I got a very small 4-watt amplifier with an 8-inch speaker, which I proceeded to cut into ribbons with a razor blade. Then I patched it up with Sellotape and stuck a few drawing-pins into it. Then I connected the whole unit up to an ordinary 30-watt amplifier. The small amp was put on full volume, while the big one was kept as low as possible. Boy! You should have heard the distortion.

'This contraption was OK for messing around with, but it turned out to be impractical on stage. So I decided to simplify matters a bit and disconnected one of the speakers on my usual amp. It buzzed a bit on normal volume, but when it was turned up to meet my requirements, it gave out a fabulous *fuzz* sound. Pete's bass does the same. When we played together at full volume, the

You Really Got Me

Girl, you really got me going
You got me so I don't know what I'm doing
Yeah, you really got me now
You got me so I can't sleep at night

Yeah, you really got me now
You got me so I don't know what I'm doing
Oh yeah, you really got me now
You got me so I can't sleep at night

You really got me
You really got me
You really got me

See, don't ever set me free
I always wanna be by your side
Girl, you really got me now
You got me so I can't sleep at night

● **'Beautiful Delilah',** Saturday Club, **August 1964**

noise was unbelievable.'

They were fortunate in finding a sympathetic producer. Shel Talmy: I worked with Ray Davies to get that sound. I was determined to get a good fat sound from the bass and the drums (with most records from the period you can hardly hear anything). I recorded the bass and drums over one or two tracks on a four-track machine and tried to build on that. It was a team effort. That's the only way to work in the studio.'

The Kinks used session drummer Bobby Graham on the finished product as time was short and Mick Avory was unused to the studio. Another session musician was used on rhythm guitar to help fill out the sound. Ray Davies: 'If Dave never plays another note, his performance on "You Really Got Me" will always give him a special place among guitar players. The sound was created in our parents' living room and ended up being copied by nearly every rock guitar player in the world.'

There may very well be echoes of 'Louie Louie' in 'You Really got Me', but only as an approach to sound and attitude. 'You Really Got Me' is that rare thing: a record that cut popular music in half. Quite apart from the influence it was to have on the Who – and thus, by implication, most 1970s power-chorded rock and heavy metal as well as punk rock – the Kinks were to offer endless permutations of this most perfect of riffs in songs like 'All Day and All of the Night', 'Tired of Waiting for You', 'Set Me Free', the ironic 'Top of the Pops' and 1981's 'Destroyer', in which the shades of Kinks present and past confront one another.

By the time that 'You Really Got Me' had sold 1 million copies, Ray Davies, Pete Quaife and Mick Avory were still only twenty and Dave Davies merely seventeen. The full weight of the music industry and its satellites descended upon them at once: for the next few months their life was a kaleidoscope of press interviews, photo sessions, television appearances, hastily arranged recordings and riotous concerts around the world. The Kinks immediately became part of the family of pop groups that mattered.

But they now faced a different challenge: whereas before they had not been allowed to develop in the way that they wanted, now they were not allowed to develop in their own time. This is an experience common to all groups or singers who have instant success, but the Kinks were particularly vulnerable. They had not been hardened, like the Beatles, by playing endless hours in seedy Hamburg nightclubs, nor did they have strong management, like the Rolling Stones or the Who. They did not have the temperament necessary to cope with all the pressure and, once things started falling apart, their back-up team dissolved into sets of squabbling factions. Euphoria quickly became nightmare, an experience that was to scar the two Davies brothers in particular.

At first, though, it was like winning the pools. Ray Davies: 'I remember walking down Denmark Street when it got to number 1. Everyone waved and said, "Well done!" That was a good moment.'

Dave Davies started on a binge that was to last for three years: 'It's a very hazy time for me, really, because I

● **Autumn 1964**

● **At London Airport, 19 August 1964**

● **The fruits of success – Pete Quaife, autumn 1964**

was always out of it. I was always getting crazy and going around the clubs and having a great time, falling over with Eric Burdon at the Scotch of St James's. I used to hang around with a guy called Michael Aldred. We used to drink Sauternes and Coke by the half-pint.'

Mick Avory: 'I just couldn't believe it. It was so sudden: you come out of obscurity, and you're somebody, and everyone's heard of you. It's quite strange. But Ray and Dave were the nucleus of it, really. I didn't feel as though it had had much to do with me.'

However, the timing of their success had a built-in problem: the music industry and its commentators were still stuck halfway between Merseybeat and the new R&B groups with their accent on self-expression and experimentation. The Kinks, with their hard R&B sound, seemed to fall between two pop generations, already misfits.

It is clear that nobody had a clear or coherent plan about how to present this new sensation. Ray believed it needed only to be said with the music, but this was not enough. The column inches and photo sessions of the time tell a story at once sad and hysterically funny: a jumble of repeated gimmicks over an unchanging backdrop of hunting jackets and sullen glares from the group. If they were not living down the allegation that they were 'doing a Stones', then they were trying to live up to being Kinks. Yet what were Kinks? They could not go for the obvious angle, sexual perversion, because in 1964 that was completely unacceptable; yet no one was able to come up with anything other than meaningless bad behaviour – most likely an entirely spontaneous reaction from the group.

Eventually Robert Wace, Grenville Collins and Brian Somerville came up with what had to be the worst yet over a drink at the Hilton; a campaign that nevertheless is now immortalized on the back of the first Kinks' LP and in most of their American press through 1965: 'The letter K has been sadly neglected in the English language for centuries. The Kinks, when they are knot making records or doing one-knight stands, are kampaigning to restore the K to its right and knoble place.' It worked brilliantly in the short term; ultimately this kampaign, like all the other gimmicks, did the Kinks no good at all.

There was yet another delayed time bomb built into the Kinks' success: the expectations and power structure of the music industry of the time. The Kinks hit at a time when the record-buying public was at its most fickle and most insatiable: during 1964 101,257,000 records were sold, an all-time peak. Singles were king: the dynamics of the market meant that you had to keep pumping the product out, regularly and seasonally, otherwise you'd be forgotten and overtaken in the scramble for the next sensation. In part this was true, and in part it was the way in which the record companies operated. After the lean years of the early 1960s producers and label managers could not believe what was happening, and they were determined, quite naturally, to make the most of the bonanza before the whole thing fell about their ears, as they confidently expected it to.

But R&B groups like the Kinks were not after profits alone; they were after self-expression. As Ray Davies said in an early, excellent interview with Alan Freeman in the December 1964 issue of *Rave* 'Being a Kink is an art, only I'm dabbling in sounds, not pictures.' This was a far cry from Helen Shapiro posing with her mum at airports. The resulting conflict of values meant that the Kinks and Ray Davies spent most of the 1960s walking a peculiarly slippery tightrope. Good for creative tension, but hardly beneficial to the psyche.

The Kinks were started on the conveyor belt: a month or so after 'You Really Got Me' went to number 1, they were rushed into the studio to record an album for which they weren't ready. But they coped. Ray Davies: 'I remember when "You Really Got Me" was a hit, we were in Arthur Howes's office when a message came through from Pye that they were going to let us make an album. They told us how lucky we were to have this privilege. The only snag was: we had to do it in two weeks. I remember that when we were doing the album I had this stupid idea: "OK, I wrote the hit, but why should I write everything?" and I decided to make an album like *Beatles For Sale*, which was a mixture of their own songs and R&B standards. I think I had only six of my own songs on that album, even though I'd written lots.'

If nothing else, *The Kinks* is the sound of that early success. It still stands up, if only for the gusto with which everything is played. The material runs from the dreadful ('I've Been Driving on Bald Mountain' and Talmy's 'Bald-Headed Woman') to the very good (Davies's 'So Mystifyin'', 'Just Can't Go to Sleep', and 'Stop Your Sobbing'). Dave Davies is featured prominently, rattling through R & B chestnuts like Bo Diddley's 'Cadillac' and Don Covay's 'Long Tall Shorty' with a confidence that is all over the album.

As soon as the album was complete, the Kinks were packed off on to the scream circuit, into a life of car crashes and rioting crowds. Ray Davies: 'For a year and a half I never heard what I was playing. It was impossible, just a wall of noise. In Scotland they threw shoes and tore our clothes off.

'I remember when we played with the Beatles, just before "You Really Got Me" was released, John Lennon used to shout "Shuddup!" through the microphone. I think they got pissed off with it. I didn't. I figured that it was part and parcel of what we were doing. It just meant we couldn't get into too many ballads.'

The Kinks had hurriedly been added to the Billy J. Kramer package tour; during a break they had to record a successor to 'You Really Got Me'. Ray Davies: '"You Really Got Me" had just started to fall. Eddie Kassner called me into his office and said, "We must have a follow-up, my boy," and I started thumping out chords – it was really easy. A few days later we did a gig in the Midlands, and we routined "All Day and All of the Night" at rehearsals. We came south and recorded it the next day, and then went up to another date.

'Burt Bacharach, whom I admired then and still do, reviewed all the singles that were around at the time. He called "All Day and All of the Night" a neurotic song. I thought I was being put down at first, but then I realized

● **With Brian Somerville, early 1965**

All Day and All of the Night

I'm not content to be with you in the daytime
Girl, I want to be with you all of the time
The only time I feel all right is by your side
Girl, I want to be with you all of the time

All day and all of the night
All day and all of the night
All day and all of the night

I believe that you and me last for ever
Oh yeah, all day and night time yours, leave me never
The only time I feel all right is by your side
Girl, I want to be with you all of the time

All day and all of the night
All day and all of the night
All day and all of the night

he was complimenting it. It's youthful, obsessive and sexually possessive, so it was a *very* neurotic song.

'We were on tour in the States recently and we heard "All Day and All of the Night" on the local rock station. It stood up very well, better than "You Really Got Me", which is a really jazzy, bassy record. "All Day and All of the Night" has got all these crashing sounds. There's a bit in the middle when I say, "Come on" and Dave yells, and the initial effect is "Get 'em off!" You see, we couldn't do anything wrong. It was done in three hours, but every one's positive, every one's come off a hit – it's easy.'

'All Day and All of the Night' is the pinnacle of their hard-rock style. Here the wrenching key changes of 'You Really Got Me' are wound even tighter, turning the song's own sexual demand into a metaphysical threat.

Others were about to take up the gauntlet thrown down by these coded curses and their state-of-the-art productions. Pete Townshend: 'I wrote "I Can't Explain" specifically to get a deal with Shel Talmy. I listened to "You Really Got Me", which I thought was a terrific record and a fantastic song at the time. Ray's early use of key changes was just brilliant.'

'All Day and All of the Night' entered the *Melody Maker's* chart at number 42 on the week ended 31 October; 'You Really Got Me', at number 40, was on its way out. Except for a two-week gap in May 1965, caused by the relative failure of 'Everybody's Gonna Be Happy', the Kinks were to have a record in the top fifty every week between 15 August 1964 and 29 September 1965: thirteen months and six hit singles. The demand for product seemed insatiable.

By the time that 'All Day and All of the Night' was in the top three, the Kinks had already been summoned to Pye Studios to do yet more recording – this time an EP, *Kinksize Session*. Ray Davies: 'That's exactly the sort of thing we shouldn't have done. "Louie Louie" wasn't as good as when we played it live. It's an awful story, but I did the vocal while I was reading the *Record Mirror.* That's how cocky I was.

'The whole EP was pretty dreadful. This lack of care was something, I think, that people wanted. We were being milked dry, really, because they thought it wouldn't last long, you see?'

And in the middle of all this, on 12 December, Ray Davies got married to the seventeen-year-old Rasa Dicpetri. Rasa Davies: 'I met Ray when I was still at school in Bradford. A girlfriend of mine was telling me about a new group called the Kinks (she was a real fan), and she said that they were going to do a show in a club in Sheffield called the Esquire. So we took the day off school and hitchhiked to Sheffield. Because my friend knew Mick, the drummer, we got in through the stage door. They were wearing their red hunting jackets and frilly white shirts. It was another world, something totally different from what I was used to. It was a small club, and everyone was very excited, shouting and screaming.

'My sister lived in London, and I used to come and stay with her in the summer. Ray had my address. When I was in London he contacted me and that's how we started seeing one another.'

● Backstage, autumn 1964

● **The Kinks with Susan Maugham (Pete Quaife's poodle is called Earl Ruthere Dino Kinkley), 28 November 1964**

Just after that time 'You Really Got Me' went to number 1 and the Kinks' lives changed for ever. Rasa got caught up in the ensuing madness: 'I didn't feel the pressure because to me it was very exciting, like a whirlwind. The only pressure I felt was when, after seeing Ray in the summer, I had to go back to school in September. Later he did a concert at the Bradford Odeon. He contacted me and told me to meet him in the park outside school on the day of the concert. But the rumour got about that the Kinks were going to be in the park, so everybody rushed up there at four o'clock. Ray was stampeded, trampled, and the headmistress, the Mother Superior, found out. I was expelled because of it. When I think about it, it was incredible, really.'

Rasa was to play an important part in the Kinks' records during the 1960s, singing harmonies on most of the big hits. She had inspired 'All Day and All of the Night' and its follow-up, released within a month of the wedding, 'Tired of Waiting for You'. Ray Davies: 'We recorded "Tired of Waiting" for our first album, but Shel wisely said, "Let's not put this on the album. Let's save this for a single." He was smart. It was originally on a demo tape I did when I lived with my sister. It was a little guitar-picking song.

'I came back on the Tube after a very late night and made the song up on the train. I told everybody I had finished the song, but when they'd put the backing track down I still hadn't written the words – I just had the "I'm so tired, so tired of waiting" part. We went to put down the lyrics the next day, and even then I hadn't finished it. We put on the "oohs" and "aahs" first, and then I did the vocals: I don't think I'd written the lyrics until I heard the sound of the "oohs" and that quiet part. I was gambling a bit. . . .

'Even then it wasn't quite finished. I remember just before we went away to Australia we went into another studio and put on the basic riff; I think people decided it needed to sound more like us'.

'Tired of Waiting' is the last of the initial trilogy of Kinks hits – all ominous, metallic, mythic statements. On the upward curve of their success they could do little wrong: after the overwhelming assault of 'You Really Got Me' and 'All Day and All of the Night', 'Tired of Waiting' shows that the Kinks could wind down and still retain their power. The energy that had exploded in the first two singles was now harnessed to an inexorable rise and fall, tension and its release, that corresponded to the frustration of the subject matter. Talmy's clean, clear production, emphasizing Pete Quaife's booming bass, pits the group's rough but elemental dynamism against Ray's newly enfranchised vocal, part pleading, part growling. As Davies himself wrote: 'The reason I change my voice in certain songs is because in every song there is a different part to play, and the vocal construction needs a different make-up every time.'

'Tired of Waiting' became the group's second number 1 in the UK and was their biggest-ever record in the USA, reaching number 6 there in April 1965. Although a simple song, it now appears to be invested with a great power, both through the perfect match of form and content and through its massive success. It hit the charts of the world at a time when its meta-frustration appeared to be a coded threat against all authority, particularly those institutions not moving fast enough to accommodate the strident demands for change.

Its release also saw the group at the crest of their upward curve: the Kinks and the team around them had been able to capitalize on, and to consolidate, the group's astonishing success. At the beginning of 1965 the Kinks were fast becoming one of the hottest groups in England. 'Tired of Waiting' was on its way to becoming the group's third top three record and they now seemed to be on a level where they could have been as big as the Beatles or the Stones. But as the pressure started to pile on, everything started to buckle, not least Ray Davies, who was having to shoulder all the song-writing responsibilities as well as being, along with brother Dave, the front line of the group. As the pressure increased, so the ground started to fall away.

Ray Davies: 'I remember a certain element of slackness creeping into the operation: managers going around in nice cars and not being at the office, the band mixing with the rock 'n' roll elite and losing its core. I saw it happening all around. Probably it was happening with me because I'd got married. I remember Brian Somerville coming up to me in Bradford when I was just about to go into the church and actually saying, "I've got tickets to South America in my pocket. If you want to take them, go ahead." In those days pop stars weren't supposed to marry.

'When we got back from Australia in February and they rushed us into the studio to record the second album, I thought, "Do you people think – it's all gonna go away? You want to rush us just to make as much money as you can in case we don't come up with anything more." That made me feel really uneasy and insecure. Maybe I didn't want to admit it to myself, but being married must have freaked me out. I made a mistake. I hate to think that I'm not very good at loving people, I mean just on a mental level, but I think I might have been in a panic realizing that there was somebody I had to look after. But then it got settled and stabilized, and I found it was a help to have somebody around.

'I remember Page said, "You know, it's a good time to get married when you're on the top" – as if it was all going to go away. But once I got those first few hits, I knew it wasn't going away.'

SET ME FREE

● **Limo life, late 1964**

It was a really fragile existence. It makes you wonder how we ever got through it.

Dave Davies in conversation, 1984

I won't take all the hand-me-downs
And make out I smile when I wear a frown
And I'm not going to take it all lying down
Cause once I get started I go to town. . . .

Kinks, 'I'm not Like Everybody Else', 1966

Within six months of 'You Really Got Me' going to number 1, the Kinks had recorded two albums, three singles and an EP. They had visited seven countries at opposite ends of the globe and had played upwards of ninety dates. They were now part of the international pop class. Yet fame was fast becoming meaningless. The Kinks were hitting what happens to other spectacularly successful groups: the escape hatch had become a nightmare just as alarming as any Ray Davies had on his sleepless nights, a hermetically sealed, claustrophobic hot-house where all manner of psychoses were able to flower.

Also they were no longer the new product on the shelves. The Kinks had become associated with a sound that was fast becoming a straitjacket. The group and Ray Davies were desperate to put it behind them. They had made it: but that was only the first skirmish in what was to prove a very long war. The rest of 1965 and the early part of 1966 is, even by the standards of the day, a mad blur of riots, fights, treachery, power struggles and very serious acts of self-destruction. The long process of attempting to gain control over their own destiny had begun: a process so long and so bloody that by the time it was fully achieved in the early 1970s the Kinks, and Ray Davies in particular, were exhausted and on the verge of emotional bankruptcy.

Yet the Kinks' strong sense of self-preservation prevailed even at their worst moments. Despite activities that would have brought most other groups to a halt, the Kinks were still able to function in the market place. A string of records in 1965 make it very clear that Ray Davies in particular was prepared to trade in worldwide success for the chance to exorcise his own demons in a series of songs that still rank among the best the Kinks have ever produced.

Eighteen days into the new year they flew off to Perth for an Australian tour with Manfred Mann. It was not pleasurable and, despite the chirpy reports that Ray Davies sent back to the *Melody Maker*, it was not a great success. The Kinks hated Australia, and the sentiment was reciprocated.

On the way back to England the Kinks stopped off in Singapore and New York City, where they taped a segment for the TV programme *Hullaballoo*. It was their first visit to the USA, right in the middle of their three biggest hits in that country: 'You Really Got Me' had reached number 7 during November/December 1964, and 'All Day and All of the Night' was climbing the charts. Ray Davies: 'The show was hosted by Annette Funicello and Fabian. They wanted us to do dance routines, so Mick and I danced with each other. Of course they banned it. They wouldn't let two men dance with each other on television.

'It was an unhappy trip. That was when we first fell out with the American union. I wouldn't join the union, and when we went back in the middle of the year they were waiting for us.'

The day after they arrived in England, it was straight into Pye Studios to record *Kinda Kinks*. Ray Davies: 'We had to do that album in a week. We came off the plane and I had an elephant leg from a bite I'd got in Singapore. We had to go straight into the studio to do the album. A bit more care should have been taken with it: I think Shel went too far in trying to keep in the rough edges; some of the double-tracking on that is appalling. It had better songs on it than the first album, but it wasn't executed in the right way – it was just far too rushed.' *Kinda Kinks* now has the distinct aura of demand outstripping supply, as the group tried out a number of styles without settling on anything satisfactory.

At this same time the group recorded their sixth single, another concerted effort to get away from the Kinks' patent sound. Ray Davies: 'We did "Ev'rybody's Gonna Be Happy" because we'd been doing a tour with a great band called the Earl Van Dyke Trio. We wanted to copy them because we looked up to them. They were wonderful, and the song was based on their style. We wanted to do something different.

'I remember we played Fairfield Halls, Croydon, on the day that it was out. I said, "I'm a bit worried about this one; I don't think it's got it," and everyone else was concerned because I was the man who was right about "You Really Got Me". Eddie Kassner said to me, "Don't worry about it. 'Ev'rybody's Gonna Be Happy' shipped 90,000 today," and I said, "Oh great." But it didn't do it. It got to number 20 and fizzled. So everyone thought, "Aha! This is what we predicted."'

Motown pastiches are not the Kinks' forte: much better is the single's flip 'Who'll Be the Next in Line?', perhaps the ultimate rejection song. Ray Davies has never sounded quite so venomous. After the relative failure of 'Happy' in the UK, Reprise took the hint and issued 'Who'll Be the Next in Line?' as the A side *after* the more Kinks-like 'Set Me Free'. Neither song did well: like their relationships, the Kinks' sound was breaking up.

More records, more dates, more riots. A mere two weeks after the release of 'Ev'rybody's Gonna Be Happy', with two of the group in poor health (Ray having caught pneumonia in Scotland and Pete Quaife having fallen down a flight of stairs), the group was caught in the worst riot of its career in the Tivoli Gardens, Copenhagen. This was an orgy of destruction that was quite spectacular even by the standards of the day, when it was common for the appearance of a major group to trigger off mass violence. Quite apart from what was going on internally, the external environment was starting to break up around the Kinks as well.

Ray Davies: 'We got to Copenhagen, went on stage and did two songs. During "You Really Got Me" the kids got up and started clapping. A lot of police ran in from outside, and the kids reacted against them. It was nothing to do with us. There was a huge fight. The Tivoli Concert Hall was mainly glass. The only thing they didn't desecrate was a statue of Jim Reeves and his record collection. Everything else was smashed to smithereens.

'They locked us in a little room somewhere. The Danish people are very proud. They get shaken very easily, and they came and looked at us as if we were dirt. A woman said, "We had the Rolling Stones last week and they were very nice boys, but you're horrible!" We got

● **'All Day and All of the Night',** Ready Steady Go, **November 1964**

blamed for it in the press, though I don't think we started it. It was big news.'

Dave Davies: 'I was pissed off because we didn't even get a chance to play. I got very drunk and very angry at the hotel, and I smashed a huge mirror behind the bar. They chased me all over the hotel. They got me in the end and put me in the nick. I was sitting there shouting abuse at everyone. It was unbelievable.'

Ray Davies: 'They cancelled the second day. Dave got pissed and threw a bottle. Within minutes (they must have been waiting), I saw this mass of police. It was like a herd of buffalo storming into the lift, and Dave was in the middle somewhere. Our road manager tried to stop them, but they hit him with truncheons, cut his face, and Dave went in for the night. We got him out, but we had to fly to England the next day to do the *New Musical Express* Pollwinners concert. We played pretty badly.'

Within three weeks the Kinks had recorded another single, 'Set Me Free'/'I Need You', and had begun their first headlining tour around the country, with the Yard-birds and Goldie and the Gingerbreads in support. Ray Davies: 'After "Ev'rybody's Gonna Be Happy" we all said, "We've got to go in and make a KINKS record," but we didn't know what a Kinks record was. So I wrote "Set Me Free". I wanted to write a song for Cilla Black, and I had to put the chunky chords on it. I hated making it. I loathed it. But now when I hear the song I listen with a lot of affection because underneath it there was a good song.'

'Set Me Free' is laboured; much better is the flip side, 'I Need You', which is perfect. For once, the Kinks were not trying too hard. Ray Davies: '"I Need You" was writ-ten as a joke. It started off as a plea. "All Day and All of the Night" was take-it-or-leave-it, but "I Need You" was the realization, without knowing it, that you do actually need somebody. But the recording session was kind of jokey. I remember that when Dave got the feedback the engineer at Pye gradually leaned further and further back in his seat, wondering what was happening. It's a good element to keep in the music, humour.'

What makes 'I Need You' work is its directness, a tech-nique which is surprisingly difficult to achieve. By con-trast with the ease of 'I Need You', the difficulty with which Ray Davies attempts to communicate his feelings on 'Set Me Free' only emphasizes the Kinks' own situa-tion, imprisoned by audience demand, release schedu-les and industry expectation.

Cooped up in their own time capsule, the four mem-bers of the group were not getting on very well with one another.

Dave Davies confirmed this in a 1966 interview with the *New Musical Express*. Over a caption dividing the Davies brothers from their rhythm section, Dave admits: 'About a year ago we hated the sight of each other. We would fly into a temper at the slightest provocation. I suppose, in a way, it was only natural when we spent so much time together.' And if Dave wasn't getting along with Pete or Mick, then Ray felt that Dave was also abdi-cating his responsibilities as the group's co-founder and the second front man.

● **Deliberate perversity – Bondi Beach, Sydney, February 1965**

Dave remembers an incident from the time: 'I kept an envelope of purple hearts in a sports jacket. I used to chain-smoke, and once I was so out of it that I burned a hole in the jacket when I was asleep; it was all smoulder-ing. The rest of the group threw me out of the car. I was wandering in a field, didn't know where I was, and I'd lost the envelope with all my pills. I was searching around the field, falling over and wondering, "What am I going to do tomorrow? I'm going to feel terrible." Then I fell into a stupor in the back of the car, and I can't remember any more.'

Yet Dave Davies's constant clubbing was not without some point. 'I think that we all influenced each other musically to some degree. You could never pinpoint it exactly. But because I was always out in clubs, I would hear everything from "A Little Piece of Leather" to Martha and the Vandellas.' As before, Dave Davies would be out doing the research while his brother withdrew and took it all in.

Seventeen dates into their headlining tour – real trou-

WONDERFUL KINKY KOPENHAGEN
APRIL 1965

● First headlining tour, May 1965

ble erupted. Dave Davies: 'Mick and I shared a house in Connaught Gardens in Muswell Hill. We were quite close at the time. What happened was that we were all travelling back in the car after a gig at Taunton, and I had an argument with Ray in the back of the car – I can't remember what it was about. It wasn't the first time we'd argued. We got back to the hotel and separated to go to our rooms. Mick and I were on the landing, and I went up to him and said, "Why didn't you stand up for me when we were having that argument? How could you just sit there and say nothing?" Mick hit me, and then the fight started. We exchanged punches, then our roadie came up and stopped it. Mick ran off shouting that I was mad.'

Ray Davies: 'The next day it was Cardiff, and we had to have separate dressing rooms for Dave and Mick. Dave had to go on stage with sunglasses because his eyes were black. When we did the first number it was fine. The second number was "Beautiful Delilah". It starts off with the drums and the guitar and then I heard nothing else. Dave had turned round and spat at Mick. As Dave turned

to do his vocal, Mick got up with a cymbal and hit him over the head with it. Dave collapsed, and Mick went off into the night. The police really wanted to get Mick. I had to tell lies to the papers. I said it was part of the stage act. I really thought it was the end of the band.'

Mick Avory: 'Dave had a quick temper in those days. We knew that was the end of that particular tour. We didn't have too many dates left, as it happened. It was horrible at the time. But everyone misinterprets it and says I hit him with a cymbal. If you hit somebody with a cymbal, you decapitate them. I only had a high hat left from my kit to hit him with, so I hit him over the head with the pedal end. Anyway it all got misconstrued. It was embarrassing, and everyone wanted to talk about it as if we hadn't done anything else.'

It is clear that the fight was an indication not of mere brattishness but of the power struggles going on within the group. Dave Davies: 'The reason why the whole thing started was that Mick wouldn't give an opinion. Thinking about it, it was the cause of a lot of friction in

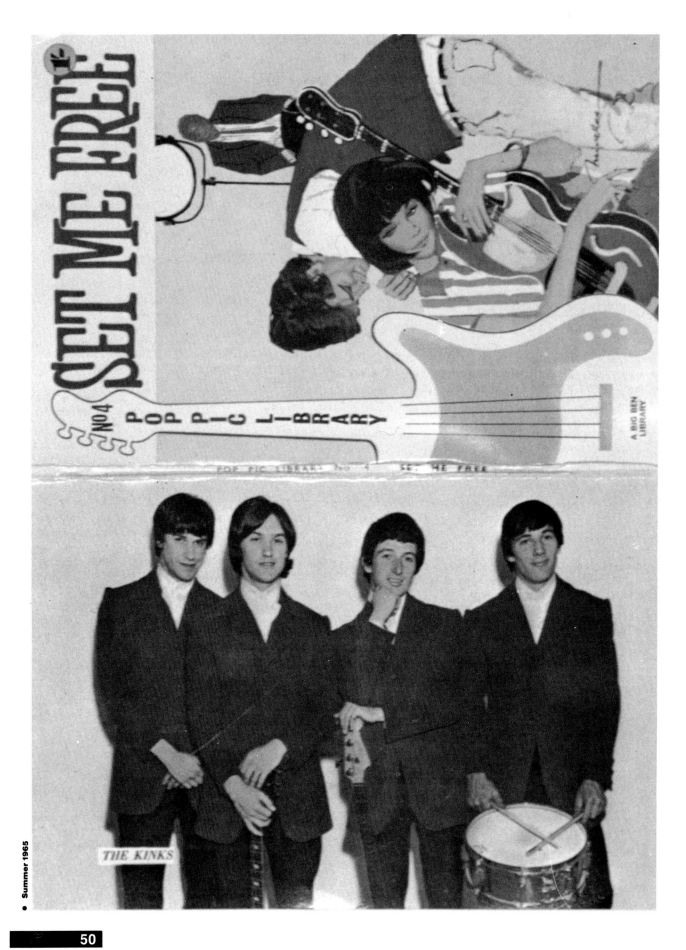

later years because there were many times when I felt that my ideas would get pushed aside in favour of Ray's simply because it was easier for the other band members to agree with him. I didn't want Mick back in the band after that, and it was only because Larry Page convinced me that we should keep the thing going in order to break America that he returned. Although Mick and I became friendly again soon afterwards, there were many occasions when he sat on the fence in rehearsals, creative situations like that when I could have used somebody on my side. He didn't want to come between Ray and myself. Although this used to go on, and ideas of mine used to get squashed, I always felt Ray's work was more important than the personalities involved, and still do.'

The remaining four dates of the tour were cancelled, as were a ten-day tour of Scotland and a date in Paris. The Kinks' reputation for unreliability was beginning to be established – a reputation that has dogged them throughout their career. At the time that was the least of their worries. The group was about to leave for its first tour of the USA, and it looked as though there were going to be no more Kinks.

Larry Page: 'That was the end of the Kinks. The Kinks will tell you, Ray will tell you, they were never going to play together again. We had this American tour coming up, and I thought, "How the hell do we get round this one?" I phoned up every member of the group and said, "I want you in my office on Friday at four o'clock." I did not let on that the others were going to turn up. Once they were there, they didn't speak to one another. There was total silence. I decided that I would steam ahead. I said, "OK, there's an American tour starting next Friday, blah blah blah. We open in New York, blah blah blah. Any questions?"'

The Kinks were in a parlous state and about to embark on one of the biggest challenges of their career. Larry Page remembers an incident typical of the disturbances of that time: 'I showed the contracts for the American tour to Ray and said, "Right, we're off to America." He should have been jumping up and down. I'll never forget it – he just said, "Mmmm, oh yeah, but I can't sign that." "What do you mean you can't sign that?" "Well, it says 'orchestra leader'." So I said, "Don't worry, we'll cross that out. Initial it and put 'group leader.' No problem." "Oh, I don't know". As I'm talking to Ray, he's got my fountain pen and he's emptying it on the floor. I'm watching it drip-drip-drip down. "Come on, Ray, we're hours late." I'm really trying to talk him into it. When he goes to sign the contract, he says, "There's no ink in the pen."

The Kinks went to America in June 1965 as big stars. Their records had been released on Reprise, a subsidiary of Warner Brothers. Pye distributed Reprise product in the UK, and Reprise had pick-up rights on Pye material for US release. They passed on 'Long Tall Sally' and on 'You Still Want Me' but did well out of the first three Kinks UK hits, which went to the top ten in America.

Quite apart from all the troubles both inside and outside the group, the American market was very different from the British one. It is no accident that two of the groups that were most consistently successful in the USA in the years after the Beatles – more so than in their home country – were packaged pop groups like the Dave Clark Five and Herman's Hermits.

Any attempt to package the Kinks was doomed to failure, although the teen press of the time had its usual valiant stab. *Flip* featured the Kinks on its June 1965 cover: 'Kinks: Kool Krazy Kooks!' ran the headline, with quotes from Dave like, 'It's great to make it both in the UK and in the US. I hope we can keep it up. It's a fab life.'

There is in existence a *Shindig* tape of the time which illustrates the problem. The show is locked into another era of presentation. *Shindig* treated pop as fluff, but the Kinks were in another orbit: they appeared to be brooding, dark, androgynous mutants leering threats like 'It's All Right' at Middle America while generally posing in the most provocative way possible. They were assured, in command and implicitly anarchic.

But the anarchy was for real. The Kinks were out of control, running wild, tearing themselves apart in a prolonged smash-up over thousands of miles of alien country. Everything had come to a head, and the Kinks' nightmare was now entering one of its most destructive phases. It was a process to be repeated twelve and a half years later, in different circumstances, by the Sex Pistols; but the Kinks survived.

They arrived in New York on 18 June. Robert Wace and Grenville Collins had not made the trip; the Kinks were being looked after by the Denmark Productions side of their management, Larry Page and Eddie Kassner. Larry Page: 'We opened in New York, where they were billed as the Kings; I got it changed. Then there was trouble all the way across America. On one date they played "You Really Got Me" – one song – for the whole act. If they were booked to do forty or forty-five minutes, Ray would play short-time on stage. I had buses going to venues with two of them at the front, two at the back and me in the middle. And Ray would sneak up the coach and start whispering. That would be the situation. It was boiling. One would go on from one side of the stage, two from the other side. We never knew, when they got to the middle, whether they'd fight or play.'

As far as Larry Page was concerned, it all came to a head on the night of the Hollywood Bowl concert. 'I'd been fighting to get Rasa over there, but because her parents were Russian, I'd had trouble with her visa. So finally we're in LA, which has to be the greatest thing for them: from a pub to the Hollywood Bowl. Not just for them but also for me. I got a call from the *Daily Mirror* in London, from Pat Doncaster, saying, "We understand that the Kinks are not appearing tonight." I said, "What are you talking about? Ray's in the next room. Of course he's going on tonight." "Can you check?" I said "I'm telling you, Pat, there's no problem. They're going on tonight." So he said, "Can you check and ring me back?" Knock, knock, knock. "Ray?" "I'm not going on tonight". I spent all bloody day coaxing them to do something that they should have been begging to do. Finally, I got them on stage. I thought, "If somebody can't appreciate success, then I want no part of it." I waited until the show was finished, then I left.'

The real tragedy of the situation is not that Larry Page was an evil manipulator or that the Kinks were totally unmanageable but that the two had entirely different value systems, which collided under the stress. What Page saw as the pinnacle of the group's career – quite correctly, as far as he was concerned – Ray Davies saw as another onerous duty: 'I believed America to be an evil place. They kept on harassing us for various reasons. I remember we were doing a television spot – I think it was for the Dick Clark show – and this guy kept going on at me: "When the commies overrun Britain, you're really going to want to come here, aren't you?" I just turned round and hit him, about three times. I later found out that he was a union official. Page and Kassner were there and, I discovered later, they fell out with a promoter on the West Coast called Betty Kaye. I'm not sure, but I think they wanted to get more money for the dates – we were getting $1,500 and we were playing the Cow Palace.'

Robert Wace: 'They failed to perform for some woman called Betty Kaye in Sacramento, and they were reported to the American Federation of Musicians, which blacklisted them.' The Kinks were not to play America again until four and a quarter years later.

● **Mick Avory, Larry Page, Mike Shepherd, Buddy Greco, Dean Martin, Los Angeles, June 1965**

● **Soho, spring 1966**

GOOD TIMES

Well, once we had an easy ride and always felt
    the same.
Time was on my side and I had everything to gain.
Let it be like yesterday,
Please let me have happy days . . .
Won't you tell me?
Where have all the good times gone?
                Kinks, '**Where Have All The Good Times Gone?**', 1965

By July 1965 ... this frenzy was only a symptom of the gathering strain beneath, as the 'swinging city' galvanized itself for a last flight into the stratosphere. Never before had London been a town so fashionably obsessed with kinks, with sexual abnormality and make-believe violence.
                Christopher Booker, ***The Neophiliacs***, 1969

● **August 1965**

The Kinks are now seen as part of the Swinging Sixties, a golden age of Boomtime, an age of full employment and seemingly endless novelty, mobility and excess, an age now perceived as remote and desirable from the viewpoint of our current depression, with its contracted and shrunken possibilities. Yet our age has a great facility for eliding timescales and rewriting history: we do not see the past with 20/20 vision, nor are we encouraged to. In fact, the Swinging Sixties could just as well be called the Satirical Sixties, a time when nothing was sacred, and harsh judgement was passed on all manner of institutions, not least the highest in the land.

This phenomenon, which had reached its political peak in about 1963 through TV programmes like *That Was The Week That Was* and the bi-weekly magazine *Private Eye*, spread into popular music over the next couple of years through the incestuousness and mobility of that particular culture. Barry Fantoni: 'All that anybody ever talked about was pop music. It was the only thing that was happening. Pop art, pop music – everything was pop. You pick up a *Daily Express* from that period and there are two pages, almost every day, of what pop people were eating, sleeping and talking. Then footballers came in, and they became stars too. Saturday night was *That Was The Week That Was* night. The whole satire thing was boosted up and you had David Frost in the hit parade with the programme's signature tune. That was all people talked about.'

This cultural mix, as well as the art school background of so many of the new musicians, gave much of the new pop music, which was reaching its full potential by the summer of 1965, a sarcastic cutting edge, which, befuddled by ears waxed with nostalgia, we no longer hear. Much of this social criticism expressed a fairly routine bohemian philosophy – songs like the Beatles

Ray Davies, Ready Steady Go, late 1965

'Nowhere Man', for instance – but groups like the Rolling Stones and the Kinks were writing songs that commented on their own situation and on the culture that they appeared to represent. The Rolling Stones, in particular, were set on a course of records, such as 'Satisfaction' and '19th Nervous Breakdown', that not only satirized the 'classless' *milieu* in which the aristocracy of pop groups now found itself but also saw through the promises and articulated the futility and selfishness that lay behind this new, golden dream – a process that reached its climax in late 1966 with the hysterical 'Have You Seen Your Mother, Baby, Standing in the Shadow?', one of the most nihilistic records ever made.

At the same time this new pop music was becoming irrevocably 'experimental' as the art school boys started to take over. The charts were periodically being invaded by odd bending noises created by chic instruments like the twelve-string Rickenbacker or the sitar, or by modish experiments like feedback, that seemed to symbolize the cultural relaxation (later tagged 'permissiveness') that had occurred very quickly among the elite and was occurring rather more slowly among the population at large.

Of all this the Kinks were both part and not part. During this period they made several records that whined and whooshed with the best of them – particularly 'I Need You' and 'See My Friends' – yet they were never given the credit they deserved for their experimentations. Ray Davies was breaking new ground with his social observation, accurate to a degree unprecedented in beat music, and with his wry commentary on 1960s culture. Yet the Kinks did not have the popularity that would bring these comments to public attention in the same way as the Rolling Stones, whose snowballing success validated their critical stance. This was due partly to timing, partly to a continuing image problem. Most of all, however, it was down to the group itself: Ray Davies in particular started to withdraw from his position as a top pop star and all that it symbolized.

As one of the key songs on *Kinks Kontroversy* had it, 'I'm on an island!' The Kinks had had mass success, but they were losing the taste for it. From this point on they were to come in at a different angle: they swapped being a great groovy beat group for a position much better suited to their temperament – one that suited them so well, in fact, that it was to become second nature: that of misfits. To ignore this fact and to lump the Kinks in, willy-nilly, with the Swinging Sixties is to underestimate both the nature of their achievement and the toll that it exacted.

Within three weeks of their return from the USA the Kinks released one of the most remarkable records of their long career, perhaps of the entire 1960s. It was a record so opaque and so subtle that only its surface could be plagiarized at the time, while its full impact has never been reproduced or fully assimilated even now.

Quite apart from anything else, 'See My Friends' was the first attempt to integrate Eastern music into pop. Ray Davies: 'We stopped off in India on the way to Australia. I

See My Friends

See my friends
See my friends
Way across the river

See my friends
See my friends
Way across the river

She is gone
She is gone
And now there's no one else
Except my friends

Way across the river
She just went
She just went
Way across the river

Now she's gone
Now she's gone
Wish that I'd gone with her

She is gone
She is gone
And now there's no one else
Except my friends

Way across the river
She is gone
And now there's no one else to take her place

She is gone
And now there's no one else to love
Except my friends

Way across the river
See my friends
See my friends
Way across the river

See my friends
See my friends
Way across the river

● **The last appearance of the hunting jackets, September 1965**

remember getting up, going to the beach and seeing all these fishermen coming along. I heard chanting to start with, and gradually the chanting came a bit closer and I could see it was fishermen carrying their nets out. When I got to Australia I wrote lots of songs, and that one particularly. You've got to write, otherwise you'd go mad. You're so far away.'

As early as 22 August 1964 the Kinks were admitting to the *Melody Maker:* 'We're always looking, searching for new sounds'. Ray Davies: 'On "See My Friends" I was interested in getting this little feedback sound, playing the notes on my twelve-string Framus and placing it near the amp, so that they'd feedback like a droning sound. When we recorded it we limited it very heavily, putting on loads of compression. That's why it's wonderfully squashed, *shhhhhh,* surging: that's the limiters pulsing, very basic but very effective.'

'See My Friends' is not only the first but it also stands as the most successful attempt to marry the sinuous, elusive textures of Indian music and an entirely alien form: the specific, effect-ridden, three-minute pop song. It works mainly because the Kinks did not go about it in the obvious way: instead of buying a sitar at the tourist shop (or even studying under Ravi Shankar), they used the instruments that were to hand. What Davies does do is capture a mood that is suited both to the plaintive texture of Indian music and to our conception of it: 'See My Friends' couples a trance-like drone with a song that is the first of the Kinks' many hymns to acceptance.

The style had immediate impact. Barry Fantoni: 'I remember it vividly and still think it's a remarkable pop song. I was with the Beatles the evening that they actually sat around listening to it on a gramophone, saying "You know, this guitar thing sounds like a sitar. We must get one of those." They were vandals. Everything Ray did they copied.'

Pete Townshend: '"See My Friends" was the next time I pricked up my ears and thought, "God, he's done it again. He's invented something new." That was the first reasonable use of the drone – far, far better than anything the Beatles did and far, far earlier. It was a European sound rather than an Eastern sound but with a strong, legitimate Eastern influence which had its roots in European folk music. On our first album there's a couple of songs that were directly influenced by that song: 'The Good's Gone', for example.'

If the form is startling enough, the content is even more so. 'We always had a camp following,' says Dave Davies now, and 'See My Friends' makes explicit the androgyny that had been a major, if unacknowledged, weapon in the Kinks' armoury of shock tactics. Dave Davies: 'My sister Gwen wore slacks one day when she came to see us. We look a lot alike anyway, and some guy mistook her for me and asked for an autograph. You should have seen his face when she spoke.'

Instead of letting it worry them the Kinks derived maximum amusement from it. When the Kinks were sharing a dressing room with Dave Dee, Dozy, Beaky, Mick and Tich on a 1966 tour Dave Dee was swishing around doing the full camp pop star number. Dave

● **Late 1965**

● **Ray Davies as City gent; the Kinks in Soho, late 1965**

Davies simply walked over and gave him a prolonged, full French kiss. The Kinks had an aristocratic view of such matters. Ray Davies in particular was quite prepared to spell out what had always been a major, if covert, force behind the music industry in an interview with Maureen Cleave: 'The song is about homosexuality. I know a person in this business who is quite normal and good-looking, but girls have given him such a rotten deal that he becomes a sort of queer. He has always got his friends. I mean it's like football teams and the way they're always kissing each other. Same sort of thing.'

But 'See My Friends' was about something deeper. Ray Davies: 'It wasn't fiction. I can understand feeling like that. As it didn't come from a deliberate I-want-to-write-a-song-about-this, it's difficult to recall the memories. It's about being a youth who is not sure of his sexuality. I remember I said to Rasa one night, "If it wasn't for you, I'd be queer." I think that's a horrible thing to say to someone of seventeen, but I felt that. I was unsure of myself, and I still find it hard to relate to guys who are out with the lads. I remember boxing and at the end of the fight the trainer came on to me and said, "You've got to work on your stomach muscles," and put his hand on me and started feeling me up. On the surface they're all really mannish, real he-men, but it exists just *there*. That really made it, for me, a bit of a lie.

'Maybe I was becoming aware of how destructive women can be, how any kind of love affair can be disruptive. The song is about acceptance: that's the way the situation is, and you must tolerate it. That's not the way I was, so it's quite mature in that sense.

'I didn't know what I was writing. I just let the words come out. The best songs happen that way. It's a different type of song from "Dedicated Follower of Fashion". I remember sitting there at the typewriter and typing it out. I couldn't have done "See My Friends" that way. I probably made it up, unaware of what I was singing, because I was more interested in getting this funny sound, yet not being experienced enough to know how to write.'

The remarkable thing about 'See My Friends' is that it goes beyond the question of homosexuality – although the Kinks weren't above playing up to that – into the area of unfulfilled sexual longing. Ray Davies was to use the same metaphor to capture a similar feeling, that of longing and loss, in another of his greatest songs, 'Waterloo Sunset'. He was also to use the drone device to get to his innermost feelings in 'Fancy'.

Two years before the reform of the legislation governing homosexuality in England the message of 'See My Friends', such as it was, did not exactly go down a treat. Ray Davies: 'I know there was resistance to it. Maybe that was a good thing; it gave it some sort of notoriety. I remember that Keith Altham of the *New Musical Express* hated the record. I talked to him about duality and people, bisexuality and things like that, and the *NME* wouldn't print that sort of thing. They wanted us to be really normal, go-ahead 'all day and all of the night' boys – you know, have a pint and piss off. But I wasn't like that.' The rest of the pop media were more concerned about the fact that the Kinks were on the way down (*Pop Weekly*) or about rumours that they were breaking up (P. J. Proby in *Melody Maker*'s 'Blind Date'). Such speculation was neither confirmed nor denied by the record's middling chart placing.

'See My Friends' was also a victim of the increasingly acrimonious power struggles going on within the Kinks' management. The time bombs planted two years before were starting to explode. First, there was trouble between Shel Talmy and Larry Page, who had recorded 'Ring the Bells' with the Kinks in America after Shel Talmy had recorded the 'official' follow-up, 'See My Friends', in London. Because Shel Talmy had an exclusive contract to record the Kinks, there was a wrangle, and 'See My Friends' was delayed.

The US market denied to them, the Kinks were packed off for more tours of the UK, Scandinavia and Europe. In September a specially recorded Kinks EP was released with a tacky cover – the group still in their hunting jackets – and an even worse title, *Kwyet Kinks*. The record inside was a bit better; it contained a couple of moves further away from the Kinks' patent style: 'Wait Till the Summer Comes Along' was the first Dave Davies composition to be recorded by the Kinks, and is convincing in its adolescent self-pity; 'A Well Respected Man' shows that Ray Davies was now finally in a position to assimilate his surroundings fully and turn out a focused riposte. Ray Davies: 'I remember exactly when I wrote it, I'd come back from that American tour, and I was absolutely worn out; I wanted to go for a holiday, but they sent me to the Imperial Hotel in Torquay. I was asked to play golf with someone, and I felt myself being accepted into the "people who had made it" category. I didn't want that, so I wrote "A Well Respected Man". I finished it when the holiday was over, and we went and recorded it all in one.

'I got a lot of it from watching people at the debs' dances that we used to play. I noticed at those dances, the more military the beat, the more they liked it, and I guess there's an element of that. Also it might have been because Grenville had worked in the City and had been shamed and denounced by his friends for leaving. That must have rubbed off a bit, but it was more of a protest effort than anything else.'

'A Well Respected Man' is mercilessly funny, positing the outward, rigid control of the middle class with its mottos – *Mens sana in corpore sano,* for instance – against a jungle of sexual and social desires that, because repressed, burst out in virulent, if comic, forms. Ray Davies: 'I did it because it gave fun back to our outfit. Everyone was smiling at each other again and happy. But it's totally different from the other stuff. I didn't think it would work at first, but it did. Pye didn't want to release it as a single because it was different from what we'd done and it was kind of a bit cowardly, but it took off in America of all places. Because I say "fags" – you know what "fags" means in America – they loved that. They just think it's really, really risqué to do that.'

Its influence was immediate. Barry Fantoni: 'The impact was enormous, of course, but not one thing that

A Well-Respected Man

'Cause he gets up in the morning
And he goes to work at nine
And he comes back home at 5.30
Gets the same train every time
'Cause his world is built on punctuality it never fails

And he's oh so good
And he's oh so fine
And he's oh so healthy in his body and his mind
He's a well-respected man about town
Doing the best things so conservatively

And his mother goes to meetings
While his father pulls the maid
And she stirs the tea with councillors while discussing foreign trade
And she passes looks as well as bills at every suave young man

'Cause he's oh so good
And he's oh so fine
And he's oh so healthy in his body and his mind
He's a well-respected man about town
Doing the best things so conservatively

And he likes his own back yard
And he likes his fags the best
'Cause he's better than the rest
And his own sweat smells the best
And he hopes to grab his father's loot
When pater passes on

'Cause he's oh so good
And he's oh so fine
And he's oh so healthy in his body and his mind
He's a well-respected man about town
Doing the best things so conservatively

And he plays at stocks and shares
And he goes to the regatta
He adores the girl next door
'Cause he's dying to get at her
But his mother knows the best about the matrimonial stakes

'Cause he's oh so good
And he's oh so fine
And he's oh so healthy in his body and his mind
He's a well-respected man about town
Doing the best things so conservatively

● **Ready Steady Go, 31 December 1965**

anybody did affected Ray, whereas quite the reverse was true; people were very conscious of Ray's ability to write songs about things which weren't necessarily love songs.'

Another profound influence that the Kinks had at the time was on the business side. Pete Townshend: 'If there is one thing I owe to Ray, it's the fact that he was so shafted in his early publishing experiences. I knew exactly what to avoid, and so did my management.' This was one thing that Ray Davies was determined to sort out, and his managers would use the fact as leverage in their own particular power struggles. Ray Davies: 'It was a mutual decision to break with Kassner and Denmark Productions. You see, I said to Grenville one day in the canteen, "Grenville, I've written all these songs and really I'm on a treadmill. I'm living in an £8 flat, and I want to buy this little house. When I come back from tour I want Rasa and the baby to have a place to live." So, graciously, Kassner arranged a mortgage, an advance, after I'd written about eight hits. We all felt that we should change publishers, and the only way to do that was to get rid of Denmark.'

The Kinks were becoming victims of what was then a standard music industry practice: music publishers would water down any money owing to the musicians through various parent companies and overseas deals. Getting rid of Denmark Productions (which meant Larry Page) was something that Robert Wace and Grenville Collins had been wanting to do for a long time. There was no love lost between the two parties. Each side accused the other of stirring it up. The Kinks' management set-up, with its two camps, had always been unstable, and once the money started coming in the Kinks had become something worth fighting over. Both sides fought with the weapons to hand: Larry Page now alleges that Wace and Collins pandered to the Kinks' bad behaviour in a way that he would not, and that made the group turn against him, while Robert Wace presents Page as a greedy businessman who would stop at nothing to tie up the Kinks completely. The deciding factor in this squabbling was the attitude of the group itself, and they plumped for the people whom they knew and liked best.

Page found this hard to understand. He'd worked hard for the group, according to his own lights, hustling covers of Ray Davies's songs. But this, of course, was entirely in Page's own interest as Ray's publisher: the more songs that were covered, the more money he made. Furthermore, the relationship had its problems, highlighted by the release, in May 1965, of Larry Page's instrumental LP of Kinks songs, *Kinky Music*. It was neither a commercial nor a creative success. Ray Davies: 'It just took the basic line of the songs. It didn't add anything to them.' And the Kinks were operating, as they always had, in an orbit entirely different from the more traditional music business world of Page and Kassner. The uncharted territory that the Kinks, along with the popular music of the time, were about to enter demanded more skilful guidance than Denmark Productions could provide, so they were out.

The Kinks broke their agreement with Denmark

● **Dedicated Followers, early 1966**

Productions and Kassner Music by taking their publishing, in the autumn of 1965, to Carlin Music and by setting up their own company called Belinda. The ensuing row meant that the release of 'Till the End of the Day' was held up and that Ray Davies got no money from his songs, apart from airplay royalties, for a good four to five years. Ray Davies: 'What Carlin did was to put all the money in escrow. I didn't earn money on any of the songs, including "Waterloo Sunset", until the case was resolved in 1970. It took that long because of all the appeals. In fact the case was about Denmark and Boscobel. It was nothing to do with the Kinks.'

In the middle of November the Kinks released their ninth single, 'Till the End of the Day'. As well as being a direct love song, 'Till the End of the Day' was another coded message about the Kinks' own situation. Ray Davies: 'It was the end of 1965, and I said, "I can't write any more. I'm really having a dead patch." Mort Schuman, the song writer, came up to my house and wanted to corrupt me. He said, "Get chords that you like and enjoy and just write a song around them." And I wrote "Till the End of the Day" that night.

'I think "Till the End of the Day" is one of my best songs. I love playing it. We've reverted to the old way of playing it; we've changed the arrangement and made it sort of ska. I probably felt a bit imprisoned when I was writing it; it was a bid for freedom. The ideas are as sexually possessive as those of "All Day and All of the Night", but in the song there's a unity between the two people. It's a song about wanting to be free and being in control of the situation – that's all I wanted to say. It doesn't say that we're going to do anything when we get through. It's just about wanting to attain that state.'

'Till the End of the Day' is another excellent example of the Kinks' ability to create, and resolve, tension in a mesh which was to be wound to its pitch in the extraordinary 'Milk Cow Blues'. Even better was the single's other side, 'Where Have All the Good Times Gone?' Ray Davies: 'The good times are gone. It's being disillusioned after the up; it's thinking twice about things. That line about "Mama didn't need no boys, Papa didn't need no toys", it was just a phoney young person's attitude towards adults because what I really wanted to say was "Papa didn't need no boys", ha ha. I sing that now. But it

● 'No wonder we had a big gay following': early 1966

is a world-weary song.'

'Where Have All the Good Times Gone?' hooks the Kinks' audience ('Won't you tell me?') into a sharp piece of self-examination and self-criticism. It's the first Kinks song to admit to an attitude that was to become even more pronounced over the next few years. Basically, Ray Davies was unimpressed with the wild flights of fantasy of the 1960s pop culture and its insistence on youth, youth, youth ('Guess you need some bringing down/Get your feet back on the ground!'). At a time when it was definitely cool to hate your parents, Davies actually dared suggest that they might have some experience that was actually worthwhile. Although critical, the song became very much part of what Ray was protesting against; David Bowie was later to cover the song for his sentimental lookback at the golden age of English pop on the 1973 album *Pin Ups*.

Both songs were included on the next Kinks' LP, released in December 1965 in England, *Kinks Kontroversy* – the last in the notorious 'K' series. It is a unified, if subdued, piece of work. The dominant feeling of the album, with song titles like 'The World Keeps Going Round', 'I'm on an Island', 'You Can't Win', is one of isolation and powerlessness: as Sandy Pearlman said in the January 1968 issue of *Crawdaddy*, 'It's suddenly obvious that all the Kinks cynicism was yet another compact rationalization in the face of the abyss. Logically the abyss renders all conclusions questionable.' But, as ever, we should beware of taking anything, even the Kinks' own seriousness, too seriously. Ray Davies: '"I'm on an Island" is a fun song. It's not a down song at all, there's quite an ironical humour coming up there, for the first time.' The message is, never take anything at face value.

Early in 1966 Ray Davies busied himself with a couple of freelance projects, writing and producing 'I'm the King of the Whole Wide World' for Leapy Lee and 'Little Man in a Little Box' for his old art school friend Barry Fantoni, then a pop personality through his successful TV show *There's a Whole Scene Going*. It is an odd feature of almost every single Kinks cover of this time that they come out sounding exactly like Ray Davies, no matter who is recording it. Both these songs are interesting, if whimsical, curios. Much more substantial was the song that the Kinks were recording at the same time, which was to be their next single, 'Dedicated Follower of Fashion'.

Ray Davies: 'I remember I threw a party – I'm the greatest "It's My Party, and I'll Cry if I Want to" type, and I always have fights. I invite people along to the party and then throw them all out. There was a guy there who was a designer. He was on about some style, and I got pissed off with him. I said you don't have to be anything. You decide what you want to be, and you just walk down the street and if you're good, the world will change as you walk past. I still believe that. I wanted it to be up to the individual to create his own fashion. Anyway I had a fight with him, a terrible brawl. I kicked him, I kicked his girlfriend up the arse. It was awful, there was blood, I was grovelling in the gutter with him – it was sad. The next day I said to myself, "Fuck all this. This has got to stop. Take it out on your work,'' and I wrote that song, typed it up straight off.

'We did a demo, which was quite good but it sounded like a demo. People were hung up with our hard electric sound. That's why the beginning is really over-dubbed to sound hard, a really powerful sound. Then it goes into this almost weedy guitar. I think the top was added to give it more power. It was put through some sort of filter. The voice sounds very trebly, more trebly than usual. I was trying to sing it, accentuating the words, just making it as clear and as exaggerated and over the top as possible. No tricks, really. You can hardly hear bass at all on that record, but somehow it gave the song some kind of charm. I wasn't pleased with it, but when we'd recorded it three times, what more could we do?'

'Dedicated Follower of Fashion' continues in the same vein as 'Well Respected Man', albeit funnier and even more vicious. It is satirical, tackling its victims from a distance, journalistically rather than empathetically. Ray Davies's better songs are those that he writes from within his characters rather than from without; this distance and lack of empathy gives 'Dedicated Follower of Fashion' a flat, two-dimensional quality that makes it, for all its glorious detail, one of a piece with the phenomenon it was satirizing.

'During that period it always seemed like the sun was shining in Carnaby Street,' says Dave Davies today, and that's where Barry Fantoni filmed a promo for the song, with the Kinks running in and out of the clothes shops. Whether Ray Davies liked it or not, the Kinks were part of that same culture, and his own attempts to find a way out of this impasse were to succeed only when he was able to relate what was going on in the outside world to his own obsessions and feelings – a process that was not in evidence in 'Dedicated Follower of Fashion' but was to occur in a later series of remarkable records.

In the meantime, 'Dedicated Follower of Fashion' was the group's greatest success for a while, reaching number 2 in the charts in March/April 1966. It re-established the Kinks as trendsetters, quite apart from exciting more controversy – Fleet Street particularly homed in on the line 'When he pulls his frilly nylon panties right up tight' – and raising, once again, the whole question of homosexuality and camp. 'See My Friends' had been too elliptical, too subtle and too personal; this time the Kinks had come right out with it in a form that everybody found easy to understand – perhaps too easy. Ray Davies: 'That song was like having your cake and not only eating it, but throwing it away as well. I remember that was the first time that anybody told me I was camp, and I couldn't understand it. I think, however, that we got a few followers that we never had before! I remember that a guy who worked for our agency came to see us on *Top of the Pops*. I was singing "Dedicated", and I could see him in the audience; when I was doing things like acting out a song, he would purse his lips and shrivel up. He thought that we were really near the knuckle for straight blokes. But I just carried on what I was doing. I didn't feel wrong doing it.'

Ray Davies drew a portrait of the Kinks for the ad that

Dedicated Follower of Fashion

They seek him here
They seek him there
His clothes are loud
But never square
It will make or break him
So he's got to buy the best
'Cause he's a dedicated follower of fashion

And when he does
His little rounds
Round the boutiques
Of London town
Eagerly pursuing
All the latest fancy trends
'Cause he's a dedicated follower of fashion

Oh yes he is
Oh yes he is
He thinks he is a flower to be looked at
And when he pulls his frilly nylon panties right up tight
He feels a dedicated follower of fashion

Oh yes he is
Oh yes he is
There's one thing that he loves and that is flattery
One week he's in polka dots the next week he's in stripes
'Cause he's a dedicated follower of fashion

They seek him here
They seek him there
In Regent Street
And Leicester Square
Everywhere the Carnabetian
Army marches on
Each one a dedicated follower of fashion

Oh yes he is
Oh yes he is
His world is built round discotheques and parties
This pleasure-seeking individual always looks his best
'Cause he's a dedicated follower of fashion

Oh yes he is
Oh yes he is
He flits from shop to shop just like a butterfly
In matters of the cloth he is as fickle as can be
'Cause he's a dedicated follower of fashion
He's a dedicated follower of fashion
He's a dedicated follower of fashion

'Dedicated Follower of Fashion'
THE KINKS

● 4 March 1966

graced the front cover of the *New Musical Express* on 4 March 1966. It now appears to be rather more revealing that he perhaps intended. All four Kinks are drawn in the most hideous Carnabetian gear possible – striped shirts, kipper ties and flowered polo necks. Mick Avory and Pete Quaife are in the background, Pete posing as he always did; Dave Davies is in the foreground, slumped in a Regency attitude of dissipation. The focal point of the portrait is Ray Davies, who is sitting up primly, glaring at the world from behind darkened and narrowed eyes. This was even nearer the knuckle, for just after the release of 'Dedicated Follower of Fashion', Ray Davies collapsed in a truly spectacular nervous breakdown. As he said to Phil McNeill in his 1977 *New Musical Express* interview, 'I was a zombie. I'd been on the go from when we first made it till then, and I was completely out of my mind. I went to sleep and I woke up a week later with a moustache. I don't know what happened to me. I'd run into the West End with my money stuffed in my socks, I'd tried to punch my press agent, I was chased down Denmark Street by the police, hustled into a taxi by a psychiatrist, and driven off somewhere.'

Ray Davies: 'But it was a comedy. It was like that film *Morgan, a Suitable Case for Treatment* when I look back on it, but at the time it was deadly serious. I remember Robert came and picked me up with a doctor. I suppose it was all a bit near the mark. That's when they told me to take up golf! And all I remember is that Dave brought a tape in, some people who were auditioning, and I fell asleep. I woke up, I swear, five days later, and they'd gone on tour.'

● **Dave Davies, Chris Andrews, Pete Quaife,** Ready Steady Go, **31 December 1965**

TOO MUCH ON MY MIND

The Kinks became less of a band, less a bundle of ambition and lust for money, fame and fun, and more of a means to Davies' fantasies. He became a social critic, or more appropriate for rock'n'roll, a social complainer. He squeezed a few hits out of the stance, but the last chart success he got in the sixties crystallized his new view of the world and dropped the commercial bottom out of the group. 'Sunny Afternoon' (1966) could have been another put-down of the English middle class, but instead the hunter was captured by the game. This was an ode to upper-class boredom. The Kinks became a classy little outfit, neurotic, long on intelligence and short on raunch, and their album sales dropped into the low thousands.

*Greil Marcus, **Mystery Train**, 1975*

The net result...apart from the most crushing credit squeeze since the war, was a freezing of wages and prices for six months, if necessary enforceable by law. It was the beginning of an explosion into reality from all those years of inflation which had been the inevitable corollary to the greatest boom the British people had ever known. And when the full details of the Government's intentions were published on 29 July 1966, it was hardly surprising that at least one newspaper should have referred back to 20 July, when the 'freeze' had officially begun as the 'THE DAY IT ALL STOPPED'.

*Christopher Booker, **The Neophiliacs**, 1969*

If 1966 can now be seen as the year in which the boom officially stopped, then it was also the end of the pop music which had been predicated on that boom. 'The Year Pop Went Flat,' stated Maureen Cleave in the *Evening Standard*, 29 December 1966, offering as harbingers a high incidence of fake profundity, the return of all-round entertainers and smoke-windowed Mini Coopers. Part of this was the consequence of the excessive milking of new sensations by over-zealous record companies, but much had to do with the ennui of both the audience and the performers. The unified culture, a mixture of upward, downward and sideways class mobility, that had been such a fertile breeding ground for these new sensations, was beginning to break up as the novelty wore off, and the mass audience that had sustained that culture was fragmenting as the money got tighter and the demands for spiritual rather than social community grew from pop's avant garde. Youth, youth, youth was no longer quite as commercially desirable as record sales fell to their lowest levels since 1955 and the bottom fell out of youth's claims for special treatment.

Yet it was during this period that the Kinks' long struggle to define their own creative and financial terms started to pay off. This time Ray Davies's protest, implicit in his breakdown, was taken seriously; as he says now, 'I think they were wary about sending me on tour in case I cracked up. I remember Bobby Wace saying when he dropped me off at the airport, after the Scandinavian tour, "Well, Ray, there's nothing more we have to worry about, there's nothing planned."' The Kinks were entering a phase in which their lives were measured not so much in riots or all manner of dramas – although they had their fair share of these during the year – as in long studio hours and a sequence of haphazardly released but unique records. On the surface the Kinks' activities, for the remainder of 1966 at least, read like the usual record of disasters – a mess of cancelled dates – yet it was also a time when they could look inward and take some care about what they were doing. Ray Davies's astute ear caught, as it always does, the flavour of the times and then sought to define his opposition to it. The songs from this period began to chart the obsessions that were to remain constant during his professional life – namely, the complexity of familial relationships, the difficulty of finding a sense of place and the primacy of class.

Ray's breakdown caused an immediate problem for the Kinks, since they were on the eve of a tour of Belgium. Robert Wace had to hurriedly arrange for a substitute guitarist, Mick Grace from the Cockneys, and Dave Davies was forced to take over the vocals for the duration of the trip. But the long-term benefit soon became manifest. Ray Davies: 'I tried not to write, but

● **Mick Grace joins for ten days, March 1966**

when I was coming out of the breakdown I started. I wrote "End of the Season", "Sunny Afternoon", "Too Much On My Mind" and "I'm Not Like Everybody Else". I was very clear afterwards because my mind had been rested, and I went into "Sunny Afternoon", which was like magic. You just know when you've made a great record. I was in California recently, and I was trying to buy a pair of plimsolls. It came through on the radio there, though I didn't recognize it until my voice came on. It was nice – people in the shop, kids, were singing along to it. It's something that registers in people's heads. They may not have been around then, but they know history. It's like the Battle of Agincourt.

'I remember we were playing with a group called Billy J. Kramer and the Dakotas, and there was a guitar player with a glass eye. The day that Labour got in, he said we might as well all stop now. No point being in this business. I couldn't understand that attitude. I thought: "You can write songs. You can be on stage. They aren't going to stop you doing that." He was more concerned with the financial aspect, and that had a big effect. Maybe I was in a reflective mood at the time. The lyric "Save me, save me, from this squeeze" was the key line. You know what that means – "Big fat mamma", the government, Queen Victoria.'

'Sunny Afternoon' is remarkable also for the return of Ray Davies's crooning vocal, first revealed on 'Well Respected Man', which uncannily captures the English upper-class accent. Ray Davies: I didn't want to sound American. I was very conscious of sounding English.

'Whereas "You Really Got Me" was really hard to get together, "Sunny Afternoon" worked a treat. We rehearsed it at the end of the day on a Thursday night and we said, "Let's not do it tonight. Let's save it for tomorrow." I remember I didn't speak until I was in the studio. I was so sure everything would go right, and I even said to Shel, "You know it's the one take, Shel. That's it."'

As far as Shel Talmy is concerned 'Sunny Afternoon' is one of the records of the 1960s with which he is most pleased. It was more than a mere pop record: it defined a season, a time in history and an attitude. Its timing was perfect; released in June, it was at number 1 in July and stayed in the charts for two months, becoming the great summer record the year that Britain won the World Cup. Yet, more important, it captured perfectly the dying curve of Boomtime in an atmosphere of boozy, resigned regret.

The song also expresses Ray Davies's fear that the classlessness of the 1960s has made him rootless. If 'Sitting On My Sofa' was a garbled curse of class resentment, then in 'Sunny Afternoon' Ray Davies acknowledges his own complicity. That is what gives the song its emotional resonance. Davies realizes that he has exchanged one kind of prison for another; he is just as much a manifestation of that dying culture as the tower block or a smart club like the Scotch of St James and worse, he has cast himself adrift – he is neither fish nor fowl. In the end, 'Sunny Afternoon' is another in the line of Kinks songs about acceptance and loss, this time it's

Sunny Afternoon

The taxman's taken all my dough
And left me in my stately home
Lazing on a sunny afternoon
And I can't sail my yacht
He's taken everything I've got
All I've got's this sunny afternoon
Save me, save me, save me from this squeeze
I've got a big fat momma tryin' to break me
And I love to live so pleasantly
Live this life of luxury
Lazing on a sunny afternoon
In summertime
In summertime
In summertime

My girlfriend's run off with my car
And gone back to her ma and pa
Telling tales of drunkenness and cruelty
Now I'm sitting here
Sipping at my ice-cold beer
Lazing on a sunny afternoon
Help me, help me, help me sail away,
You give me two good reasons why I ought to stay
'Cause I love to live so pleasantly
Live this life of luxury
Lazing on a sunny afternoon
In summertime
In summertime
In summertime

● European product, 1965–6

about not sexuality but social placing, the feeling captured perfectly in the song's stately, perennial fade.

Barry Fantoni: 'His parents were people that were like my own. They were working-class which means that they were the mirror images, the *Doppelgangers,* of the extreme upper classes. Customs and ways of doing things were highly ritualized, organized and, for that reason, much more interesting. As long as they didn't try to break out, they were safe. Ray broke out and has been unsafe ever since. That's the problem. He feels perhaps a sense of betrayal because the one thing he would constantly say to me was that his songs were the kind that people would sing in the way they sang "Roll Out the Barrel". I remember a Christmas party at his house. Everyone was singing his songs, and it was the nearest I've ever come to seeing him display genuine emotion about his work. There were almost tears in his eyes. Subsequent events show that clearly that hasn't been the case. Popular songs of that kind happen only in a particular kind of ethos, and "Roll Out the Barrel" will forever be 'Roll Out the Barrel'. I don't think our generation will ever sing songs in quite that way.'

To emphasize the point, the Kinks put another solution to the same problem on the 'Sunny Afternoon' flip: 'I'm Not Like Everybody Else' expresses the logical summation of the art school attitude. Sung mainly by Dave Davies, written by Ray, the song captures well the way in which the two brothers worked: if the physical presence of 'I'm Not Like Everybody Else' is Dave's, then its intellectual and spiritual presence is Ray's. It could be a routine piece of pop breast-beating, yet the Kinks sound quite at the end of their tether. The crude instrumentation and simple fury of the song winds up in a holocaust of noise. For the final time in the 1960s Ray and Dave Davies gathered up all their multitudinous resentments and threw them in the face of the world with a violence that transcends the petty bohemianism of the subject matter, a violence that was not to be repeated for a good ten years, until the beginning of punk rock.

Just after the release of 'Sunny Afternoon', when the song was climbing up the charts, the Kinks had the latest and the most serious in a long line of accidents. Ray Davies: 'We were playing Morecambe Pier, up near Blackpool, and I said, "Pete, come out in the car with us," because he used to come to gigs on a scooter. He said he would come back in the van with Pete Jones because he wanted to talk to this girl. They had a crash on the way back. I didn't know about it until the next morning, when I watched Robert Dougall reading the news before *Grandstand*. He said, "Two of the members of the Kinks pop group are severely ill in hospital after a crash up north." Grenville heard about it, and he said, "Oh, good, good, anyone dead?" That was his way. I was a bit shattered by it. Then it made me more positive to go on.

'We had to find a replacement quickly, as we were going to do *Top of the Pops*. I was in a rehearsal room at Carlin Music and a guy called Bill Fowler, who was our plugger, brought in this guy who looked like he'd just walked off a building site. Handsome-looking boy. I said

● Pete Quaife as mod - early 1966

● John Dalton joins: Ready Steady Go, June 1966

"Who are you?" He said "Oh, I'm John Dalton. I've come to audition." I said "Have you got a bass?" He said "Yeah." "Play me a scale of D minor" (which was all we needed for "Sunny Afternoon"). He played it, and I said, "All right, you're in."

John Dalton: 'Then they said, "Do you fancy *Top of the Pops?* Do you fancy doing it tonight?" I said, "You're joking!" I must have looked so nervous. They tried to fit me out because I'd turned up there in a pair of jeans, which weren't very fashionable at the time. I think they got me one of Pete Quaife's coats, which came halfway up my arm, and I borrowed a pair of the road manager's trousers and some shoes and went on like that.'

Ray Davies: 'To my great delight we knocked the Beatles off number 1. They'd been there for just a week – that's one of the joys of my life'. Now it was time to renegotiate the deal with Pye. The Kinks and their management had long been frustrated with the deal but had been unable to do anything about it. Ray Davies: 'It was 1966, and I was sitting in the canteen at London Weekend Television, and I suddenly realized I'd got these hits and I hadn't got any money. I'd had to get a loan from Kassner to buy a house, and I was paying that back. I was getting something like £30 a week. I think Grenville said, "It's because our deal is so bad. The only person who can probably renegotiate it is Allen Klein, who's doing something for the Rolling Stones." So I agreed to go and see him in New York. I went over with my accountant. He sat me down in his office and said, "OK, Ray Davies, what do you want?" I said, "Money. What do you want?" He said, "I want the Beatles." It's rumoured that he offered Epstein a cheque for a million dollars. I think it was a straight enough answer to his question because that's the only reason I'd be sitting down with him, since everybody knew he was like the archetypal villain in a film.'

Klein's reputation in the music industry of the time was notorious. The publishing and recording contracts which had groups like the Rolling Stones and the Kinks tied down were anachronistic in relation to the hitherto unforeseen amounts of money now being made. No matter how watertight a contract, Klein would find a breach and use it as a basis for renegotiation, usually on vastly improved terms. Although in his eyes the Kinks were small fry, Klein did the trick with Pye Records, albeit at a price.

The negotiations with Klein dragged on for three months, throughout the late summer and early autumn, causing several gig cancellations and holding up the release of what was to become one of the Kinks best LPs, *Face to Face*. There was another uncertainty that kept the number of gigs down: after his crushed foot had healed, Pete Quaife decided to leave the Kinks in September 1966. In the event, his departure was a temporary one, but for some time his place was taken by Dalton.

Like other major 1960s groups, the Kinks were becoming creations of the studio, spending more and more time getting the product right and augmenting the basic four-man group sounds with sound effects and other instruments – mainly the harpsichord and various other keyboards played by Nicky Hopkins.

Dave Davies: 'I always remember that the birth of songs would be Ray at the piano. He would say, "What do you think?" and Rasa and I would start singing harmonies. I remember the early songs being very much like that. I don't know how Ray feels about it now, but I always felt that Rasa was a good influence on Ray at that point because she acted as a kind of catalyst between me and Ray. We're very, very different. I was always the one who was out having a good time, and Ray was much more reserved and thoughtful. I never used to think about it until I was about eighteen or nineteen, whereas she was in the middle of it and had a creative impact.'

Shel Talmy: 'I always remember the Kinks as being professional in the studio. I respected their opinion and they mine. They'd just come in and record. I think the studio was an oasis of sanity by comparison with what was going on outside.'

Face to Face finds the Kinks at their most baroque. Its brittle, complex sheen mirrors the exotic hot-house atmosphere of British pop at this time; it comes with the same sweet, if slightly sickly, atmosphere of *Revolver.* But perhaps even more than in *Revolver,* the fresh air is let in at regular intervals.

The Kinks were far too canny, at that stage, to get trapped in form. The record with its dreamlike, drugged languor, could be the sound track for the upper-class Chelsea party that ends the film *Blow Up*. Ray, like David Hemmings, is wandering through the English class system, alienated yet fascinated, lost yet captured. By the time of *Face to Face* Ray Davies was able to express vocally a wide variety of points of view charting his own ambivalences, which were beginning to be articulated fully in his songs.

Ray Davies has always been one of pop music's most defended personalities, but here the mask slips in a series of songs that reveal, behind his characteristically elliptical and understated style, some central conflicts. 'Rainy Day in June', with its thunderstorms, uses the weather as a metaphor for a violent change of mood. Ray Davies: 'It was from my fantasy in the back garden. I love rain and the moistness after a storm, and it was about fairies and little evil things within the trees that come to life. The springboard line was "There was no hope or reasoning, that rainy day in June." It's a confrontation with reality in a sense, except it's in a fairy tale.

'Too Much on My Mind' is disturbingly self-evident, as is 'Rosy Won't You Please Come Home', which posits Ray Davies as a mother of a girl who, 'since she joined the upper classes, doesn't know us any more'. Rasa Davies: 'Rosie, his sister, lives in Australia. I remember he'd gone to Australia when I was expecting Louisa, and he obviously became very sentimental about the whole thing. He wrote "Rosy Won't You Please Come Home" because he was very close to her.' The song also expresses Ray Davies's own regret and loss at leaving home for his new, classless life, but, as the song makes quite clear, 'changing his mind' is not a viable option.

'Fancy' stands as one complete statement of Ray

Fancy

*Fancy
If you believe in
What I believe in
Then we'll be the same
Always*

*Fancy
Just look around thee
If you will fancy
All the girls you see
Always*

*My love is like a ruby
That no one can see
Only my fancy
Always*

*No one can penetrate me
They only see
What's in their own fancy
Always*

● **Pye Studios, April 1966**

● Live, April 1966

Dead End Street

There's a crack up in the ceiling
And the kitchen sink is leaking
Out of work and got no money
A Sunday joint of bread and honey
What are we living for?
Two-roomed apartment on the second floor
No money comin' in
The rent collector's knocking, trying to get in
We are strictly second-class and don't understand

Why should we be on Dead End Street
People are living on Dead End Street
Have to live on Dead End Street
Dead End Street

On a cold and frosty morning
Wipe my eyes and stop me yawning
And my feet are nearly frozen
Pour the tea and put the toast on
What are we living for?
Two-roomed apartment on the second floor
No chance to emigrate
I'm deep in debt – now it's much too late
People want to work so hard we can't get a chance

People live in Dead End Street
People are dying on Dead End Street
I'm gonna die on Dead End Street
Dead End Street

Davies's philosophy. Ray: 'I remember writing ''Fancy'' really late one night. I think I wrote the song after ''Sunny Afternoon'' came out because I had this silly old Framus guitar that I played on all those records. I had the wrong strings on it, but it had a nice quality. It was a picking sound, and I could sustain one note, as Indian music does. I didn't intend it to be that way, really. A friend of mine didn't like the words ''Fancy all the girls you see''. They were too specific for her. But I question that because sometimes you got to make people feel at ease, just put something normal in. It's not a rule, but sometimes it's wrong to be totally off the wall. The song deals with perception. I think love is like something that you hold. You've got to put love in your hand like *that*, but you must never grasp it. That's the secret. If you grasp it, it goes away. It's got to be allowed to shine. That line ''My love is like a ruby that nobody can see'', it's a bit possessive but it's charming. And ''No one can penetrate me'' – what can I say about that? A virgin! It's inside me, really. When I started writing that it was at the time when people really wanted to find out what was wrong with me. All my life I've been able to keep them out.'

Face to Face was put out with what now seems like the perfect precious pop art sleeve, a riot of multi-coloured psychedelic butterflies. Ray Davies is not particularly enthusiastic: 'I didn't like that sleeve. I wanted the cover to be black and strong like the sound of the LP, instead of all those fancy colours. I was starting to let things go and accepting things that I shouldn't have.'

Face to Face brought the Kinks some credibility, but it didn't sell, and you can't eat credibility. It was time for another hit single. The Kinks recorded 'Dead End Street' with John Dalton and released it in the middle of November, two weeks after the LP. Ray Davies: 'I wanted to write a song, a modern-day depression song, like the songs of the American Depression, because I felt that's what was happening around me. It's a jovial song, really, in a minor key. It's about people who've got no way out, saying, ''What's gone wrong? We were promised the good life – what are we living for?''

'It's all about people who weren't chic enough and didn't have access to drugs. It's about two people who were possibly living in Wakefield. Rasa came from Bradford. She was born in Germany, and her parents were in a displaced persons camp. I think I picked up a lot of it from them. I used to go up to Bradford a lot, and her dad used to talk to me about hard times. I wasn't being fooled by all the euphoria that was around; people were taking a lot of drugs because they didn't want to see. I was trying to see things, but people rejected it; even though it was quite a big hit, they rejected the idea of it.

'There's a nice trombone sound on ''Dead End Street''. Originally it was a French horn part and it sounded really pompous. The recording that Shel had done was wrong. I went back in on the Friday night, and we redid it. We used two basses on that, Dave playing the ordinary one and Dalton playing a Danelectro, which is a really trebly sound. If you listen carefully you can hear two bass guitars. I play the stodgy piano for which I am famed. Then we got to the ending: the horn player whom we normally used was a guy called Albert Hall. Albert was doing a gig that night, and I thought, "Well, what about a trombone?" So we sent Grenville and Robert out to the pub. We found this guy called John Matthews and we dragged him in. He learned the part, and then we asked him to improvise at the end. Shel came in the next day and heard the new version. Thinking it was his, he said, "It's great. I don't know what you want to do!"'

In 'Dead End Street' Ray Davies works through his obsession with the upper class, gets it and his own position in perspective and comes out the other side. A year and a half on Ray reaches back to his time spent with Rasa in that tiny Muswell Hill flat – and even further back, to his working-class youth – and pulls out a remarkable song, which is perhaps the only one of the period to capture what was actually happening (as opposed to what people wished was happening) in an age of delusion. While most of the pop world was chasing the premises of Boomtime into a new Nirvana, a false reality based on drugs, Ray Davies saw the reality behind the situation – a Britain where unemployment figures were rising rapidly, a Britain where LSD meant £sd, and not enough of it.

The song derives its deep resonance from the tension between the plaintive beginning and the angry chorus, with its clenched-fist yells. Its reeling, carnival fade-out suggests that, like Arthur Seaton in the film *Saturday Night and Sunday Morning*, the Kinks weren't going to let the bastards grind them down.

The song's flip side, like those of so many other Kinks singles of this period, is equally remarkable. 'Big Black Smoke' is a splendidly Dickensian tale about the frailest, purest girl in the world, who is seduced by the bright lights of the big city and is 'dragged down by the big black smoke'. The song is perfect: the booming, descending bass lines chart this particular pilgrim's progress while church bells and town-crier yells from Dave make explicit the chaos and squalor implicit in the song's title, a phrase originating from early Victorian times. Here the Kinks reinvent the potent myth that surrounds the great English social commentators of the eighteenth and nineteenth centuries, Dickens and Hogarth – connections hinted at by the Kinks' first costumes.

Ray Davies: 'It's a very London song. It's about the evils of the big city. I was just fascinated with the line "She put on her pretty coloured clothes", which is about a girl who comes to London and ends up as a prostitute somewhere like Euston. I knew a girl who was like that. She died of junk. She ran our first fan club. It was a bit about her, really. And I liked the way that Hogarth really tells things the way they are in his pictures. Possibly the song came more from Hogarth than Dickens – a lot of visual ideas.'

Ray Davies's visions were becoming increasingly cinematic in their complexity, atmosphere and scope, and even at this early stage he was aware of their visual potential. Late in 1966 the Kinks made a pop promo for 'Dead End Street', in and out of coffins near Camden Town. The film was banned by the BBC, but the record still shot up the charts, reaching number 5 over the

● **Pye Art Department sleeve,** Face to Face

● The first depression song, 'Dead End Street', in Rock Dreams, 1973

● **Pete Quaife returns, November 1966**

● **The Melody Maker Eleven, March 1967**

Christmas season. In retrospect, 'Dead End Street' and 'Big Black Smoke' represent the pinnacle of Ray Davies's career as a social commentator, dealing as they do with subjects with which very few people were concerned at the time.

For a brief period Ray Davies and the Kinks were off the treadmill: they had won their battles, and the frenetic touring had stopped; and Ray Davies was able to use the extra time to record what he wanted in the way that he wanted. In his 1977 interview with Phil McNeill he remembers the few months around the time of 'Waterloo Sunset' as 'one of the happiest times of my life. I had my friends; I used to play football on a Sunday; life was music and writing, touring with the band.'

After several months of inactivity the Kinks released a couple of singles within a month. The first of these had been recorded especially for the large market that the Kinks had in Europe, 'Mr Pleasant'/'This is Where I Belong'. Although as good as most other records at the time, it pales by comparison with the second of the Kinks' three releases from this time, 'Waterloo Sunset'. Ray Davies: 'I woke up singing it in my sleep. I used to put a notebook by the bed, which made things impossible for poor Rasa. I woke up singing it like Frank Sinatra. It was in a swing mode – that was how I first heard it. Then I went to the piano and played it. I thought it was quite nice, yet so different for us I thought twice about doing it. I wanted to write a song about a Liverpool sunset because of the death of Merseybeat and all that. Then I thought, I'm a Londoner, why all the tributes to Liverpool? I have a real passion for London and it was also a very personal song.

'I was in hospital, at St Thomas, for an operation when I was a kid. I nearly died. I had a tracheotomy and the balloon burst. I was attached to a machine and I had a nightmare and pulled all the things out of my arms. Then two or three or four days later I couldn't speak because of the operation. Two nurses wheeled me out on to the balcony, where I could see the River Thames. It was just a very poetic moment for me. So I thought about that time – I wanted to write a really great London song.

'There's no memory of that song that isn't a pleasure. I went over to Dave's and I played him the chords and said, "What do you think?" He said, "It's really good. What are you gonna to do about the middle?" I went back and the first thing I did was write the middle – simply, "chilly chilly evening time". Then we went into the studio and tried it. Shel wanted to do it a certain way and we used Nicky Hopkins on it, but it just didn't happen. So I went secretly to Mick and Dave because I wanted them to play in a certain way. I played acoustic really loud and got Mick to beat hard. It's the only record where I think Dave is playing an arrangement because he didn't know what to play on it. So I got guitar, bass and drums down first. Then I got Dave working on the middle. When the time came to put the vocals on, I did it in one take, double-tracked part. Then I got the back-up singers there – Rasa, Pete and Dave. I think I sang as well. It was just wonderful. When it came to the final "Waterloo Sunset" line, I think it was Rasa who suggested the really high har-

● **Late 1966**

● Mid-1967

monies as a peak.'

Dave Davies: 'We spent a lot of time trying to get a different guitar sound, to get a more unique feel for the record. In the end we used a basic tape-delay echo, but it sounded new because nobody had done it since the 1950s. I remember Steve Marriott of the Small Faces came up and asked me how we'd got that sound. We were almost trendy for a while.'

Ray Davies: 'When the record was finished, and it was coming out, I got Rasa to drive me down to Waterloo Bridge to see if the atmosphere was right. This was at night time. Ever since then it's become my centre. I've never worked with a song that has been a total pleasure from beginning to end like that one.'

The true achievement of 'Waterloo Sunset' is to turn the everyday – for what is more mundane than commuters? – into something of wonder and mystery. It is an elegiac masterpiece of recaptured experience. Like 'Sunny Afternoon' and 'You Really Got Me', 'Waterloo Sunset' traps a moment in history and a mood: Ray Davies's uncanny ear catches in this record a sense of possibility that was more expansive and more profound than most of what the new psychedelic groups – many of whom, like the Doors, Love and Jefferson Airplane, were freely to acknowledge the Kinks' influence on their work – were able to come up with.

At that time that was not thought to be important. More interesting was the story that Ray Davies was planning to 'do a Brian Wilson' (lead singer with the Beach Boys) and retire from live performances with the Kinks. This was speedily retracted, and with true perversity the Kinks recorded a scream-drenched live LP – to be released seven months later – exactly at the time when their touring was falling off.

Live at the Kelvin Hall catches the Kinks on a good night, full of smashing guitar chords, audience sing-alongs and hits recorded in the then favoured amphetamine style. This was becoming an exception rather than the rule. Barry Marshall worked with the Arthur Howes Agency at the time: 'Basically because the Kinks were unpredictable, there were fights and problems, and nobody ever knew if they were going to show up. When they did, it was often rather untogether and a bit of a shambles. So Ray got into the community singing thing with the audience to cover up things while they put their gear back together again. Once they got going, it was fine. I remember Bill Fowler used to feed Dave cups of tea on stage until Dave realized he was awake.'

Waterloo Sunset

Dirty old river must you keep rolling
Flowing into the night
People so busy, make me feel dizzy
Taxi lights shine so bright
But I don't need no friends
As long as I gaze on Waterloo sunset
I am in paradise
Every day I look at the world from my window
The chilly, chilliest evening time
Waterloo sunset's fine (Waterloo sunset's fine)

Terry meets Julie Waterloo Station
Every Friday night
But I am so lazy don't want to wander
I stay at home at night
But I don't feel afraid
As long as I gaze on Waterloo sunset
I am in paradise
Every day I look at the world from my window
The chilly, chilliest evening time
Waterloo sunset's fine (Waterloo sunset's fine)

Millions of people swarming like flies
Round Waterloo underground
But Terry and Julie cross over the river
Where they feel safe and sound
And they don't need no friends
As long as they gaze on Waterloo sunset
They are in paradise
Waterloo sunset's fine (Waterloo sunset's fine)

BAD DAYS

The thing you have to remember about the Kinks is that until 1967 they weren't even house-trained.

Robert Wace in conversation, 1984

The recent Festival at Monterey made an important statement; it therefore becomes trivial to discuss the merits of the acts which are performed there, or the validity in the appearance or non-appearance of certain acts. The Kinks were not present, neither were they missed. For they were surely there in spirit.

*Andy Wickham, sleevenote, **The Live Kinks: An Orgy for Ears**, 1967*

● Summer 1967

By the middle of 1967 the Kinks appeared to be hitting another peak, but several factors were eating away at their success. First, they still lacked the management or the record-company support that could capitalize on and develop this new position. Indeed, they were to spend much of the second half of the year involved in the litigation between Boscobel Productions and their erstwhile managers, Denmark Productions.

Also the musical climate had changed: the focus had shifted from singles to LPs, from the metallic precision of 1965-6 to the loose, ragged edges of 1967. More important, it had shifted from the UK to the USA. The Kinks were debarred from this new source of energy and revenue. Because of their four-year ban they were consigned to the backwater of UK and European chart success, and even that could not be guaranteed. The Kinks had become profoundly out of sync, a position they may well have liked in theory, but which in practice nearly meant the end of the group. Although their songs' subtleties might reflect the prevailing pop mood in the UK at the time, it was no match for the napalm tactics then *de rigueur* in the USA.

The Monterey Festival is notable not just for all the future corpses that litter it but also for the musical bludgeoning that goes on throughout every set. From Janis Joplin to Jimi Hendrix, from the Who to Otis Redding, all overact, overstate and oversimplify. Monterey was the beginning of stadium rock.

However, the next thing that happened surprised everybody. A month after 'Waterloo Sunset' Dave Davies had a massive international hit with his first solo record, 'Death of a Clown'. Dave Davies: 'That was a tune which I wrote on the piano at my mum's house.

'I walked in one day, sat down and played it. Ray suggested a few ideas for a session, and we just did it. Everybody liked it and Robert pushed for getting it out as a single. But I was really depressed then. I remember writing minor chords, very reflective of my melancholic periods. Sometimes I would have liked people to leave me alone, so that I could just sit down and not have to entertain people socially. I suppose I was expected to always be up when I didn't really feel like it. "Death of a Clown" was a gesture: "Leave me alone, I'm not a performing seal."'

Superficially, it was business as usual for Dave. As Keith Altham wrote in a May 1967 interview in the *New Musical Express*: 'We are, of course, worried about Dave! Ray's younger brother has grown big bushy sideboards like privet hedges and taken to wearing a Noddy hat about the London clubs. One attempt was made recently to set fire to his sideboards with a gas lighter but the whiskers withstood the flame.' However 'Death of a Clown' sets Dave's fierce intensity against a tune and a subject worthy of it. The echoed bar-room piano and strummed guitar matches perfectly Dave's hoarse vocal and the coded lyrics of self-pity couched in Dylanesque phrases; topped by the astonishing appearance of the Charles II dandy in full flight, it could hardly fail.

The record at last brought Dave Davies – always the glamour of the Kinks but until now in his brother's sha-

● **'Death of a Clown' on** Top of the Pops, **August 1967**

● **August 1967**

dow – into the spotlight. His solo career was launched, followed later on in the year by 'Susannah's Still Alive', which is one of the Kinks' best productions of the period, with its massive piano and bass riff.

Ray Davies: 'I remember I was in the bar at *Top of the Pops* when Dave did "Susannah's Still Alive". He looked stunning. He had a good leather jacket on, and his appearance was the focal point of the show. I was there with Richard Green who said, "He could be wonderful." But it wasn't handled properly.'

Their management had other things on its mind; in May Boscobel Productions were the defendants in a suit brought by Denmark Productions following the Kinks' defection to Belinda/Carlin late in 1965. Denmark alleged that Boscobel had broken the original management agreement made in 1964, but Boscobel counter-attacked by alleging that Denmark had in fact broken the agreement through Larry Page's breach of professional duty when he left the Kinks in the lurch in Hollywood in July 1965. The old enmity between Larry Page and the Boscobel team, Robert Wace and Grenville Collins, which had led to the break in 1965, resurfaced in the courts and in print.

The Kinks had to relive that disastrous 1965 tour of America in court. Dave Davies: 'I remember I had to give evidence. I was really nervous and I didn't want to give evidence, so I said, "I've got a sore throat and I can't speak." The barrister said to the judge, "If the court pleases, Mr Davies has a very bad throat today, so he will be speaking very quietly." And I ended up shouting. I was pointing at Larry Page in the dock and shouting and everybody was laughing. It was total uproar. It was wonderful.'

The case dragged on into appeal throughout 1968. Ray Davies: 'I had a very good judge, Judge Widgery, who went on to be the Lord Chancellor. Denmark's case was presented so cleverly: they were fighting it as a breach of management agreement. On the second day Lord Widgery said, "I know nothing about the music business but this is about publishing. It is not about management." He said in his summing up that we should fight it on infancy, because Dave was under twenty-one when he signed the contract. We decided in the end that it had to be a draw. All I can remember was that I was in the witness box for two days and I wasn't supposed to speak to anyone. I felt like a real criminal.'

Eddie Kassner: 'What happened was that the judge said in the first case (which became a lawbook case) that the contract was invalid because Larry abandoned them over there in Hollywood. Then we went to appeal and we got the right to keep the songs; we made an arrangement with the lawyers that all songs published or recorded until that time (that means up to and before 'Till the End of the Day') belonged to us for the copyright term and that new songs would go to Carlin. As you know, the copyright term is fifty years after the death of a composer; that's international copyright law.'

Besides these star court appearances and Dave Davies's solo career, the Kinks were starting to diversify. Ray Davies was already announcing plans to write a TV

Death of a Clown

● Summer 1967

My make-up is dry and it cracks on my chin
I'm drowning my sorrows in whiskey and gin
The lion tamer's whip doesn't crack any more
The lions, they won't fight and the tigers won't roar

So let's go and drink to the death of a clown
Won't someone help me to break up this crown
Let's all drink to the death of a clown
Let's all drink to the death of a clown

The old fortune teller lies dead on the floor
Nobody needs fortunes told any more
The trainer of insects is crouched on his knees
And frantically looking for runaway fleas

So let's go and drink to the death of a clown
Won't someone help me to break up this crown
Let's all drink to the death of a clown
Let's all drink to the death of a clown

show for the Kinks – an ambition which was not to come to any kind of fruition for a good couple of years – and, more important, he had begun to produce the group full-time on the departure of Shel Talmy. Talmy now insists that his contract with the Kinks had run out, but it is clear that he was also in the way of Ray Davies's own definite views about how things should be done. Talmy's decisive approach had been vital for the Kinks when singles had to be recorded in a day squeezed between one-nighters, and his own sound had been an important part of the Kinks' success. But now that they were the creation of the studio, with all the time in the world, he was becoming superfluous. Ray Davies had re-recorded the last two Kinks singles behind his back, and nobody noticed, least of all Talmy.

Ray Davies now feels that his taking over production was a mistake: 'I feel I shouldn't have been allowed to produce *Something Else*. What went into an album required someone whose approach was a little bit more mundane.'

Davies's assessment is correct: despite some of the best songs the Kinks were ever to write, *Something Else* is less than the sum of its parts. It reflects its piecemeal recording: it is a patchwork quilt of the old upper-class Kinks of 1966, the crystalline pop group of 1967, and the whimsy that was to follow in 1968.

The Kinks were withdrawing into their own world, a process caught by the Art Nouveau nostalgia of the sleeve and the dreadful boosterism of the sleevenotes: 'Welcome to Davies land, where all the little Kinklings in the magic Kinkdom wear tiny black bowlers, rugby boots, soldier suits, drink half-pints of bitter, carry cricket bats and ride in little tube trains.'

The album kicks off nice and smooth, with one of Davies's sharpest homoerotic songs, 'David Watts'. Ray Davies: 'David Watts is a real person. He was a concert promoter in Rutland. We played a concert up in Peter-borough, and he seemed like a regular army type. He said to us, "Look, boys, it's a bit of a shithouse out here. Why don't you change in my house?" I said, "Oh thank you, Mr Watts." But I did notice he had white socks on. Anyway we did the gig, and afterwards he said, "Would you like to come back for a little celebration?" I said, "Yeah, why not? We're not doing anything. We'll be home in a couple of hours." We had a few glasses of pink champagne and all these men kept arriving, all the not-able people in Rutland, escorted by little boys! Mick and Dave homed in on the situation and Mick started danc-ing. Mick's trousers fell down, and I said to David Watts, "Don't you fancy that big hunky drummer?" He said, "Get lost, sweetie, it's your brother I'm after." I thought, "This is the chance to get Dave set up."

'We had bottles and bottles of champagne and I said, "Dave, listen, I know you don't write a lot of songs and I'm a bit worried about the future. Get clued into this – I think he's in love with you." Dave went out to the gar-den, where they had some swings, and I said to David Watts, "Well, you might be all right. He's my brother, and I'm very protective of him. If there's a liaison between you, a friendship or an affair, I want to ensure that Dave

● **'Autumn Almanac',** Top of the Pops, **November 1967**

Autumn Almanac

From the dew-soaked hedge creeps a crawly caterpillar
When the dawn begins to crack
It's all part of my Autumn Almanac
Breeze blows leaves of a musty-coloured yellow
So I sweep them in my sack
Yes, yes, yes, it's my Autumn Almanac
Friday evenings people get together
Hiding from the weather.
Tea and toasted, buttered currant buns
Trying to compensate for lack of sun
Because the summer's all gone

Oh! my poor rheumatic back!
Yes, yes, yes, it's my Autumn Almanac

I like my football on a Saturday
Roast beef on Sunday's alright
I go to Blackpool for my holidays
Sit in the open sunlight
This is my street and I'm never gonna leave it
And I'm always gonna stay
If I live to be ninety-nine
'Cause all the people I meet
Seem to come from my street
And I can't get away
Because it's calling me
Come on home, come on home

Oh! my Autumn Almanac
Yes, yes, yes, it's my Autumn Almanac

gets half of the house!'' They sat there on a swing together, holding hands! But Dave didn't fancy him, it's as simple as that. David Watts was a bit shattered by it. But we became good friends and we often went to his house when we passed it on the road. Whenever he heard the song he said, ''You bums writing that song. You bums!'' He is a wonderful man, one of the greatest people I've ever met.'

Dave Davies confirms the story, merely adding, 'I think I should have had some say in the matter!'

Ray Davies: 'The song was about admiration, like for a prefect or a sports captain. There was a boy called Denton at school who was the head of football. He had all the best girls after him. It's just like Flashman. ''David Watts'' is all about winning the favour of this guy.'

The album's other gem was the extraordinary 'Two Sisters'. Ray Davies: '''Two Sisters'' is a classic song. It's got a couple of heart-wrenching lines in it – I love to come up with those. What I'll do is play a little game like chess and make mediocre moves, then I'll come in with a killer. ''When she saw her little children she decided she was better off'': you're waiting for the end to get the hook line, you see. ''Two Sisters'' is about Dave and me in a way – I was the dowdy one.'

Despite the fact that *Something Else* was as good as any other record released that year, the Kinks failed to establish themselves in the new album market. *Something Else* sold least well of all the Kinks' LPs to date, only reaching number 35 in the charts in October of that year, just when their new single, 'Autumn Almanac', was going up the charts for its three-month run.

Ray Davies: 'It was a very up song about a man, a contented little gardener, who does his job and says to himself, ''When the winter comes I sweep all the leaves up and put them in my sack, my autumn almanac.'' We used to have a hunchback gardener called Charlie. There is one line, ''Oh my poor rheumatic back'', because I suffer from a spine problem. So I thought I would throw that in for the people who knew me.' What other groups were to use as frills, the Kinks were to use as form.

There was a vogue at the time for running various recorded instruments backwards to spice up what were otherwise conventional pop songs. Ray Davies decided to construct a whole song this way: first he wrote the middle – 'I go to Blackpool for my holidays' – and then he reversed the tape. The sound that came out was like 'Autumn Alman-I-ac', and that formed the basis for the rest of the song. Ray Davies: 'I was going through a period of trying to experiment with reverses and words and vowels. That was what was good about that song. I thought it was the best single. There was a guy at the BBC who said, ''You're going to be known for a long time for that song. Brass bands will play it.'' It would be nice on a brass band. I felt I really had achieved another step, just like I did with ''Waterloo Sunset''.'

But the success of 'Autumn Almanac' meant that the Kinks' course was set in this brave new world. Whether they liked it or not, they were a singles group and, as everybody was beginning to know, singles were for teeny boppers. Soon even this market was to fall away from them.

Six months after 'Autumn Almanac', the Kinks emerged from a long hibernation with a new package tour and a new 45, in a concerted attempt to consolidate this apparently new market. It was ill-judged. 'Wonderboy' is one of the most opaque and, in John Mendelsohn's phrase, 'one of the most irresistible of the Kinks' popcorn singles'. It is certainly one of the campest; but its effete la-la-las and characteristic sloppiness hides an extraordinary Ray Davies lyric. Ray Davies: 'That was one of John Lennon's favourite Kinks songs. What the song is about is looking at a child for the first time and wondering what's going to happen in its life – how fucked-up it's going to be when it gets into the world. "Wonderboy, some mother's son" is probably the line that triggered it off. We were about to have our second daughter, Victoria: maybe I wanted a boy.

'I also thought I'd experiment as a song writer because I was a big fan of those older writers like Cole Porter and Irving Berlin. I had the two things happening and I'd thought I'd experiment. On paper, as it's written, it's one of my favourite songs.'

'Wonderboy' now arrives with a characteristic Davies disclaimer, but in truth it juggles its ambiguities brilliantly. A profoundly serious song, it is couched in candyfloss; Ray Davies's characteristic confusion about what the world is comes up against the incontrovertible fact of birth. His simple joy at the event is balanced by the song's devastating pay-off. In the end the song captures an essential human feeling: that feeling of loss that lies at the heart of any love affair, whether parental or sexual. In its concentration upon the subject of early childhood, it is not surprising that it was John Lennon's favourite song, for it was he who spent most of his career trying to work out these crucial first five years of our lives.

The record was not a commercial success: it peaked at 35, the Kinks' worst chart showing since their first hit. By this time they were embroiled in their package tour, with a classic bill: this year's pretty boys, the Herd, closeted with last year's brickies, the Tremeloes, with the Kinks cast as dirty old men. It was a disaster. Ray Davies: 'Everyone was panicking because "Wonderboy" wasn't sounding like a hit record. Among the management and the agent, Danny Detesh, there was definitely a sense that the band wouldn't go on for much longer. I remember Danny came backstage when the record flopped and said, "Well, you've had a good run. You've enjoyed it." As if it was all over for us. It was an uncomfortable tour to do as the Tremeloes were on an up-swing. They'd had a couple of silly hits, and we were never very accomplished on stage. We felt uncomfortable, particularly because we hadn't had any chart records and that affects the way you play.'

The two EPs released to capitalize on the Kinks' tour both flopped, and the general feeling in the business was that the Kinks had had it. This pessimism was temporarily relieved by another wonderful Kinks 45, 'Days'. Ray Davies: 'I remember playing it when I was at Fortis Green the first time I had a tape of it. I played it to Brian, who

Wonderboy

Wonderboy
Life's just begun
Turn your sorrow into wonder
Dream along, don't sigh, don't run
Life is only what you wonder
Day is as light as your brightest dream
Night is as dark as you feel it ought to be
Time is as fast as the slowest thing
Life is lonely
Wonderboy
Wonderboy
Everybody's looking for the sun
People strain their eyes to see
But I see you
And you see me
And ain't that wonder
Wonderboy
Some mother's son
Life is full of work and wonder
Easy go life is not real
Life is only what you conjure
Wonderboy
And the world is joy
Every single day
It's the real McCoy
Wonderboy
Some mother's son
Turn your sorrow into wonder
Dream along
Go have your fun
Life is lonely
Life is lonely
Life is lonely

Days

Thank you for the days
Those endless days
Those sacred days you gave me

I'm thinking of the days
I won't forget a single day
Believe me

I bless the light
I bless the light
That lights on you
Believe me

And though you're gone
You're with me
Every single day
Believe me

Days I'll remember all my life
Days when you can't see wrong from right
You took my life
But then I knew
That very soon you'd leave me
But it's all right
Now I'm not frightened of this world
Believe me

I wish today
Could be tomorrow
The night is dark
It just brings sorrow
Let it wait

Days

NEW SINGLE

THE KIN

WONDERB

7N17468

PYE DISTRIBUTED BY PYE RECORDS (SALES) LTD.
A.T.V. HOUSE GREAT CUMBERLAND PLACE LONDON W.1

 The last package tour, April 1968

★SEE THEM ON TOUR★

Sat.	April	6	Granada, Mansfield
Sun.	,,	7	Granada, Walthamstow
Mon.	,,	8	Granada, Bedford
Tues.	,,	9	ABC, Exeter
Wed.	,,	10	ABC, Gloucester
Thurs.	,,	11	Capitol, Cardiff
Sat.	,,	13	Newcastle City Hall
Sun.	,,	14	De Montford Hall, Leicester
Mon.	,,	15	Town Hall, Birmingham
Tues.	,,	16	ABC, Northampton
Wed.	,,	17	ABC, Peterborough
Thurs.	,,	18	ABC, Chesterfield
Fri.	,,	19	ABC, Chester
Sun.	,,	21	Empire Theatre, Liverpool
Mon.	,,	22	Odeon, Manchester
Wed.	,,	24	ABC, Cambridge
Thurs.	,,	25	Granada, Slough
Fri.	,,	26	Central Hall, Chatham
Sat.	,,	27	Bournemouth Winter Gardens
Sun.	,,	28	Coventry Theatre

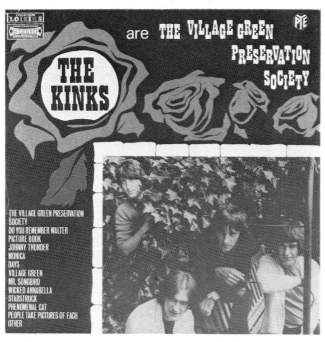

THE VILLAGE GREEN PRESERVATION
SOCIETY
DO YOU REMEMBER WALTER
PICTURE BOOK
JOHNNY THUNDER
MONICA
DAYS
VILLAGE GREEN
MR. SONGBIRD
WICKED ANNABELLA
STARSTRUCK
PHENOMENAL CAT
PEOPLE TAKE PICTURES OF EACH
OTHER

● **The French** Village Green, **November 1968**

used to be our roadie, and his wife and two of his daughters. They were crying at the end of it. Really wonderful – like going to Waterloo and seeing the sunset. It was a signature on a piece of work. It's like saying goodbye to somebody, then afterwards feeling the fear that you actually are alone.'

'Days' ventures to suggest that the loss that occurs at the end of a relationship is there all the time anyway, and that all lovers leave a part of themselves, like barbs, inside each other after they part. Further, like 'Wonderboy', it suggests that loss is at the heart of every human relationship, and that every human meeting is overshadowed by its parting. 'Days' has a strong forward drive and a gorgeous melody; it now appears, like 'Wonderboy' and the LP that was to follow, too potent and acute for the newly polarized pop audience. After a long period when they could do no wrong, the Kinks could do no right – exactly at the time when, artistically, they were reaching a peak. On the other side of the extraordinarily moving 'Days' was the perfect hard rock of 'She's Got Everything'. This was the return to the horniness of 'You Really Got Me', but the Kinks had learned a few tricks in the intervening three and a half years. 'She's Got Everything' has a more considered spontaneity, with everything taut yet loose, and represented a perfect white dance record in a year when people were not dancing very much.

Dave's solo career, meanwhile, was grinding to a halt. A tour had been projected in January but had been frustrated by internal disagreement, and a third single, 'Lincoln County'/'There is No Life Without Love', had disappeared without trace in the middle of 1968. Both sides, like most Kinks recordings of this period, are very good indeed: 'There is No Life Without Love' is charming, while 'Lincoln County' is a ferocious, 'I'm coming-home-from-jail' type song. Apart from Dave's customary impassioned delivery, much of its depth derives from the inclusion of a true childhood story. Dave Davies: 'I was in love with this girl at school and I bought her a scarf as a birthday present. ·I walked halfway to her house, but for some reason I just couldn't give it to her, so I hid it in a hole in the wall and thought, "Oh sod it, she wouldn't like it anyway." And I went home. An hour later my mum, who had been out and had walked down the same road, came in saying, "Look what I found – this really lovely scarf! It's really beautiful." She wore it, and I never said anything. Probably to this day she doesn't know about it. I just pulled on the experience when I wrote that song.

'I felt that because "Death of a Clown" had done so well I was being pushed by the record company and the management to get on and make more records, which is probably what I should do, but I always have to believe that it's *me* doing it. I felt I was losing control of things. I rebelled against myself – the usual paradox.'

Over the past year the Kinks had amassed a large backlog of material from their burrow at Pye Studios. But this very profusion was to create a glut at exactly the time when the Kinks' commercial standing, and thus their ability to release product, was being called in question on both sides of the Atlantic. In Britain the Kinks had not had a top ten hit for nine months, since 'Autumn Almanac' and 'Something Else' had met with a marked lack of success. In the USA the situation was even worse – 'Sunny Afternoon' had been the group's last single hit in 1966, and both 'Face to Face' and 'Something Else' had sold disastrously.

Within three months of one another, three different albums were scheduled for release in the USA and Britain, all containing the bulk of the tracks that would eventually surface on *The Village Green Preservation Society*. The album that Davies wanted eventually came out in November, but the delays and confusion were symptomatic of something deeper. Ray Davies: 'There were two points in my life, in my career, when I should not have been allowed to put records out: then and in 1973 to 1975. I was searching and a bit lost. I was upset about not going to America. And I moved to a house up in Elstree which was a big manorial mansion. As soon as I moved into that house I wasn't really happy.'

On the record all of Ray Davies's resentment at the youth culture whose highwire he had walked for so long, and which had caused him to forsake his roots, came bursting out in a series of feelings and anecdotes pulled together by the record's conservatism. Ray Davies: 'It all started off in 1966, when I wrote a song called "Village Green": "Now all the houses are rare antiquities, American tourists flock to see the Village Green." I said in a *New Musical Express* interview that I wanted to be Walt Disney, and I think that's what I wanted to achieve. "Village Green" meant nothing to me except in my fantasy. It was my ideal place, a protected place. It's a fantasy world that I can retreat to, and the worst thing I did was to inflict it on the public. I should have left it in my diary.

'It's a very intimate album. That's the problem. Paul Schrader once said to me, "When you get a good story, you get a personal problem, then you turn it into a metaphor." I didn't do that. I just got the personal problem. But in a way "Village Green" is a metaphor. I still listen to it, and it's still the most durable record from that period.'

The record works today because the fantasy reflects Ray's confused state. *The Village Green Preservation Society* is a sustained world ("It was my own Wizard of Oz land," says Ray) with a series of disparate songs linked by a coherent theme and mood. Ray's depressed state gives the album an emotional unity and a depth that, because of their changed working practices, the Kinks were unable to repeat in their later attempts at this format in the 1970s. Apart from the main statements of the record's wistful theme – 'The Village Green Preservation Society', 'Do You Remember Walter', 'Picture Book' and 'Village Green' – the record contains a clutch of great rock songs: the snappy 'Star Struck' (a single in the US and on the Continent), the original 'Johnny Thunder' and the perfect 'Big Sky'.

Ray Davies: 'That's one of my favourite songs. My publisher, Carlin, had asked me to go to the Cannes Music Festival, and I spent an evening with all these people doing deals. The next morning at the Carlton

Big Sky

Big sky looked down on all the people
Looking up at the big sky
Everybody's pushing one another around
Big sky feels sad when he sees the children
scream and cry
But the big sky's too big to let it get him down

Big sky's too big to cry
Big sky's too high to see
People like you and me
One day we'll be free
We won't care
Just you see
Till that day can be
Don't let it get you down
And when I feel that the world's too much for me
I think of the big sky
Then nothing matters much to me

Big sky looked down on all the people
Who think they got problems
They get depressed and they hold their heads in their hands
And they cry
People lift up their hands and they look up to the big sky
But the big sky's too big to sympathize
Big sky's too occupied
Tho' he would like to try
Then he feels bad inside
Big sky's too big to cry

One day we'll be free
We won't care
Just you wait and see
Till that day can be
Don't let it get you down

Last of the Great Steam-Powered Trains

I'm the last of the good old puffer trains
I'm the last of the blood-and-sweat brigade
And I don't know where I'm going
Or how I came
I'm the last of the good old-fashioned steam-powered trains
I'm the last of the good old renegades
And all my friends are middle-class and grey
But I live in a museum
So I'm OK!

Hotel I watched the sun come up and I looked at them all down there, all going out to do their deals. That's where I got the "Big Sky looking down on all the people" line. It started from there.'

With 'Last of the Great Steam-Powered Trains', the Kinks had finally recorded the old R&B staple, Howlin' Wolf's 'Smokestack Lightning'. This song states clearly Ray's own attitude to his isolation, physical and cultural. Ray Davies: 'I hated the hole I was in here; in Britain you were either a hit machine or you didn't exist. That was the choice I had.'

Although the record contains some of Ray Davies's best songs, full of his customary wit, melody and observation, it hit a very serious problem. Quite simply, *The Village Green Preservation Society* was appallingly out of sync with the time, as Ray Davies explicitly acknowledges in 'Last of the Steam-Powered Trains'. Pop had polarized to the extent that if you were not a bubblegum group, you had to be 'underground', which, like most pop movements, was Stalinist in its exclusion of all dissenting voices. Free love rather than virginity was high on the agenda, and it was time to tear the walls down rather than to slap a preservation order on them. 'Revolution' and 'heavy' were the operative words; action, not observation, was what was required. In the face of such cultural imperatives, the Kinks' wry, understated belief that things did actually continue came over as chintzy as a floral teacup. And at this point in pop it was smart to break the crockery.

Yet the album was not without its long-term effect. Ray Davies: 'The strange thing about that record is that although we couldn't go to the States, Americans eventually picked up on it because of the war in Vietnam. We got a call from the Warner Brothers President, Mo Ostin, saying, "This album is great, you should come over and try to promote it." But of course we couldn't. Our hands were tied. We were locked out.'

The Kinks' next move took them even further away from the mainstream. On 20 October they begun a booking at the Fiesta, Stockton, in their cabaret debut on the supper-club circuit. They continued with two further dates in 1969, one of which was at the Batley Variety Club. The reason for this peculiar step was the Kinks' usual perversity (misfits as always) but, more important, economic necessity.

As their agent of the time, Barry Marshall, says: 'They'd run out of steam with the one-nighter circuit. They'd run out of people who would book them because they never showed up. So they did Stockton at £2,000 for a week, and that money meant something.' Mick Avory: 'It didn't work for us because we were a band that should have been playing in clubs or to a rock audience. We couldn't really perform in front of the type of people that you get at cabaret clubs because they want everything polished, not played too loud, you've got to play within their confines. We never really had that approach to the music.' At the time, playing cabaret was tantamount to an admission of defeat as far as the smart end of pop was concerned.

By the beginning of 1969 the Kinks were old, tired

● Cabaret Kinks, late 1968

and terminally unhip. During the first two or three months of the year Ray Davies busied himself with writing songs with the Kinks for a series of television shows. Work began on the project *Arthur*, an hour-long drama for Granada to be written by Ray Davies and the Kinks with Julian Mitchell. Another drama contact, Ned Sherrin, who had been a major force as the producer of the TV show *That Was The Week That Was*, brought in Ray Davies to write and record one song per week for a series of six BBC television shows featuring Eleanor Bron called *Where Was Spring?*

Various songs from this period have surfaced on record, including 'When I Turn Out the Living Room Light', 'Where Did My Spring Go' and 'Did You See His Name', a song about a man whose arrest for shoplifting is reported in the local paper and who subsequently commits suicide. Ray Davies: 'I had the brief for a song on Thursday, wrote it on Friday and it went out on Saturday. There is a story attached to that. My GP, Doctor Aubrey, was an old-school doctor, in the Boer War and all that. He used to look at me under his glasses and he'd say, "I know what's wrong with you. You're shirking." "No, I've got a bad leg, sir." "You're shirking. Show me the leg." He was really good. He also said to me, "You know what you're going to be when you grow up, my boy? You'll be a preacher."

'Anyway, I was looking through various stories for "Did You See His Name" in the local paper because I had to write a story about a man with a tragedy in his life. I saw an obituary for Doctor Aubrey, and it made me feel a real shit for getting stories from ordinary people.'

After some more cabaret dates the Kinks decided to gear themselves up for another single and another tour. The new song, 'Plastic Man', was a poor harking back to the old satirical themes. Ray Davies: 'I hate it. It was a desperate attempt. Somebody said that we'd got to have a record out to do the tour, and that's what they got. I like

"King Kong" on the other side, though. I wish we could've recorded that properly.' 'Plastic Man' excited controversy from the word go. The song's halting lurch up the charts was given the death blow by the BBC, which objected to the insertion of the word 'bum' into an already cheeky lyric.

But all this paled into insignificance when, three days after the release of the record, Pete Quaife announced to Mick Ledgerwood in a *Disc* exclusive that he was finally leaving the Kinks. 'I'm leaving and that's it. I told Ray I was sorry but I couldn't take any more. I was fed up playing pretty bubblegum music. I'm sick of standing on stage and playing two notes per bar. I want to do something more productive. There's no enmity. It's just that the other Kinks and I are going in different directions.'

Pete Quaife's position with the band had been uncertain for quite some time. After his car crash in June 1966 he had left the group for the first time. Ray Davies: 'Then Pete married this rich girl from Denmark and went to live there, where he was a big noise. I knew he was unhappy with the group because he felt that I was hogging it. He thought the band was finished, but he came back after the hits and we literally fired Dalton to accommodate him. Pete made "Waterloo Sunset", "Days" and "Autumn Almanac", but the old jealousies were creeping back in again.

'I couldn't have done it without Pete. In the early days I was quiet and worried about the way I looked because of my teeth. Mick was a jerk, Dave was an angry wild kid, and Pete was an ambassador. But the first time I ever really fell out with Pete was when he wrote "Daze" on the tape box of "Days". I said, "Don't be a sod. This song means a lot to me.'

It now seems clear there was a long-standing rivalry between Ray Davies and Pete Quaife, who had been in the same form at William Grimshaw. Dave Davies: 'I've got a picture somewhere of a 100-yard race with Pete and

● **Pete Quaife and Dave Davies listen 'critically' to World Service session,
27 November 1968**

Ray. It's taken from the tape, and Ray's just there in front of Pete. That must have had some bearing on the way they saw each other. Ray probably didn't notice it too much, but there must have been a lot of friction, competition.

'Pete and I got on really well together because he was totally off the wall and I was like that as well. I don't think Ray enjoyed a lot of the publicity we got, but we loved it in the early days, prancing around, wearing silly clothes. Maybe the truth of it in the end was that Pete fell out of love with us musically. He formed a band with some Canadians. How could he do that? He lived on the Coldfall Estate in Muswell Hill.'

Pete Quaife's departure was something more than just a nuisance. Ray Davies now sees the cover of *Village Green Preservation Society* as the last picture of the group: 'When one of the founder members leaves the band is dead. Once you lose the thing – the four originals getting together, going through it together, forming the band together – once that goes, the group is a different group. That picture signs it off.'

Pete Quaife's final departure marks the end of the first part of the Kinks' story. Afterwards they became an entirely different group of people with different aims: the original classic format of the four-man pop group had disappeared along with the time that had spawned it.

The Kinks had seen the unified pop culture with which they had grown up fragment and fall away from under them. Ray Davies had used the security of his commercial success to further his artistic aims, only to find that he was not, in fact, on an island and that artistic integrity without commercial success was a bitter pill to swallow. The Kinks, first and foremost, had defined themselves as a pop group, and their working life was necessarily circumscribed by an essential commercial discipline. Whether they liked it or not, they had to change as the context of pop changed; they had to try to adapt their skills and preoccupations to the demands of a voracious business fundamentally unsympathetic to the complexities that they were trying to get across. If they had broken up at this point, they would now be hailed as the purest band of the sixties, with a perfect career trajectory – from hit to cult. Instead the Kinks were to become survivors: and survival meant cracking the huge American market. This was a process that took ten years to come to fruition – with the top ten success of 'Low Budget' in 1979 – but it exacted a high emotional and artistic price.

● Village Green **photo session, Hampstead Heath, summer 1968**

SHANGRI-LA

The music press built up a mythical world of 'rock' in which music was 'progressing' at unimagined rates, leaving all its predecessors behind like prehistoric curiosities. Championed in Britain by the *Melody Maker*, the groups made pilgrimages to America where *Rolling Stone*, FM radio, and audiences at live concerts welcomed them even more enthusiastically. Hearing the 'far-out' lyrics and 'spaced-out' solos of the Doors, Jefferson Airplane, and Grateful Dead, the British musicians returned to Britain fired with enthusiasm to be even more experimental and adventurous. Although there were many parallels between the development of music in Britain and in America in this period, there was one fundamental difference which had repercussions that lasted for at least the next fifteen years. In America, the leading underground bands all signed direct to major record companies, enabling those companies to reinforce their hold on the American record industry and effectively to drive out virtually all the indie companies. The result was a drift into conformity, sterility and repetition that destroyed much of the momentum of the previous fifteen years.

*Charlie Gillett, **The Sound of the City**, 1983 edn*

In October 1969 the Kinks toured America for the first time in four years. Since their last visit the country had changed, and so had their status: from being co-headliners with the Beachboys at the Palace of Showbiz, the Hollywood Bowl, they were now second-billed to Spirit at a hippie venue, the Fillmore East. This Icarus-like fall from grace was not lost on the group. Ray Davies: 'It was really embarrassing staying at the Holiday Inn and then going down to the cheapest supermarket to buy food. We'd had seventeen hits, but that was the state it had got to.'

None the less, in America at this time British was best, as a new generation of UK groups took up the promise offered by the better organized American music business and its larger market. Yet although Englishness was being sold wholesale, it was a particular kind of sensibility that was in demand. The England that was being marketed was not the closely observed country of Ray Davies and the Kinks, with its implicit recognition of this island's complex fabric, but a simplified distortion of America. Like a refracted image, English groups like the Who, Ten Years After and Jimi Hendrix were selling America back to itself. Taking black American music as a basic premise, and then, ironically, building on a form invented by the Kinks in 'You Really Got Me', they concocted a music that was dazzling in its technical virtuosity but, beyond showing an audience what it wanted to see of itself, often meaningless. These successful groups realized that what their new audience (typified by the larger venues) wanted was gestures that could fill those vast spaces: often this was to mean simplification that verged on self-parody. If the Monterey Festival was a musical nuking, then Woodstock threw everything but the kitchen sink into a bludgeoning holocaust. This was the game that the Kinks had re-entered; to survive, they had to become an American group. But at the time they simply did not fit. Pete Townshend: 'Their view of life, at this time, which was not to fight but rather to acknowledge, to sit back, to oberve, to see the humour in situations – how could the Americans possibly relate to that?'

Before the Kinks returned to the USA they had a few matters to resolve. The most urgent was the lack of a bass player. There was only one choice as a replacement for Pete Quaife, and that was the man who had done it before: John Dalton was re-hired within a couple of days. Most of the rest of the year was taken up with the writing and recording of *Arthur* and plans for the October tour of America, two projects that were later to become intertwined. At the time of 'Plastic Man', however, Ray and Dave were involved with separate concerns – Ray was producing the Turtles' LP *Turtle Soup*, and Dave was still playing about with his solo LP. Apart from the new material that was released on singles, various other tracks had been recorded for possible inclusion on this mythical product: 'Shoemaker's Daughter', 'Are You Ready Girl', 'She's My Girl', 'Do You Wish To Be a Man', 'Crying', 'Groovy Movies' and 'Mr Reporter'. Neither the album nor any further collection of Dave Davies's material was released at this time: Dave's peak as a solo performer had been in late 1967, and he had failed to capitalize on it. At this stage he appears to have been disinclined to push his solo career any further; he felt that the sessions for this collection of material had been too rushed and that the group had not been involved enough.

These projects, however, would become irrelevant as the Kinks' autumn push took shape. In the meantime they still had to live. Their new agent, Barry Dickens, details the depths to which they had sunk. 'The first thing I did was to send them to Sweden. They ended up playing two shows a night all over Sweden. It was the only place I could get them into to make them money. They've got these big amusement parks where they have bands playing; people pay a pound and they get all their amusements and can see a group as well. It was safe because the Kinks didn't have to draw anybody: people went in there anyway. Just like Disneyland.'

Another port of call was Lebanon. Ken Jones had joined the Kinks the year before, as their road manager: 'We were the first band to play Beirut, in May 1969. We were supposed to play for three days in the Hotel Finosia, which has a 2,000-seat ballroom. It was put back two weeks because it was just about the time they were starting the wars among themselves, although it was then just skirmishes. It was a bit of a disaster: we didn't get the rest of our money; we had to pay our hotel bills; and part of the equipment was left in Beirut.'

Just at this point things were starting to happen in America. Warner/Reprise decided to put its money where its mouth was, and the problem with the American Federation of Musicians was resolved. Robert Wace flew over to New York City and Los Angeles to finalize an autumn tour, and the Kinks undertook to behave themselves and act like sensible young businessmen. Ray Davies: 'We had to sign a document for the AFM saying that we'd done something we didn't do to give us clearance. We promised to be good boys.'

The Kinks were set to open in New York in October, and a new LP, *Arthur*, was released a week before. *Arthur*, subtitled *The Decline and Fall of the British Empire*, was an ambitious project comprising both an album and a one-hour TV drama on which Ray Davies and Julian Mitchell had been working for some months. *Arthur* refers explicitly to Ray Davies's childhood: 'When I was a child I lived with my sister Rose, my brother-in-law Arthur and their son Terry. Arthur was a very strict man; he was part of the generation that was disillusioned with Britain. His brother was a fighter pilot and got the VC, but Arthur was grounded because of his eyes. Nothing quite worked out for Arthur.

'Arthur was wary. I could see his guts turning over watching television; he'd drawn plans of this new village they were building called Little Elizabeth in Adelaide, Australia. His life was dedicated to going. Rose was terrified but she loved him and backed him up. There was one point when Terry was doing quite well at school and wanted to stay in England, but he decided to go with his Dad.

'When I got to Australia Arthur said to me, "You know, I like that record you wrote about me." I was honoured, actually, because he liked very little. His sternness was something I'd never experienced before.

'He took me for a drive one day and he said, "I've got your sister well insured because I'm going to die soon." And lo and behold, he died when I was back in England, in October 1973, the worst year of my life.'

In *Arthur* Ray Davies delivers the goods: his preoccupations with family, class and the whole sweep of English post-war society are brought into sharp focus. The plot, as Julian Mitchell explains in the sleevenotes, concerns

Arthur Morgan, who lives in a London suburb in a house called Shangri-la, with a garden and a car and wife called Rose and son called Derek who's married to Liz, and they have these two very nice kids, Terry and Marilyn. Derek and Liz and Terry and Marilyn are emigrating to Australia. Arthur had another son called Eddy. He was named for Arthur's brother, who was killed in the Battle of the Somme. Arthur's Eddy was killed too, in Korea. His other son, Ronnie, is a student and he thinks the world's got to change one hell of a lot before it's going to be good enough for him. Derek thinks it's changed a bloody sight too much – he can't stick England any more, all those bloody bureaucrats everywhere, bloody hell, he's getting out. Ronnie and Derek don't exactly get on.
The Granada TV story...takes place on Derek and Liz's last day in England. Nothing very much happens – everyone has Sunday dinner together, then Ronnie turns up and the men go to the pub, where Ronnie gets all worked up about the capitalist system, while Liz and Rose talk about the past. Arthur takes them all to the boat, and they have a picnic on the way. All the time Arthur's remembering his life. It's a sad day for him, seeing them off.

The plot is static. It is not about action but is rather an examination of various people, their ages and attitudes. Because it is scripted, it allows the songs the freedom to breathe: they are there as amplifications of mood and texture rather than as narrative devices. The fact that they stand up on their own has a lot to do with Ray Davies's growing maturity as a writer, his ability to express different points of view and the care that the Kinks took to get the songs right. John Dalton: 'I can remember getting more satisfaction out of hearing *Arthur*, the finished product, than any other album we've made. It seemed to take a long time, but when it was actually finished I thought, "It was well worth it." It was simple as well; there were only four of us on it.'

Dave Davies: 'I remember the highlight for me was

Yes Sir, No Sir

Yes Sir, no Sir
Where do I go Sir
What do I do Sir
What do I say

Yes Sir, no Sir
Where do I go Sir
What do I do Sir
How do I behave

Yes Sir, no Sir
Permission to speak Sir
Permission to breathe Sir
What do I say, how do I behave, what do I say

So you think that you've got ambition
Stop your dreaming and your idle wishing
You're outside and there ain't no admission
To our play
Pack up your ambition in your old kit bag
And you'll be happy with a packet of fags
Chest out stomach in
Do what I say, do what I say
Yes right away

Yes Sir, no Sir
Where do I go Sir

What do I do Sir
What do I say

Yes Sir, no Sir
Permission to speak Sir
Permission to breathe Sir
What do I say, how do I behave, what do I say

Doesn't matter who you are
You're there and there you are
Everything is in its place
Authority must be maintained
And then we know exactly where we are
Let them feel that they're important to the cause
But let them know that they are fighting for their homes
Just be sure that they're contributing their all
Give the scum a gun and make the bugger fight
And be sure to have deserters shot on sight
If he dies we'll send a medal to his wife

Yes Sir, no Sir
Please let me die Sir
I think this life is affecting my brain
Yes Sir, no Sir
Three bags full Sir
What do I do Sir, what do I say
What do I say, how do I behave, what do I say

Arthur. Ray was writing about real things, and I felt that this was what we should be doing.'

In *Arthur* the Kinks took their four-man-group format as far as it would go. Each song works both separately and in the context of the album as a whole. By this time the Kinks were able to pull off a wide variety of moods and subjects without being either pompous or trivial. The repertoire ranged from the lackadaisical 'Drivin', through the intense fury of 'Brainwashed', to the wistfulness of 'Young and Innocent Days' and the exuberance of 'Victoria'.

Most expressive is the vocal of Ray Davies, which veers from the upper-class parody, 'Yes Sir, no Sir', through his Mickey Mouse vocals on 'Australia' (a sharp reminder of the humiliations of the 1965 tour) to the quietly intense outrage of 'Some Mother's Son', which takes up the 'Wonderboy' line and turns it into one of the most moving anti-war songs ever. It is all the more powerful because of the constraint and complexities of its points of view. As in 'Where Have All the Good Times Gone', Ray Davies is not afraid to point out that instead of being on the wrong side of the generation war, parents may have some worthwhile experiences of their own.

However, the album was too subtle for a pop world polarized within itself and against the world outside: 'intolerant mockers of the little man' was a general feeling. Ray Davies does fall into one classic trap by identifying Arthur Morgan as 'little' in the album's centrepiece, 'Shangri-la'. But what the critics missed was the obvious empathy expressed in the song's twists and turns, particularly the angry middle break, and the joyous support of the album's final song, 'Arthur'. This is not the adolescent satire of 'A Well Respected Man'. What lifts 'Arthur' above cheap jibes is the Kinks' emotional involvement with the subject matter.

Arthur was the Kinks' big shot: a mature multi-media package that was intended to be the first full-length drama to be scored by a successful pop group, that would stretch the boundaries of pop music itself and that in the end – although this was not the intention at first – would have provided strong artillery for their second invasion of the USA. For on 17 October the Kinks flew off to the rock groups' Shangri-la.

The Kinks had exploded into the consciousness of American teens in 1965 with three straight top ten singles, but only a year later the pieces were being tidied up and swept away. The damage done to their reputation by the 1965 tour, plus an increasingly specific English viewpoint in their songs, meant a curve of declining single success, halted temporarily by 'Sunny Afternoon' but down to the wire with 'Mr Pleasant' and 'Waterloo Sunset'. Their albums did even worse.

The pop press is always a reliable guide to changes in the weather, and from the start the American teen press, like its English counterpart, had always had a problem with the Kinks: they weren't that cute; they weren't that malleable; they weren't even that outrageous. They didn't give great copy, nor did they have fascinating love lives. Nobody had much of a handle on them, and apart from a few introductory articles explaining their name (usually based on the 'K' Konceit) magazines like *16* and *Hit Parader* contented themselves with reprinting old Keith Altham articles or just not bothering. For as the Kinks faded, so began the inexorable rise of Paul Revere and the Raiders, featuring Phil 'Fang' Volk.

As sales declined their records became increasingly hard to get. Doug Hinman was an American fan: 'For all intents and purposes, the Kinks vanished here by the beginning of 1967. I honestly can't recall ever hearing a Kinks song on AM radio from '67 to '69 or on FM until '69 (excepting an occasional "oldie" hit). You couldn't find their 45s in the stores after "Mr Pleasant", or even order them specially, should you be lucky enough to know a new title existed. They just didn't fit in during this period. Most people assumed they'd broken up long ago.'

But although the Kinks had disappeared from the teen comics, they were the subject of a great deal of attention from the emerging underground press: magazines like *Crawdaddy*, *Mojo Navigator* and *Rolling Stone*. This critical interest slowly but surely laid the foundations for their re-emergence. The process of rediscovery had reached a pitch of hysteria by the fall of 1969, and they arrived in America on the crest of a wave of hype and genuine interest.

Much of this feeling is manifest in a promo package released by Warner/Reprise at that time, 'God Save the Kinks'. 'They were desperate to find a package for us,' Ray Davies now says, and it is hard to view the contents of this lavish box any other way. It contained (1) a 'God Save the Kinks' badge, slightly too large; (2) a consumer guide to all the Kinks' records, which used words like 'raunchy' (for the early stuff) and 'nostalgic' (for the later stuff); (3) an official souvenir, some 'grass' from the 'Daviesland Village Green'; (4) a pin-badge Union Jack; (5) a jigsaw puzzle of *The Village Green Preservation Society* rear sleeve; (6) a silly card; and (7) an LP called *There, Now and Inbetween*, with the *Something Else* picture of the Kinks at their most foppish, superimposed on a nostalgic picture of the English countryside in the 1930s. The crowning glory was the endorsement by Hal Halverstadt of the creative services group of Warner Brothers Seven Arts Records, Inc.: '. . . Which leads us to believe that the Kinks may not have had it after all. And that their recent and mighty contributions to the rock scene may one day be appreciated by the record-buying public at large. And that the Kinks are to be supported, encouraged, cheered. And saved.'

Although the package may now seem ridiculous, in fact Warner/Reprise had done a good job of capitalizing on the Kinks' underground reputation, and more than just die-hard Kinks fans were waiting for them to return. *Arthur* was released to rave reviews and heavy promotion on both coasts. What neither the audience nor the Kinks had realized, however, was how much America had changed in five years. Huge amounts of money had been pumped into the music business throughout 1966, 1967 and 1968, and the Kinks, only just surviving on the scampi-and-chips circuit and rock-bottom European gigs, seemed Mickey Mouse.

Doug Hinman was one of those who had waited for four years: 'Sitting reasonably near to the stage, I could see the old metallic-sparkle drum kits still with their old logo. Up close I noticed what a beat-up little trooper of a kit it was, and how small it was by comparison with the huge kits used by the opening acts. The tom-tom shell was smashed and shoddily repaired. The amps were the only contemporary equipment on stage – obviously leased for the tour. Out came the guitars: Ray's old Telecaster, beat to hell and, last but not least, Dave's legendary Flying V. After the announcement out came the band, straight into their wall-of-sound rave-up to "Till the End of the Day". Sloppy but energetic, electric and magic. The sound was not great – the singing was too low in the mix and probably slightly off – but the enthusiasm of the crowd virtually erased any fault. Dave was very visual, rocking out. Ray, emaciated in his red striped polo shirt, was frail and unsure, tentative. Mick looked basically the same. In retrospect, they seemed cleanly split between being an old-style pop act and a contemporary live band.'

Ray Davies basically confirms this impression: 'The first gig we played was at the Fillmore East. Bill Graham announced us. We were terrified because we had new amps which we'd hardly used and we were working with wedges. All through that tour we really had to work on our sound, and John Dalton was bearing the brunt of it. At one point John said, "If I'm not good enough, I'll leave." It was a very hard tour.'

A week later, they were playing the Kinetic Playground at Chicago, where they were second-bill to the Who. This must have been particularly galling, for the Who had been lower down the bill from the Kinks in July 1964, when 'You Really Got Me' was on the point of release. This time the tables were turned: the Who had already put in two and a half years' hard ground work and had become everything that the Americans expected from a British group – hard, flash and bombastic. Everything the Who were doing right the Kinks were doing wrong. The band's frustration built up. Ray Davies: 'There was a lack of confidence on our part and on the part of the management. It was very unfulfilling. We enjoyed playing the tour, there was a buzz about it everywhere we went, but it just didn't happen. Dave got pissed off. He smashed an exit sign at the hotel so he wouldn't have to play again, and we had to go home for a rest. It was probably the nearest we had come to breaking up since Mick smashed him over the head with a cymbal.'

Even more galling was the reception that *Arthur* was getting. With typical Kinks timing, the record had been released six months after the Who's *Tommy* – an ambitious double album built around a central narrative. At the time this was called an 'opera' by the Who's assiduous publicists, who were busy touting *Tommy* into the top ten on both sides of the Atlantic. With its mystical/sensational preoccupations and its musical pyrotechnics *Tommy* was much better suited to the demands of the pop market in both countries: *Arthur*, by comparison, was too muted, too real, and its concern

● **Memorabilia from Warners'** God Save the Kinks **package, summer 1969**

for the old was desperately unfashionable. Ray Davies: 'Arthur was a labour of love. I was angry with a society that had built me to be factory fodder; I wasn't angry about older people because I could see that they'd been victims of it.'

Although well intentioned, Warner/Reprise compounded the problem by selling the wrong kind of Englishness. What young Americans wanted was not 'The Village Green' or the pinstripes, teapots and semi-detached houses on the *Arthur* sleeve but long hair, suede fringes, and 'far-out' guitar solos – things the Kinks were unable to provide. *Arthur* went into the charts at 92 and disappeared.

The Who associations followed the Kinks throughout that tour. John Dalton: 'Once we brought out *Arthur*, everyone said, "Oh they're copying *Tommy*." I tried to explain it wasn't copying *Tommy* at all. Ray had had the idea years and years before that.'

Ray Davies: 'I never really considered *Tommy* any threat. I'd heard it. Anyway it was a wave that was bound to happen to the Who, and what happened to us was inevitable because we were on a downward curve.'

Worst of all, the TV presentation of *Arthur* was cancelled at the last minute. As Ray Davies said to John Mendelsohn in a contemporary interview, the reason for its cancellation was: 'a mixture of things. One, the budget went over, and at that time Granada TV were cutting costs. Then it was affected by the political incompatibility between the producer of the show and the people upstairs. Also, I don't think he even knew how to do it. If they'd given me the freedom they'd promised me in the beginning, I could have done it.'

Arthur's commercial failure and the cancellation of the TV show had a disastrous impact on the Kinks and Ray Davies in particular. They had made their best shot, and it had been met with indifference and incomprehension. Losing the programme meant that Ray Davies was to pursue the idea of a concept album/TV drama to death right into the 1970s. Eventually, he actually got to do it – ironically, with Granada TV – in 1974-5 as *Soap Opera/Starmaker*. But by then it was far too late.

The Kinks were on a downward curve again. Three singles from *Arthur* were released in England. Two of them, 'Drivin'' and 'Shangri-la', had great Dave Davies B sides ('Mindless Child of Motherhood' and the Byrds-like 'This Man He Weeps Tonight'), but only the third, 'Victoria', was a minor hit in both Britain and the USA.

The Kinks' second tour of America, in January/February 1970, did little to improve their position. On their third tour of the US Doug Hinman remembers: 'They seemed to be losing their momentum in the US. Perhaps this is a biased impression, since it was not a particularly glamorous gig: an old-style ballroom in an out-of-the-way, dying mill city (Lowell, Massachusetts). This was one of the legendary drunken gigs that were to become their calling card over the next few years. It was clearly a nowhere gig, and I think they knew it.' But again the Kinks were to pull the rabbit out of the hat.

When I get to the word C-O-L-A, cola…are there any men in the audience this evening? I want all the men, all the boys, to sing, 'C-O-L-A, cola.' And when I get to the word L-O-L-A, lola, I want all the women, and all the people who think they're women, and all the people who used to be women, to sing, 'L-O-L-A, lola.' And all those people who can't sing, I want you to clap your hands and join along. And if you can't clap your hands or sing, I can't suggest anything.

(Ray Davies, introduction to 'Lola', Winterland, San Francisco, February 1977)

Ray Davies: '"Lola" is a long, long story. A subject for a glossy paperback. It's the kind of torment that anybody in that situation goes through. I was desperate to make my marriage work. It's all too easy to say that you're imprisoned by the people who love you. But I was making myself a prisoner, and I wasn't able to do my job properly, that's all it is. I remember Rasa got very upset when she said that "Lola" was the first single she hadn't sung on. I remembered an incident in a club. I think Robert Wace had been dancing with this black woman, and he said, "I'm really on to a thing here." And it was OK until we left at six in the morning, and then I said, "Have you seen the stubble?" He said, "Yeah," but he was too pissed to care, I think. I'd had a few dances with it…him. It's kind of obvious. It's that thrust in the pelvic region when they're on the dance floor, and they're never quite the same as a woman. So it's a combined disguise. But "Lola" is a love song.

'At the turn of the year, I felt very dejected, very depressed. I was offered a part in a play and I took it. It was called *The Long-Distance Piano Player*, and it cleared me of all music. I came back refreshed and energized. I had two songs, "Lola" and "Powerman". We rehearsed in the front room of Fortis Green for weeks and weeks. Then we went in and recorded it. We did one version and Bob Wace said, "What you need is a really arresting beginning, like you used to have on 'You Really Got Me'." So I got the first few chords, strummed the guitar, then started the lyric. That's listening to people again, taking advice.'

Robert Wace: 'From time to time I used to go up to Ray's house and listen to some of the songs he'd written. He just played them to me on the guitar, and you had to find the diamond among them. If he had something that he thought was very good, he'd hold it back. He might play a tiny bit of it and then go on to something else, and say it wasn't finished or something like that. He played me a bit of this song, and I said I really liked it. So they went in and recorded it. I listened and I said, "It's terrible, really terrible." They'd done it like a country and western song. I made them go in and re-do it.'

In 'Lola' Ray Davies picks up all his sexual ambiguities and throws them in the face of the world, but this time with a good belly laugh. 'Lola' is a great shaggy-dog story, performed by all the group with an irresistible drive, giving Ray Davies plenty of opportunity to purse his lips and slur his vocals. Clues are littered throughout the song ('I'm not the world's most physical guy', 'Girls will

be boys and boys will be girls') until the payoff that sets thousands of genders bending: 'I'm not the world's most masculine man – but I'm glad I'm a man and so is Lola.' Now, who is a man?

'Lola' went top five in the UK and top ten in America. It restored the Kinks, brought them a whole new audience and transformed Ray Davies's persona. It was the first pop song, three years after legalization in the UK, to deal at all with any kind of homosexuality, even if it was cloaked by the ambiguity of transvestism. It was done so charmingly that no one could take offence. If it remains a more overt statement of Ray's equivocal sexuality than 'See My Friends', then that is because Ray had to overstate in order to win his audience. In June 1970, that was of paramount importance.

If 'Lola' spelt out what others like David Bowie would turn into careers later on in the 1970s, it also brought in a couple of people who were to become an important part of the Kinks' team during their years of touring. Ken Jones: 'I said to Ray many years ago, in 1969, "Why don't we get a little piano so you can do 'Waterloo Sunset' on the piano instead of the guitar?" He said, "That's not a bad idea," so we got the piano and consequently we wanted a keyboard player. So we were in Morgan Studios, and John Gosling walked in with a cape, one of those military-type capes, and his hair down to here, and I said, "Fuck me! It's John the Baptist!"'

John Gosling: 'My audition was the recording session for "Lola". I was given chord sequences, pieces of paper with chords written on them. I sat down and played them and when "Lola" was finished, I recognized it was one of the ones I'd played on. I just followed the chords and that was it, out it came.'

The Kinks also acquired a new PRO, Marian Rainford: "The first time that I met Ray was on 26 May 1970. He spent most of the afternoon gnawing his way through the brim of his straw hat."

With these people on board, the 1970s Kinks were set. They had a new profile and a new pitch in the market place. During the summer they busied themselves with recording their next LP, which had the unwieldy title of *Lola versus Powerman and the Moneygoround, Part One*. Ray Davies: 'The LP is the struggle of a band really deciding to fight back.' *Lola versus Powerman and the Moneygoround* represents another step in the Kinks' battle for the right to determine their own destiny. All the myriad resentments that had accumulated throughout the 1960s are laid bare stage by stage, from being struggling musicians ('Get Back in Line'), to getting the accoutrements that are necessary for a career ('Denmark Street'), through the lift-off of success ('Top of the Pops'), through the rip-offs that are endemic once success has been achieved ('The Moneygoround'), to the furious desire for freedom that underlined the Kinks' own feelings throughout this album.

Lola Versus Powerman and the Moneygoround is a distinctly cautionary tale: it is a story of love and lust versus power and self-interest and, by implication, the story of the Kinks versus the music industry. Naturally, there was no contest, and the picture of the Kinks that

Lola

I met her in a club down in old Soho
Where you drink champagne and it tastes just like cherry-cola
see-oh-el-aye cola
She walked up to me and she asked me to dance
I asked her her name and in a dark brown voice she said Lola
El-oh-el-aye Lola La-la-la-la Lola

Well I'm not the world's most physical guy
But when she squeezed me tight she nearly broke my spine
Oh my Lola la-la-la-la Lola
Well I'm not dumb but I can't understand
Why she walked like a woman and talked like a man
Oh my Lola la-la-la-la Lola la-la-la-la Lola

Well we drank champagne and danced all night
Under electric candlelight
She picked me up and sat me on her knee
And said dear boy won't you come home with me
Well I'm not the world's most passionate guy
But when I looked in her eyes well I almost fell for my Lola
La-la-la-la Lola la-la-la-la Lola
Lola la-la-la-la Lola la-la-la-la Lola
I pushed her away
I walked to the door
I fell to the floor
I got down on my knees
Then I looked at her and she at me

Well that's the way that I want it to stay
And I always want it to be that way for my Lola
La-la-la-la Lola
Girls will be boys and boys will be girls
It's a mixed up muddled up shook up world except for Lola
La-la-la-la Lola

Well I left home just a week before
And I'd never ever kissed a woman before
But Lola smiled and took me by the hand
And said dear boy I'm gonna make you a man

Well I'm not the world's most masculine man
But I know what I am and I'm glad I'm a man
And so is Lola
La-la-la-la Lola la-la-la-la Lola
Lola la-la-la-la Lola la-la-la-la Lola

emerges from the album is clearly not a happy one: songs like 'Denmark Street', 'Powerman' and the album's centrepiece, 'The Moneygoround', rely either on a neurotic drive or on a manic jauntiness which only just covers their frenetic spleen; the non-plot songs, like 'This Time Tomorrow' and 'Long Way from Home', express an alienation and disillusionment that verges on the cosmic: 'Yeah, we've got to get out of this world somehow/We've got to be free, we got to be free now.'

This generalized disgust persisted in the album's future 45, 'Apeman'. Ray Davies: 'When "Lola" was a hit I came back from the tour of America and I picked up Victoria, who was one year old, and I cried because the only song she could sing was "Lola". We drove down to Cornwall and I got the idea for "Apeman" in the car. It was very easy to write – it just went "I'm an Apeman" with that piano.' In 'Apeman' Ray Davies developed the slurred calypso voice that was first in evidence in 'Lola'. (It was also around that time that the Kinks began singing what is still an audience staple, the 'Banana Boat Song': 'It had become a camp little extra which I always liked. I had the Stan Freberg version, which I thought was marvellous. I really rated Stan Freberg.') Luckily, the humour of 'Apeman' rescues the LP from a pervading mood of bitterness; the same humour is apparent in 'Top of the Pops', in which Ray Davies brilliantly recaptures his own youthful innocence.

Dave Davies has a couple of songs on the album which polarize its contents neatly. 'Rats' is an angry rocker with simplistic lyrics, but 'Strangers', with its lovely tune, is one of the best songs that Dave has ever written, though it reveals a worldweariness astonishing in someone so young – at the time of the album Dave was only twenty-three: 'Where are you going? I don't mind/I've killed my world and I've killed my time/So where do I go, what do I see/I see many people coming after me . . .'

The album's other masterpiece is 'Get Back in the Line'. Ray Davies: 'That song is inspired by the film *On the Waterfront*. In the last scene the guy is beaten up but he gets back on the line – the work line – and says: "Everybody works today." It's also to do with the embarrassment of getting dole money. I've experienced that very little. I went to get my employment form for a student job, and I got in the wrong line by mistake. I stood in the unemployment line. My dad had been unemployed a lot. He said, "I don't ever want you to see me standing in that line." It means a lot to me, that song. I sang it up at Newcastle, just sang it alone, when we were last there. It got the biggest applause of the evening.'

This is not the album that one would expect from a group coming off a massive international hit. Clearly, the chaotic first six years of the Kinks were finally catching up with them; they were tired, disgusted and, implicitly, losing their capacity for emotional responsiveness. They were paying the price of being at the cutting edge of one of the most unpleasant industries in the world. 'Powerman' savages the music business with a bitterness not seen again for seven years, when punk rock temporarily blew its shoddy pretensions and workhouse practices right open. Yet this bitterness only emphasized

● 12–15 November 1970

the Kinks' own manifest lack of power: they had made their bed, and they had to lie in it or get out. 'Powerman' thus now appears to be an album unravelling at the seams under the weight of its own contradictions. The Kinks were in a permanent state of confusion. In its various forms this state was to continue through the 1970s.

In the meantime the Kinks' resurgence was continuing: 'Apeman' went top five in England, the last single to do so; unfortunately in the USA it hardly featured at all. Just when they should have been capitalizing on their new-found American success, Ray had been distracted by one of the Kinks' most irrelevant projects, the score for an undistinguished film called *Percy*. Ray Davies had already dabbled in film music, writing the theme tune for *The Virgin Soldiers*, which was produced by his old colleague Ned Sherrin. *Percy* was more ambitious. The Kinks knocked out a soundtrack LP consisting mainly of instrumentals, which also included three songs of note, the country and western parody 'Willesden Green', the passionate 'God's Children' and one of Ray Davies's most achingly lovely songs, 'The Way Love Used To Be.'

At this time relationships with Robert Wace and Grenville Collins were not at their best. Robert Wace: 'We didn't see the funny side of *Lola versus Powerman and the Moneygoround*. We were very, very upset about that, but we just decided to ignore it.' On a personal level, however, there was a deeper unease: the Kinks and their managers were getting tired of each other.

At a time when the Kinks needed a strong team around them to help capitalize on their new-found success once and for all, it was lacking. As if to attest to their loss of momentum, the rest of 1970 and the beginning of 1971 were a catalogue of frustrated projects: two LPs, *Lola Versus Powerman and the Moneygoround, Part Two* and *Songs I Did for Auntie,* were scrapped after some work had been done. Most of the first half of 1971 was taken up with various tours: the Kinks actually made themselves visible about Britain before going to Australia, Europe and, inevitably, America during March and April. But whether they liked it or not, the success of 'Lola', the single, and *Lola Versus Powerman and the Moneygoround* (which went top forty in America early in the new year), had delivered them straight back into the hands of the powermen.

Ray Davies: 'While we were on tour with *Powerman and the Moneygoround,* which was a big hit at the time, I went up to Warner Brothers and people started calling me "Ray, babe". I didn't like that; I was being treated as a piece of gold yet again.' The Kinks' contract with Pye Records in England and Warner/Reprise in the States was coming up for renegotiation. The bidding was lively, as the Kinks were, in music industry parlance, 'hot'. But neither Warners nor Pye was really in the running.

Ken Jones: 'Ray felt that if we were going to be a worldwide act, we'd got to go with a worldwide company. RCA, being a worldwide company, seemed a good answer.'

Ray Davies: 'We wouldn't commit to sign to anybody. It was rather a nice time, lots of meals. Bob Wace and I used to love going to all these functions and being met by people who really wanted the act. RCA wanted us so bad, I just said to Robert, "Ask for another hundred thousand pounds." And they offered it.'

The Moneygoround was about to whirl even faster.

UNREAL REALITY

I've been travelling on this road
I get the feeling it's getting on
I keep moving on
I keep rolling on
But does anybody know my name?

Dave Davies, *'You Don't Know My Name'*, 1972

If the Kinks and their audience are suffering now, it is from a deep sense of frustration and futility that occasionally borders on stagnation.

Tim Jurgens, **Fusion**, *April 1972*

By 1971/2, the Kinks were getting out of sync again. 'Lola' had re-established them in the US and the UK, but their status was still marginal, and the group's own behaviour at this point was not calculated to improve it. Despite some good product and assiduous promotion in the early days at RCA, the Kinks' contradictions were starting to tear them apart (in particular Ray Davies) just at the time when there was neither the back-up nor the culture to support them.

It was a bad time in popular music. The excitement of the 1960s had long since passed, as had its utopian promises. What was left was a vacuum well-documented by Charlie Gillett in *The Sound of the City*: 'here was pop music and its audience settling down at home with the mortgage to pay, and kids to put to bed. Good night, America.' For the people who'd been through the sixties and survived, the going was difficult. Pete Townsend: 'Ray and I went through exactly the same thing – scrambling for concepts which might allow us to do what we knew we could do, which was to write songs, and to make them in some way bigger and better – maybe turn them into a novel or a movie or musical or something that would become world news.'

This drive contrasts with the fragility of the Kinks' own success and the corner in which it put them. As Marion Rainford remembers: 'They were going through a very funny stage in relation to the music of that time. There was all this very heavy rock music. Everybody was terribly cool, everybody listened to the music. You went to a concert to sit and listen, and on stage it was "everybody listens to *my* music." The problem with the Kinks was that the people who didn't know them and hadn't seen them before would go to a concert and find that they couldn't just sit and listen to the music. They were expected to join in and respond. Because it was uncool, we were getting some very funny press around those first two or three years. It was a bit like confronting a serious concert audience who were expecting Beethoven but were suddenly told they were going to get Gilbert and Sullivan. Down comes the song sheet and, right, every-body join in. But the real Kinks audiences knew what was expected of them.'

The Kinks were already basing themselves in the US, where they were promoted as a campily nostalgic party band. This fitted in with the song best-known to their new audience and the new conception of them as a classic pop group. In the seventies wasteland, the sixties were already being revalued, and the Kinks' records that had flopped in the mid-sixties were now hailed as masterpieces by critics like John Mendelsohn. This nostalgia was strengthened by the 'backward-looking', 'Olde Englishe' preoccupations of their material.

If RCA got the design team of the moment – Higgis, Wade, and Farrell – to design the sleeve of *Everybody's in Showbiz*, then Reprise countered by putting the Queen's Horseguards and Beefeaters on the *Kink Kronikles*, the best compilation of the group. To a limited extent, this was successful. The Kinks caught the tide of a mini-fashion that had begun in New York and had spread to the UK. Indeed, they could be regarded as among its major instigators. As Peter York writes in *Style Wars*:

> To a generation and a sub-group already seeing double through pop art, and thus in the vanguard of the double-think revivals that marks the sixties – the art nouveau, deco, moderne, ultra-kitsch *et al*. – was added another devastating factor. Camp. In a very acute article in the *Village Voice*, John Lombard showed how the assimilation of camp, once largely a homosexual sensibility, had begun to affect the marketing of all sorts of thing sold to non-queer people in America . . . Camp and pop put together produced what I call art necro; a quick-change revivalism which became very big business around the turn of the decade, when, as John Lombardi says, people were looking for something *silly* to take their minds off depressing things.

The Kinks fitted the bill. Ray Davies had changed from the nervous performer who had returned to the United States in 1969:

> Now Ray fluttered on stage, to the delight of the audience, waving his arms and wiggling his ass. He cooed into the microphone and carried on like a music-hall performer trying to do Mick Jagger, Oscar Wilde, Ondine, and Ernie Kovak's 'Percy Dove Tonsils' all at the same time. It was *very* campy and it knocked out most of the audience except for a few people with puzzled grins who didn't know quite how to react. Halfway through the first number it became obvious that Davies was very, very high on

● The first photo session for a year: the Flask, Hampstead, 17 December 1971

● Everybody's in Showbiz **retro sleeve, August 1972**

something more euphoric than audience feedback. In fact he was having trouble standing up.
*(Richard Nusser, **Village Voice,** 8 April 1971)*

So far so good. But below the surface there were distinct problems, a considerable dislocation between all the silliness and the changes that were actually occurring in the group. The Kinks themselves had changed. Where they had once been a four-man unit, or at least a unit with a two-man front line, Ray Davies was now becoming increasingly isolated as the producer, writer and performer. Dave Davies, on his own admission, was withdrawing: 'I think I became more thoughtful after "Lola" – just the fact of growing older, growing up. I became much more interested in philosophy, yoga and all those things. I used to practise my guitar a lot. I never used to practise in the sixties. I'd just go out and play. When you are searching like that, I think you tend to go inwards. It's what I now call my monk period.' With Dave's withdrawal, the balance of power in the group shifted to Ray, especially since John Dalton, John Gosling and Mick Avory were content to go along with the flow.

This increasing pressure on a day-to-day level also came at a time when Ray was becoming more and more ambitious, both creatively and commercially. Albums were the big money-spinners and the main creative form: tired of the singles treadmill, Ray Davies and the Kinks needed no persuading to concentrate on them instead. But Ray Davies's filmic ideas led him to think of grandiose concepts, most of which were finally frustrated by the difficulty of co-ordinating the visual input. Basically, at this stage, the music industry just was not ready. It would be ten years later, with the dawning of the Age of Video, that thanks to their persistence the Kinks would finally profit from what they had presaged.

These ambitions led the Kinks to expand their five-man unit with first a horn section and later various girl singers. From a definable group they became a troupe with Ray at the head – a lot of fun but a logistical nightmare. Also, in 1972 Ray Davies knocked down the last walls between him and his goal of self-determination. The relationship with Boscobel was finally severed – in the wake of the usual litigation – and a warehouse was bought in Tottenham Lane, Hornsey, for use as the Kinks' own studio. This achievement was a summation of all that he and the Kinks had fought for throughout the 1960s and 1970s, but the struggle had been too damaging. Unable to trust anybody, and with ambitions way beyond the writing of the three-minute pop song, Ray Davies was over-extending himself drastically.

RCA were anxious to make a big splash in the market place: the Kinks were one of the main strings to their bow, the other being David Bowie. Fag rock was in, as was evidenced by the turn-out at the Kinks' signing party in New York, which featured Alice Cooper, Andy Warhol and entourage, and the Cockettes, the San Franciscan troupe of transvestites who had adopted the Kinks as mascots. But their new LP, *Muswell Hillbillies*,

Muswell Hillbilly

Well I said goodbye to Rosie Rooke this morning
I'm gonna miss her bloodshot alcoholic eyes
She wore her Sunday hat so she'd impress me
I'm gonna carry her memory 'til the day I die

They'll move me up to Muswell Hill tomorrow
Photographs and souvenirs are all I've got
They're gonna try and make me change my way of living
But they'll never make me something that I'm not

'Cause I'm a Muswell Hillbilly boy
But my heart lies in old West Virginia
Never seen New Orleans, Oklahoma, Tennessee
Still I dream of those Black Hills that I ain't never seen

They're putting us in identical little boxes
No character just uniformity
They're trying to build a computerized community
But they'll never make a zombie out of me

They'll try and make me study elocution
Because they say my accent isn't right
They can clear the slums as part of their solution
But they're never gonna kill my cockney pride

'Cause I'm a Muswell Hillbilly boy
But my heart lies in old West Virginia
Though my hills are not green
I have seen them in my dreams
Take me back to those Black Hills
That I ain't never seen

showed that they were concerned now with something quite different.

The theme of the album was very specific: the forceable removal of the working class from the inner-city areas by the town planners. This had been going on in Britain since the war, uprooting whole communities and creating man-made deserts at the heart of once-great cities, deserts which still remain. One family that had been moved was the Davies family, from Caledonian Road to Muswell Hill. Ray Davies: 'That inspired me to write *Muswell Hillbillies*. I took the idea from the Beverly Hillbillies, who were just pokey little farmers until they struck oil and were sent to live in Beverly Hills.

'In the beginning it was written as a play, a script for a film. It was about the rehousing that was going on at the time. Mum and Dad lived in Islington and they were happy there. I don't know what happened, but they had to move out of the city. Anyway, my image of it was getting on a truck like the Beverly Hillbillies and putting all the stuff on the back. That was the start of the film. Maybe Dave and I were just two little scruffy kids in the back.

'What was great about my parents was that they'd never tell us about the money problems they had; those were always covered up. My Dad loved a pint and he loved to dance; he used to dance like a black man. His name was Frederick George. That's how the idea started out.'

The front cover of *Muswell Hillbillies* shows the group in a pub at Archway, in north London, called the Archway Tavern. Ray Davies: 'I remember at that time the pub had the worst country and western band in the world. They were Irish, trying to play country music. I wanted us to mimic that. Obviously it was more rock 'n' roll because we were doing it, but my vocals were slurred. Also, I was trying to use an off-mike technique, particularly on "Acute Schizophrenia Paranoia Blues". That's a genuine story, again about my dad – "Even my old dad lost the best friend he ever had/Apparently his was a case of acute schizophrenia." He used to love throwing parties on a Friday night; he'd come down and dance and sing all the old songs. He sang like an Indian, a Red Indian, and I think that's where I got my instinct from.

'"Have a Cup of Tea" is my gran. We all used to go round to her with a problem. She was like a fairy godmother. She lived until she was ninety-eight. She lived in a street called Blundel Street. It's not there any more. She used to go to a pub, the Copenhagen, walk all the way herself, order a gin and Guinness, drink it and go home every night until the day she died. You could sit with her when we had rare gatherings that weren't parties and she knew everything. You could see it – she just knew where everybody was at. It was a real privilege being with her. I just wish she and her knowledge could be around now.'

Muswell Hillbillies unravels 'Dead End Street' in loving and exact detail, even down to the repeat of that earlier song's central line, 'What are we living for?'. Its twelve songs cover every aspect of the Kinks' working-class roots: from madness, resignation, anger, alcohol, holiday travel, dieting, crime, to the universal panacea – tea. There is no physical escape: the only possible escape is mental: defiance.

Muswell Hillbillies stands as a great and brave record. With careful listening, the rigorous authenticity of its conception, subject matter and execution turns it into a metaphor for the Kinks' own situation: The long road from 'You Really Got Me' through 'Sunny Afternoon', *Arthur* and *Powerman* ends here. Ray Davies is not an introspective writer but a social critic, highly aware of place and community. *Muswell Hillbillies* is the Kinks' own *Plastic Ono Band*, but, unlike John Lennon and his obsessive soul-searching, Ray Davies looks into his own childhood and works out what it means in terms of its social context and the lives of other people – a mature and remarkable achievement.

However, the album was regarded as disappointing by an audience which had come to expect from the Kinks either the 1960s revisited or the music of a good-time band. Although launched in a blaze of publicity, *Muswell Hillbillies* did only moderately well in the charts, reaching 100 late in 1971.

In a final flourish of working-class independence, Ray Davies fired the last remaining link with the sixties aristocracy, Robert Wace, on 30 December 1971. It was the end of an eight-year association. John Gosling: 'Ray was desperate to get a lot of things done that just didn't seem to be getting done when Robert and Grenville were around, and he thought, "Right, I'll do it myself." It's the old thing – if you want something done, do it yourself. I can understand Ray's attitude at the time, because I have it now. I trust things to other people and they never come up with it. But I think it damaged us.'

The internal structure of the group was changing: Ray Davies was becoming increasingly isolated. As Janis Schact reported in the November 1972 *Circus*, 'He doesn't spend much time off-stage with the other members of the band because he is sure they change when he walks into the room, that somehow and for some unknown reason they are intimidated by his presence.' Dave Davies was withdrawing. It was now up to John Gosling to be the group's raver, to live out the reality behind the Kinks' then current myth. Kinks concerts were awash with alcohol. John Gosling: 'It was freedom to me to go out on stage and play to a lot of people with a band that was well known. I enjoyed myself to the hilt. It was a bit difficult to adjust at first. I just used to hit the bottle, throw as much evil stuff down my throat as possible.

'We had a reputation for it anyway. Dave used to drink a lot; Ray probably didn't. He often abstained because he knew somebody had to keep himself together. At this time in the States we had a nickname, the "Juicers," and at every gig we did, the walls of the dressing room would be lined with cans of beer.' However, despite the rave reactions – as evidenced by Lillian Roxon: 'At Carnegie Hall on the second night, they were shouting "Ray Davies for President". I haven't seen anyone rush the stage like that since Mick Jagger last came into town' –

Celluloid Heroes

Everybody's a dreamer and everybody's a star
And everybody's in movies, it doesn't matter who you are
There are stars in every city
In every house and on every street
And if you walk down Hollywood Boulevard
Their names are written in concrete

Don't step on Greta Garbo as you walk down the Boulevard
She looks so weak and fragile that's why she tried to be so hard
But they turned her into a princess
And they sat her on a throne
But she turned her back on stardom
Because she wanted to be alone

You can see all the stars as you walk down Hollywood Boulevard
Some that you recognize, some that you've hardly even heard of
People who worked and suffered and struggled for fame
Some who succeeded and some who suffered in vain

Rudolf Valentino, looks very much alive
And he looks up ladies' dresses as they sadly pass him by
Avoid stepping on Bella Lugosi
'Cause he's liable to turn and bite
But stand close by Bette Davis
Because hers was such a lonely life
If you covered him with garbage
George Sanders would still have style
And if you stamped on Mickey Rooney
He would still turn round and smile
But please don't tread on dearest Marilyn
'Cause she's not very tough
She should have been made of iron or steel
But she was only made of flesh and blood

You can see all the stars as you walk down Hollywood Boulevard
Some that you recognize, some that you've hardly even heard of
People who worked and suffered and struggled for fame
Some who succeeded and some who suffered in vain

Everybody's a dreamer and everybody's a star
And everybody's in show biz, it doesn't matter who you are
And those who are successful
Be always on your guard
Success walks hand in hand with failure
Along Hollywood Boulevard

I wish my life was a non-stop Hollywood movie show
A fantasy world of celluloid villains and heroes
Because celluloid heroes never feel any pain
And celluloid heroes never really die

You can see all the stars as you walk along Hollywood Boulevard
Some that you recognize, some that you've hardly even heard of
People who worked and suffered and struggled for fame
Some who succeeded and some who suffered in vain

Oh celluloid heroes never feel my pain
Oh celluloid heroes never really die

I wish my life was a non-stop Hollywood movie show
A fantasy world of celluloid villains and heroes
Because celluloid heroes never feel any pain
And celluloid heroes never really die

the Kinks' status in the US was still marginal. It was a question, as it had been so many times in the group's career, of commitment. Marion Rainford: 'They didn't like going to the States for very long. I mean, most groups would go over there and spend three months, but the Kinks would refuse to do that. They didn't like leaving their families.' The Kinks were still stuck in mid-Atlantic, attempting to keep their hands in both in England and the US and refusing to commit themselves to the move that success in the US demanded.

By the summer they were still clinging by their finger-tips to their UK chart status. Their first single for eighteen months in Britain, 'Supersonic Rocket Ship', had entered the charts. Whether hip or not, the survivors were back on *Top of the Pops* for the last time in ten years. And when the Kinks appeared on the programme it was the opportunity for all manner of spectacularly bad behaviour: Ray decided to pour beer all over Slade, while John Gosling fell off the rostrum.

Their next album, *Everybody's in Showbiz, Everybody's a Star*, is another ambitious project that went off at half-cock: as ever, the Kinks were unable to match ideas with practice. *Everybody's in Showbiz* is the Kinks' 'road' album: their impressions, both descriptive and emotional, of the life they were forcing themselves to live. Half the album is about what it took to keep them on that road, and the other half asks the question: why are we doing it? – a question, one suspects, not answered to the Kinks' own satisfaction.

America had lured Ray Davies out of his shell. His occupation of the centre stage, together with the increasing experience of the group, had forced his once flamboyant brother into the shadows. Dave's own uncertainties and prolonged hangover in the wake of the sixties didn't help: 'I've always had that melancholic streak, I don't know where it comes from. My mum always said that I was born old. I've always felt either really young or really old, and I alternate between those two.' Dave's problem of identity, both within the group and without, comes bursting out in 'You Don't Know My Name'. His withdrawal, whether voluntary or forced, changed the power structure of the Kinks irrevocably. The Kinks were now Ray Davies's group, and this was to cause rumblings that still reverberate today.

The centrepiece of *Everybody's in Showbiz* is 'Celluloid Heroes'. Like Kenneth Anger's contemporaneous *Hollywood Babylon*, Ray Davies attacks the central paradox of stardom: the fact that illusion becomes reality and vice versa. In this song he contrasts the permanence of the celluloid with the transience of the people who make it glow. The song's killer hook finally forces Ray Davies to confront the un/reality of his own situation. To the question 'Why?' comes the answer 'There's no choice.'

In contrast to the emotional confusion of the studio set, the live recording stands as a testament to the Kinks' own success and to the new community of which they had become part. Ray Davies: 'It was left over from the glamour period. Suddenly all these transvestites, the Warhol set, started turning up at our gigs, and I thought

I'd go the whole way and sing 'Mr Wonderful' and other songs like that.'

The live album reflects the constant drinking that was occuring at Kinks concerts – symptomatic of the apparent closeness between performers and audience. There's a revealing bit of audience/performer interaction: " 'I need you!' " shouts a fan, to the simpering response: 'Thank you, so nice to be wanted. Ah!' The Kinks were definitely not the crunching, hard rock band of the early sixties or even the pure pop group of the late sixties but rather a traditional party band. They had lost one audience and gained another, and in doing so the Kinks were living out the *Muswell Hillbillies* fantasy (that bad Irish group in the Archway Tavern) for real.

Central to this transformation was the addition of the brass section, the Mike Cotton Sound, that had joined them for the *Muswell Hillbillies* tour. The brass sound on both albums dominates, to the extent of being out of control. This works fine on the live sides but is often obtrusive in the studio set. Ray Davies: 'It wasn't quite right, but I loved having the trad music in there and it was used sparingly. It was rock 'n' rolly trad music. I wanted a rhythm section, but I didn't want it to be Stax. It was a morale thing. The group was suffering because it didn't have a manager. I think there was a lot of insecurity, but the shows came over with sheer bravado.'

Ultimately *Everybody's in Showbiz, Everybody's a Star* is highly confused. The Kinks were successful, yet wondering what success was for. Also, it was a marginal success: they'd lost the original community of Muswell Hill only to find another, yet this new community, however much fun and however sustaining, was no substitute for the original one. The swagger of both albums conceals a deeper malaise that John Gosling hints at: 'In those albums in the early part of the seventies I don't think Ray knew where to turn. He seemed very confused. He didn't know what the public wanted at all. He knew what he could do and what he was good at, but he didn't know if it was going to sell records. I think that caused a lot of inner turmoil in Ray and that made him very difficult to work with at the time.'

Everybody's in Showbiz – 'a good, meaty rock album' in Kinks terms – functioned adequately in the market place, reaching number 70 during the autumn. But a harbinger of the Kinks' increasingly marginal status can be found in a vitriolic review of *Showbiz* by Mike Saunders:

Well, this does it. If dismal albums this year from the Beach Boys, Stones, Hollies, Procul Harum, Lou Reed, Van Morrison, Arthur Lee and Creedence Clearwater hadn't publicly closed the lid on the last remains of sixties rock, the Kinks' new album irreversibly nails it shut. *Everybody's in Showbiz* is abysmal beyond belief, a totally worthless album from the same group that was responsible for so many rock 'n' roll masterpieces of the sixties.

Saunders goes on to deliver his prescription for a cure:

With Led Zeppelin on the verge of re-establishing themselves as one of the handful of truly great groups in rock today, the field of metal mania is stronger than ever. And if rock 'n' roll ever revives, it's probable the heavy metal genre will play a large transitional role in such a development.

The Kinks, with their vaudevillian frailties, were no competition for the ruthlessly reinforced strengths of the new heavy rock groups, which were finally rationalizing a musical barrage of the sort that had gone at Woodstock. The relationship between these groups and their audience was one of dominance and submission. Any sense of community was not between the group and the audience but within the audience itself. The group was way out there, way out of reach. Given all this wattage, the pub cosiness of the Kinks was beginning to seem positively old-fashioned. Furthermore, the small success of the 1972 Reprise compilation *Kinks Kronikles* showed that the Kinks were still seen as a sixties group. *Celluloid Heroes* wasn't a hit on either side of the Atlantic, yet despite all the mistakes of the last project Ray Davies plunged the Kinks into more grandiose schemes with the single-minded tunnel vision of the obsessive.

The first project was to mount *The Kinks are the Village Green Preservation Society* as a West End stage show, augmenting the new eight-man Kinks with six extra horns, six extra singers, a light show and proper staging. Immediately the show started to go over budget, and there were production problems as well. In the end the concert was only a qualified success, but Ray Davies was spurred on to make plans for the realization of his full vision: a three-album extravaganza called *Preservation* which would take this small West End musical on tour throughout Britain and the Americas on the conventional rock circuit. Given the state of both the music industry and the Kinks, this now seems a staggeringly ambitious plan, vainglorious even. Davies says tersely: 'Yeah, I was cracking up then. I should have had a manager to tell me, "Don't do anything, go away for six months." That was a nasty time. But the shows were great. The Kinks were really like the Kinks.'

Nevertheless, spring 1973 saw the Kinks much in demand, reaping the benefit of their three-year build. In England they did yet more TV for the BBC and played a sell-out concert at the Royal Festival Hall on 8 June. In the States their mini-tour at the end of March played to capacity audiences everywhere. And in May another Kinks project came to fruition with the official launch of the Kinks' new recording studio, Konk in Hornsey. The princely sum of £70,000 had been sunk into converting the old warehouse in Tottenham Lane into a sixteen-track studio with Dolby reduction unit, a Neve desk and a baby grand. 'It's nice to have your own recording studio and nicer still when it can be put to commercial use as well,' ran Marion Rainford's press release.

Apart from the label which was to follow later that year, Konk was the Kinks' final act of self-determination.

White City Festival, 15 July 1973

Ray Davies's burning resentment of the corners into which he had been pushed during the 1960s – which at the time had been directed at himself in songs like 'I'm Not Like Everybody Else' – was now being channelled into attacks on the proper enemy, the music business itself. Apart from the essential means of production (the record company and pressing plants), he had now gathered everything under his wing, publishing, management, studio, even the leadership of the group – everything, that is, except himself.

That spring, despite the sell-outs, the Kinks were on a downward spiral. A contemporary review of the February 1973 gig at Southampton by John Hardie captures the mood: 'The brilliance, the flash of contact, the charge of hearing a fine band at full stretch – these were missing. . . . For a few moments I thought the Kinks were going to blow it.' It was at that time that the eddies of the past ten years were collecting into a whirlpool whose quickening waters were, slowly but surely, dragging Ray Davies down. John Gosling: 'His personal life was going through a bit of a chaotic time. I think it overwhelmed him. If everything else had been fine, then he'd have been OK. But signs of strain were beginning to show – pairs of glasses with no glass in them, that sort of thing.'

Roy Hollingworth, who was one of the only music journalists to champion the Kinks during this time, saw signs of stress coming from a different quarter: 'The business end of rock 'n' roll is terrible. No matter what you are or who you are, whether you're an unknown or a celebrity, you're a product and you're treated as such. I know Ray hated all the wheeling and dealing and the wheels within the wheels, which was nothing to do with the music. I think he had a lot of songs tied up with people he didn't necessarily want them tied up with. I think once a musician has to start thinking about business, the reality can be crippling.'

On 20 June the final blow fell: Rasa Davies walked out with Victoria and Louisa. During the 1960s Rasa had been kept firmly in the background, despite the fact that she had sung some of the gorgeous harmonies on the Kinks' best records. But in the early 1970s things were getting worse. Rasa Davies: 'I really felt that I was getting nowhere with my own life. Ray was very busy working. It's something I could cope with today, I'm sure, but I couldn't cope with it then. I had two small children and I was always alone. I used to get very lonely. I threw myself into studying all sorts of different things, but it wasn't enough somehow. I was seeing less and less of Ray, as he was away a lot. When he was at home, he was very into himself and working, writing a lot. He makes himself busy all the time. It's as if he's got this thirst; he's got to be busy. He's unable to relax. His mind is working all the time, I'm sure, even when he's sleeping. I think Ray's just got to be on his own a lot of the time. He's a loner. I think he needs somebody there in the background. But who's going to be in the background and cope with the way he is? If somebody wants to be with somebody, they want to *be* with them. The marriage just crumbled.'

A week later Ray Davies took an overdose of drugs and was admitted to Highgate Hospital. Two weeks after that,

on 15 July, still not having heard from Rasa or the children, Ray Davies and the Kinks were forced to perform with Sly and the Family Stone, and Edgar Winter's White Trash, at the White City Stadium.

It was a bastard day, and a bastard festival. Damp, and friendless White City. Ray shot hurriedly across the stage in white bags and blazer, smiling quickly and took up his usual stance. The set was hurried but he moved a small audience more than it was moved all that day. He had them clapping. And they sang, and you could hear them. And he was the only person to do that. Ray Davies swore on stage, he stood at the White City and swore that he was 'fucking sick of the whole thing', he was 'sick up to here with it', and those that heard shook their heads. Mick just ventured a disbelieving smile and drummed on through 'Waterloo Sunset'. The place sang.

*(Roy Hollingworth, 'Thank You For the Days, Ray', **Melody Maker**, 21 July 1973)*

This article ended with an appeal to Ray to reconsider his decision.

Ray Davies: 'I did try to kill myself that day. I took what must have been uppers, the whole bottle. I went to Whittington Hospital and I said, "My name is Ray Davies and I'm dying." And they laughed. I had my stage make-up on and a clown's outfit, and they said, "Oh, we believe you. Why don't you just write down the names of two people who are next of kin?" I wrote the first one. The second one I couldn't see. I fell over and they knew they had a real case. They dragged me into the ward, got the stomach pump and made me throw up. I remember such terrible guilt. They brought in a real junkie and all I can remember is seeing his boots, sad boots on the next bed. I felt like a complete prat after that. Dave was so good to me; he took me in and looked after me. I remember sending Dave out for some records. At college I had rejected a lot of classical music, but through Paul O'Dell I became fascinated by Mahler. I said, "Dave, will you get me records by Mahler?" and he said, "How do you spell it? Is it like Robin Marlar, the cricketer?" Anyway he brought these records back. I put one on – it was Mahler's Ninth, his last symphony, his version of the end of civilization. I could relate to that. I decided that I was going to leave the music business completely.'

SOAP OPERAS

THE POINTER SISTERS: YES, THEY COULD COULD

RAY DAVIES:
A WHOLE NEW
ACT FOR
THE KINKS

PLUS
PETER TOWNSHEND
MOTT THE HOOPLE
EUROVISION CONTEST
LED ZEPPELIN

● **The cover of** Rolling Stone, **1974**

It's ridiculous. They had all those hits when they were just in their twenties, from which they'd seen precious little money. But it's also a fine irony, and not untypical, that when Ray struggled to control his own destiny and shrugged off all the managers and all the publishers and got a complete handle on his own record deal, the stuff dried up. It was such a psychotic effort to get complete control of his own life – and out came *Schoolboys in Disgrace* and *Preservation Soap Opera*.

Tom Robinson in conversation, 1984

I'm the magic maker
I'm the image maker
I'm the interior decorator . . .

Ray Davies, 'Everybody's a Star (Starmaker)', 1975

If the whirlpool had sucked Ray Davies down, the rest of the Kinks were also dangerously adrift. Their leader's breakdown, if not entirely unexpected, was catastrophic. Yet because of the product commitment under the RCA deal and the momentum of their own career, there was nothing for the Kinks to do but survive – a feeling that is celebrated in various songs of this period. At the same time, the Kinks committed themselves to a course of ever more ambitious, ever more convoluted stage shows and albums which took them further away from their roots and brought them to the verge of artistic and commercial bankruptcy.

Neither the music business nor the Kinks' own internal structure could deal with the demands of 'rock theatre', yet there remained few alternatives. If the pop culture of 1971 and 1972 had been dire, then by 1973 – 4 it was even worse – split irrevocably between 'weeny boppers' on the one hand and 'heavy' album buyers on the other. As far as the industry was concerned, it was in a state of stasis, with the balance tipping finally in 1975 – 6 towards the tightly controlled cartel that runs it today. In this new age you were nothing unless you went platinum, and the Kinks were hardly in this league.

However, they carried on playing constantly across the States: since 1969 the Kinks have toured every year, an unrivalled feat for any group of their period. It was this assiduous application that built the ground work for their success in the late 1970s. But at the time the Kinks were running ragged, and on close inspection the razzle-dazzle of the tours looked threadbare. Ray Davies had managed to pull himself back from the brink, but his problems were not resolved: in seeking to control his business, he'd forgotten what it was there for in the first place. Like the industry as a whole at this period, the business side, not the music, was running the Kinks.

● **The brothers at Konk Studios, late 1973**

● **Ray Davies and one alter ego:** Soap Opera **at the New Victoria Theatre, 16 June 1975**

The decision to combine theatre and pop music could only produce a collision of values in that market place. Because of the different communities out of which they operate, and the different sets of audience expectations, theatre and pop rarely mix well at the best of times. If anybody could have pulled it off, it was Ray Davies, with his theatrical background at art school, his involvement with television drama and a long history of sustained plot from the *Arthur* album onwards. In the 1960s Ray Davies and the Kinks had tapped the collective unconscious in a series of brilliant records: this knack had now deserted them as Ray Davies became increasingly isolated from the world outside and pursued his ambition to merge pop music with other media.

But the art was not there; the money was not there to make it happen; and, with hindsight, the vehicle was not there either. What Ray should have been making, if only he'd known it, was what we now know as the pop promo, that perfect match of narrative, image and music.

The product of the new format was not to appear until the end of the year, but in the meantime Konk was playing an increasingly important part in the Kinks' lives. Dave Davies: 'I really wanted to get the studio together. I spent a lot of time setting it up. In actual fact, I did some engineering on some of the *Preservation* tracks, so I was getting into that as well. I've always been interested in that side anyway. I'll always remember spending this period as a semi-recluse.'

It was at this point, while the Kinks were in limbo, that Dave began to find his feet again, only to feel them slipping away once more. John Gosling: 'I think Dave always felt he'd been overtaken. A lot of the stuff that he recorded at Konk was never released, although it was far superior to the stuff we were doing with the Kinks on *Preservation*. It would have done him a lot of good to see those tracks come out.' Dave would have to wait another seven years before the release of his first solo album.

The rest of the year was spent finishing *Preservation, Part I*, the opening round of the whole *Preservation* project. *Preservation, Part I* grafts a simplistic plot on to the mood of the original *Village Green Preservation Society*: a sylvan Ray Davies fantasy land is threatened by the forces of rampant capitalism, exemplified by Mr Flash. Remembrance for things past dominates the album, but whereas the original *Village Green* worked as a sustained metaphor for the Kinks' isolation from their own roots, *Preservation* shows those roots unravelled, stripped bare.

'I'd really like to wander from country to country, as a sort of tramp. I'd have a bank account I could draw on in the different countries when I needed it, but I would like to do what I wanted and be free to watch people and life,' Ray Davies said in a *Disc* interview on 5 September 1964. Two of the better songs on this album are both sung by the tramp, a character with whom Ray Davies has evidently long identified. 'Sweet Lady Genevieve' is an achingly direct love song with a gorgeous melody, while 'Sitting in the Mid-Day Sun', a sequel to 'Sitting by the Riverside', continues perfectly the series of Ray Davies's hymns to nature and laziness. But the album fails as a whole because what was once implied by a line, a guitar phrase, a gesture or a mood is now explained to death. All the contradictions that had been contained in a three-minute single like 'Dead End Street' are now dissected until the tension that gave those early songs such resonance has utterly disappeared.

Despite Ray Davies's admission now that he should not have been let near a studio during this period, the Kinks, undaunted, plunged straight into more recording. Within six months they had come up with a double album, *Preservation, Part II*. This was at a time when they were still touring non-stop and Ray Davies was personally involved with prolonged negotiations to establish the new Konk label.

Preservation, Part II was released by RCA in July, a mere seven months after *Preservation, Part I*. This double LP, which shows distinct signs of over-ambitiousness, strain and haste, attempts to tell the story of:

> a world-travelled tramp, who returns to his village green, a small strip of terrain in a sleepy backwater, to renew the friendships of his youth and settle down. He expects to find it unchanged. Instead he finds a corrupt and dictatorial regime run by Flash and his gang of spivs who are terrorizing the population and lining their own pockets. But the people have had enough and a military coup brings Flash tumbling down. Face to face with his own conscience, he eventually repents his evil ways and is conditioned to take his place in the new society.

The cover photo illustrates a waxy-faced Ray Davies in Max Miller garb surveying a post-holocaust landscape; on the reverse he and the rest of the Kinks are busy acting out various characters from the plot. Ray Davies: 'I was Max Miller, one of my idols from music-hall days. Max Miller kept his audience in touch with reality. He was just a comedian, a rebellious comedian, and he couldn't get work for a lot of the time because he was too naughty to cope with.'

From the record it is difficult to guess where Davies's and the Kinks' sympathies lie: certainly Flash is much more developed as a character than Mr Black, the usurper, who is merely a cipher. In the end Davies is asking: when extreme, which is worse, corruption or purity? Hardly revelatory, but at least the album does not deliver easy judgements.

Ray Davies: 'Humour is a good element to keep in music. I think what happened in the *Preservation* record is that the humour changed. A lot of people thought it was humourless because it was dealing with a very black subject. But it was really a sort of black comedy.' Of all the show albums of the period, this is the one that is the hardest to take without the stage performance or the film. There are several reasons for this. The plot is tighter than that of *Part I* and needs explaining: this is disastrous in musical terms, for, as on the Who's *Tommy*, the album's weakest tracks are those in which things are made explicit to the point of banality in order to push the action along. Hokey announcements break up the flow; many of the album's songs skitter in Thespian speech over a wide variety of styles; and the Kinks are unable or temperamentally unwilling to play with their usual gusto. In concentrating so hard on content, Ray Davies was losing the form.

The Kinks were no longer a rock 'n' roll band; they had become a troupe, playing arrangements rather than songs. Mick Avory: 'Those songs were away from the group-type sound because there were so many other musicians on them – different singers, different brass sections, etc. We got a bit detached from the group itself. You felt like you were doing the music for a particular project rather than the band. Now when we work out a song we think how would the Kinks play it. But it was almost like doing film music in terms of concept.'

What good songs there are – 'When a Solution Comes', 'He's Evil', 'Artificial Man' and the jug-band 'Mirror of Love' – sound like demos for the finished product. John Gosling puts his finger on the cause: 'A lot of it was bland and over-produced. It was remixed over and over again. I think it was a bad thing, having our own studio, having that amount of time to try things out. It was destructive rather than constructive.' John Gosling also reveals that there was some friction within the group at that time: 'We used to see it as Ray Davies manipulating the band to do a Ray Davies solo album. There was quite a bit of resentment now and then. Everybody probably needed more of a free rein. From my point of view, I felt that given a bit more of a chance, musically the songs could have been great. The songs that were good were very, very good. I was quite happy to go along with the way that Ray wanted them done, but we were still holding back.'

During the spring the Kinks (or rather Ray Davies, Dave Davies and Tony Dimitriades) had formed a record production company, Konkwest Limited, and its product outlet, Konk Records. The Kinks, finally, had their own label. Ray Davies: 'I thought it would be a great idea to have a little label so we could put out 5,000 records of a new band. In the seventies you had to be a megastar to get a record deal. I thought we could get these little bands, almost like having a football team. That's what I really intended it to be.'

One of the first artists to be signed to the label, along with solo singers Claire Hamill and Andy Desmond, was Café Society, a soft vocal group featuring Ray Doyle, Hereward Kaye and Tom Robinson. Tom: 'We had a residency at a place called the Troubadour in Earls Court every other Tuesday night, and Alexis Korner was guesting for us that night. Ray Davies, John McCoy (who was a manager friend of ours) and Dimitriades came down to see us. Ray got up and did a little jam with Alexis, and then he invited us into the studio to do a sound test. That would have been about December 1973.

'There were two contracts. There was a recording contract and then we were told about this other thing called "publishing", which gives you a bit of extra money, and we agreed. To be fair to Tony Dimitriades, he did say, "You must show this to a lawyer," but we didn't

● **The** Preservation **troupe, 1974**

know how to find a lawyer. We didn't even have a full-time manager. In the end I telephoned somebody and said, ''Well, we've got this contract. Do you think it's all right?'' And he said, ''Well, what does it say in it?'' I went through the main points, and he said, ''Well, that sounds OK.'' It was signed, but it was never gone through.' Café Society were making the same mistakes that the Kinks had made over ten years before.

While all this was going on Ray Davies had plunged himself into writing and staging yet another play with songs, *Starmaker*, for Granada Television. He was coming up with ideas so fast that *Starmaker*, with all its songs and dialogue, was recorded the week that *Preservation, Part II* was released.

The Kinks hit the usual problems that face musicians when they start working in TV: for a start, the pace of pop groups and TV studio crews are entirely different; also the Kinks fell foul of an insufficiently equipped sound department. John Gosling: 'We had a problem with *Starmaker* because they spent two days on the visuals and about six hours, if that, on the sound. So the sound was very inferior – it was a terrible mix. But I think Ray had started to get the acting thing out of his system.' There were other problems as well. Ken Jones: 'When we did the TV in Manchester Ray was the actor and the star, call it what you like, and the Kinks were the musicians. Dave was in a bad way again. I agreed with Dave because I thought to myself, I wouldn't let anyone treat the Kinks this way.'

Starmaker shows Ray Davies trapped in the hall of mirrors in which he'd been pacing for the last ten years. Many of his songs have expressed actual dilemmas – sexual, social and cultural – but on *Starmaker* he zeros in on the implicit theme of the *Everybody's in Showbiz* studio LP, with its unreal reality and doubts about the nature of stardom and the impossibility of escaping it. *Starmaker*, transmitted on 4 September, initially sets up the star as playing an ordinary person (for research purposes, of course), but the identity of that ordinary person, Norman, takes over so that you don't know which is the real person, the star or Norman. Is it the star's fantasy or Norman's? If it is Norman's fantasy, was it ever real?

It is a beautifully poised guessing game that is also fun, but reviews were mixed. Some critics thought that the show's subject was condescending, while others claimed that Ray Davies was simply revolving his ideas like a hamster on a treadmill. But there were others who thought differently. Pete Townshend: 'It's just shocking to realize that it happened and it did nothing. I remember seeing it and thinking, this is either going to be completely ignored or it's going to be huge. It was totally and completely out of time. It was like seeing the last episode of *The Prisoner* but being lived out by somebody. Ray was both the puppet master and the puppet, precariously living out the audience's experiences, crying and laughing in public. It was unbelievable.'

And then it was *Preservation* live. After a well received show at the Royalty in London on 16 November, the Kinks went off to the States. Ray Davies: 'I was being

pressurized. They kept saying, ''Do you want to do another tour around America?'' And I said, ''Yeah, I'll do it if I can do my show with it.'' It was a sad attempt to get the show done as a musical on stage. There were some good things in it, but the whole thing did degenerate.'

Mick Avory: 'It was like an amateur theatre thing but fun to do. And audiences felt they were part of it as well. They came to the Kinks' concerts because we'd only do them in little theatres – the show wouldn't come across in big places. It was a really good thing to do for a while. And it was a way of progressing and keeping the Kinks together. But finally, you have to get back to the group again.'

No sooner had the Kinks toured with *Preservation* than they changed tack yet again, this time to work up the *Starmaker* material into the *Soap Opera* package. Ray Davies: '*Soap Opera* was wonderful. I was a man who was imagining I was an accountant imagining that he was me.'

Soap Opera finds the Kinks, yet again, sustained merely by the force of Ray Davies's own obsession with an album which dramatizes what appears to be a severe identity crisis. The *Preservation* albums had reflected Davies's confusion – about his own class and politics, about where he was in the world and about what he had to do with it – with the central figure of the tramp as his own escape clause. *Soap Opera* picks apart the *Everybody's in Showbiz* thread and its unreal reality, and unravels it in various shades of grey.

Ray Davies had now been a pop star for over ten years and had survived longer than most in a highly competitive business. Yet the prolonged struggle to adapt to shifting artistic and market criteria, on top of the insecurities which had driven him into that way of life in the first place, had taken its toll, quite apart from his appalling one-man fight against the music industry.

The comparative conviction of the last song makes it quite clear what Ray Davies's stance is in relation to his own conundrum: 'They can't stop the music playing on.' Pop music in the seventies was no longer an arena for the artistic vision and social comment which had affected people's lives so strongly in the sixties but simply a self-contained world with its own little rituals and follies. It was not something that could get better or worse; it was just there, its own universe. The Kinks were caught like flies in amber. There was nothing they could do but flaunt their gestures and carry on. *Soap Opera* is not easy listening: apart from the camp humour with which Davies infects some of the songs, and the snatches of dialogue with June Richie, the album's theme affects the music and the melodies are tired, directionless and second-hand. The Kinks sound and feel alienated from everything.

Where *Soap Opera* worked was on the stage, particularly in the States, where the Kinks began to pick up a new, younger audience. The long touring was beginning to pay off, and just as *Soap Opera* reflected the alienation of its creator and star, so it reflected the alienation of the American audience, for many of whom pop music was the only lifeline in a culture without community.

● **Mr Flash,** Preservation **tour, December 1974**

• Ray Davies, 16 June 1975

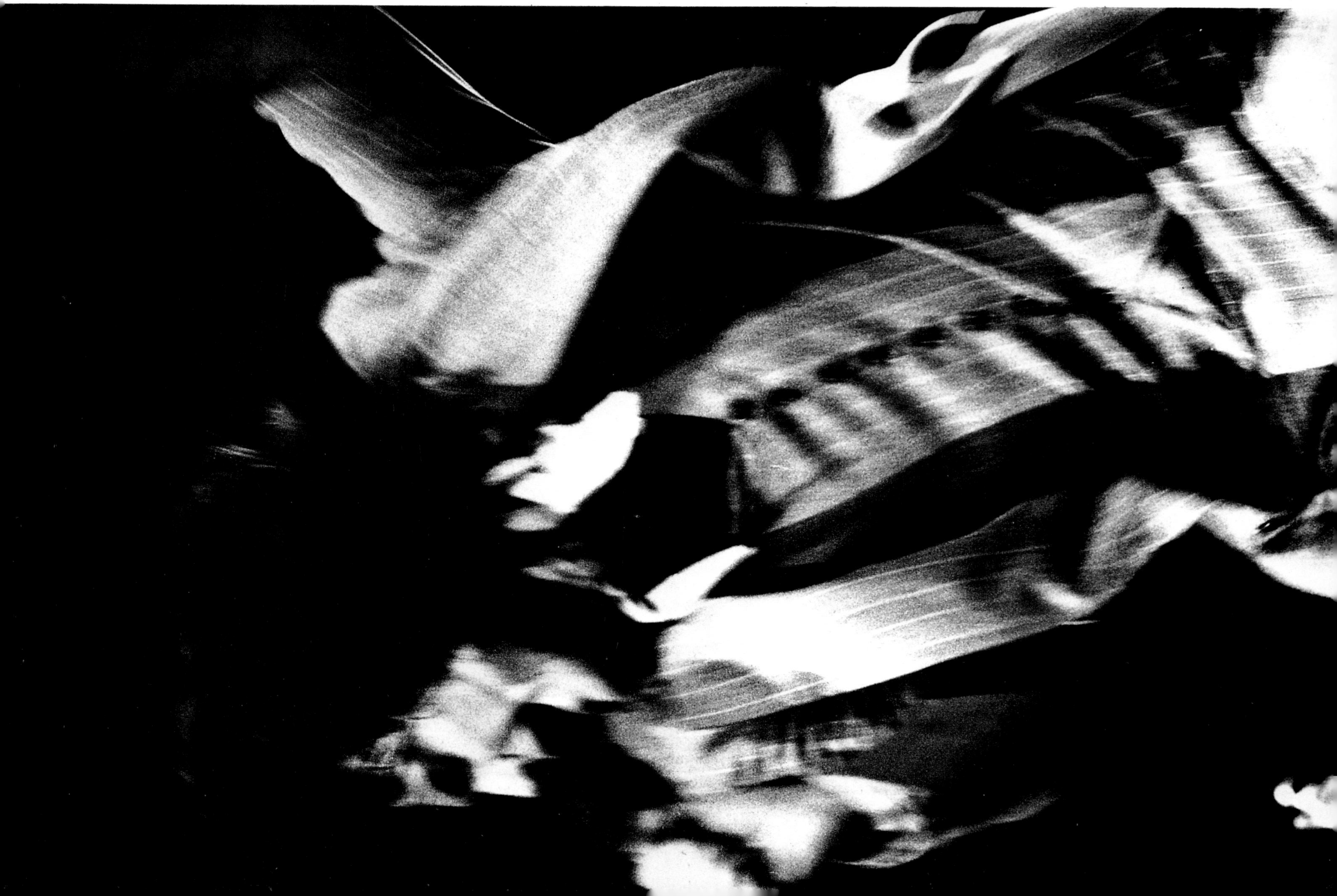

They could just well imagine the reverse of Davies's own conundrum: that they were in fact pop stars imagining their own reality. The *Soap Opera* tour, however, saw dissension among the Kinks building up. John Gosling: 'Dave and I used to talk about it on the plane coming over: "Wouldn't it be just great if we could be an ordinary rock band?" We both resented the fact that we were using a lot of extra people and that sometimes the extras would be at the focal point of the stage. I found myself sitting behind the lot. I'd been here for five years and I was backing three girls! I used to get really wild, and Dave felt the same. We used to have little outbursts.'

This discontent was evident at home as well. Ray Davies was reacting to the world with the haste of a man driven. Frantic writing schedules and the Kinks' own punishing efforts to keep afloat on both sides of the Atlantic meant that not enough time was spent on Konk – at least not in the eyes of some.

Café Society, with Tom Robinson, were trying to finish their first album for the label. Tom Robinson was forced, both by nature and by the group situation, into the role of catalyst as far as dealing with Konk was concerned: 'The album took a year – not a year of constant work, I hasten to add, but a year of waiting to get in the studio. Ray toyed with it. It was really like a rich man's toy, a record label to produce other acts and based, I don't doubt on good intentions. But it was really frustrating: we were never actually allowed to get on with what we could do. It was always a matter of getting studio time and actually persuading the company (in fact Ray) to agree that something should happen. You could never get anything defined. It was always, "Oh well, we'll go into the studios soon. We'll do it one day next week." And come Thursday you'd call up and say, "Wasn't it going to be this week?" "Oh no, the Kinks are in America this week." It was very frustrating. What Ray did do was to let us support the Kinks a couple of times. I learned everything I know about how to deal with the audience just from watching Ray Davies from the side of the stage.'

By this time Davies was on to the next, and final, concept album, *Schoolboys in Disgrace*, which traces Mr Flash back to his adolescence in a sequence designed to illustrate his (and, of course, Ray Davies's own) motivation for his subsequent actions. The record and show, premiered late in 1975, were the strongest Kinks products for a while: Davies had caught the dissension among his own ranks in a concept and a series of songs designed to match the Kinks' sense of humour and musical predilections.

Ray Davies told Judith Simons of the *Daily Express* in March 1976: 'I approach my albums like a newspaper article: take a theme, research and develop it. The song with the most social significance on this record is "The Hard Way", based on friends' visits to the Youth Employment Officer and the way they were pushed into jobs they did not want. By the age of seventeen some of them were sad people, already bitter, regretting not having worked harder at school or developed skills. My own favourite is the most autobiographical, "The Last Assembly". On my last day at school I was ill, yet I

struggled in for that last assembly. I'd spent much of my school days skipping lessons. At one time my truancy was so bad, I was sent to a psychiatrist. I was the first boy in the family after five girls, so I had everything I ever wanted. There wasn't anything significantly wrong with me. I was simply trying to be individual.'

Some of *Schoolboys* is as personal as Ray Davies ever gets. The 'plot' reads distinctly like some of Dave's escapades on Hampstead Heath (for example, Flash is found *in flagrante delicto* and summarily expelled from school). But for once the plot is not of primary importance: the album shows the Kinks back on form with good hard songs, played clearly by just the five Kinks for the most part. The brass section is relegated to its former function of punching out chorus lines. The dragging tempos and pastiches of *Soap Opera* are gone. Many of the songs, like 'Jack, the Idiot Dunce' and 'The First Time We Fall in Love', are in a style that goes back to what Dave Davies, and indeed the rest of the group, were listening to at school – rock 'n' roll; others, like 'I'm in Disgrace' and 'The Hard Way', go back to that mid-1960s 'chunky Kinks sound'. *Schoolboys* is a return to form by a group and a man who had plumbed the depths and were now on the way back up. Songs like 'No More Looking Back' and 'The Last Assembly' show Ray Davies squaring up not only to his own adolescence but also to subsequent events, notably his failed relationship with his wife and, to an extent, his audience.

On *Schoolboys in Disgrace* Ray Davies implicitly accepts the permanent adolescence that being involved in popular music entails: 'I want to be a little boy. How can I be a little boy when I have to leave school? All right, I'll go to college. Oh, that's going to end soon. How can I continue to be a little boy? Join a rock 'n' roll band.' Furthermore, *Schoolboys* marks the end of the period of self-examination identified by the concept albums. For the 1960s had taken their toll on both brothers: whereas Dave, the extrovert, had withdrawn during the 1970s, Ray, that most defended of men, had carried out his soul-searching in public.

But the old sureness of touch was beginning to return. Change was in the air, and the new optimism of the group and the stage shows reflected it.

Ken Jones: 'We had a back-projection screen, and Ray would come on stage in a mask as old Mr Flash, and on screen would come Dave, Mick and John as schoolboys, and they would walk across the screen. Then Ray would disappear and come out again as a schoolboy. Then he would come out with a gown and cane – he was the head – and two girls in boaters and short skirts and stockings and suspenders would sing with him. It was fantastic, there's no question about it. It was wonderful what they did on stage.' Ray Davies: 'It was real repertory rock.'

Schoolboys was also the last album for RCA, which quickly brought out a shoddy 'greatest hits' package called *Celluloid Heroes*. The Kinks were about to make a major shift. Their record sales and status, despite growing interest in the press, had sunk to a dangerous level in Britain. The endless series of reissues that had

139

● **The Kinks with Clive Davies: Arista signing party, June 1976**

been streaming out of Pye Records since 1971 had hung the old 1960s image of the group like a millstone around their necks. In Britain everything the Kinks did was judged (as to some extent it still is) by reference to their sixties records, which, thanks to their continuing quality and the degenerate nature of pop at the time, were by then being called 'classics'.

But in America sales and status were rising. Since 1973 the Kinks had virtually ignored Britain, and their five-year slog was beginning to pay off. After a dip with *Preservation, Part I* their sales went into the fifties with *Soap Opera* and into the forties with *Schoolboys in Disgrace*. Ray Davies: 'They urged us to keep going. We decided to concentrate on America because we'd had that ban and we felt cheated. We thought we'd got to put that right because we're good. Besides, Britain in the seventies was piss-poor. Nothing was happening – absolutely nothing. That's why when the so-called 'new wave' came along in 1977 it released a new energy in me. It also got rid of all those pop people.'

Ray Davies made two decisive steps early in 1976: he rented a flat in New York, and he started negotiations to sign the Kinks to a new record company, Arista, whose president, Clive Daves, had a knack for signing prestige mavericks. The Kinks were about to become an American group.

ROCK 'N' ROLL FANTASY

Hello you, hello me, hello people we used to be
Isn't it strange, we never changed
We've been through it all yet we're still the same
And I know it's a miracle, we still go and for all we know
We might still have a way to go . . .

Kinks, *'Rock 'n' Roll Fantasy'*, 1977

I always shun the idea that I might be accepted, because maybe if I was, I'd stop searching. I want the right to change.

Ray Davies, **Newsweek**, 26 June 1978

The Kinks' decision to commit themselves totally to America in the early summer of 1976 was a smart move. Ken Jones: 'If your ambition is to let everybody know who you are, what you're saying, and to let them know about your music, you have to go to America – that's a fact. If you crack it in America, so to speak, you'll sell millions and millions of records and millions and millions of people will know about you.' The Kinks were now at that stage of their career when Britain could not – and would not – sustain them, either artistically or financially. Not only is the British market small (albeit highly influential) but it is also committed, for a number of reasons, to a high turnover of product and ideas. The Kinks had lasted five years in the British market, from 1963 to 1968, and they'd had enough. Ray Davies's move to New York and the Kinks' signing to Arista marked their final commitment to a market into which they had been trying to break since 1969. The Kinks, that most disorganized of groups, were now obliged to play the numbers game, where success is measured by the three zeros after your sales figures.

Although they share the same language, the British and the American music business could not be more different, in terms of both the way in which they operate and what the audience expects from them. In the UK the music tends to be called 'pop', in the US 'rock'. The semantics underlie the different places that popular music occupies in the two cultures. Britain is a tiny country, with centralized media pouring out information about popular music with intense rapidity and concentration. The blanket coverage that any successful group will receive makes for a success that is quicker but far more unstable. Britain is the hot-house from which the seeds of much pop culture are dispersed throughout the world. The country will know about a new group within days of its first significant success, but this also means that the pop audience will be prepared to cast it aside just as quickly for the next sensation. Furthermore, in 1976 Britain was undergoing a cultural revolution of unparalleled ferocity: according to the rigid rules of punk

rock – rigid because in a cultural desert there was no choice but to stand your ground and scream, 'This is mine!' – nobody could have long hair (except the Ramones), nobody could wear flares and nobody was supposed to be over twenty-five. How could the Kinks compete with this, even if they wanted to?

If Britain is small but trying to expand, America is a huge country trying to reduce itself to a manageable size. This is reflected in the differences between the pop audiences. In Britain you go to a concert and the attitude expressed is 'Look at me! I'm different! I'm not like everybody else!' In America it is much more likely to be 'Look at us! Hey, we're the same!' Pop music does not express a single community in England but rather a myriad of diverse, potentially warring tribes; in America it is the source of a different sort of identity, a way of ignoring those empty spaces in a community that is illusory but nonetheless almost real because it is believed in so strongly.

Because it is more about coming together, and because of its size, America is a much slower-moving market. But once 'cracked', it is more sustaining. The length of time that it takes an artist to wind up is commensurate with the time taken to wind down. This is difficult for the British to comprehend, since for every American pop cycle there are at least ten in the UK. Yet America allows an artist to grow and keep his position in a way that Britain rarely can. But America needs constant attention: tours have to coincide with the release of albums and must be scheduled carefully over the fifty states in order to achieve the desired effect. This calls for big industrial muscle, and the record companies are far more powerful in the US than they ever could be in the UK. Basically, if you are not signed to a major label and do not have thousands of dollars pumped into promotion, touring and all the other things that grease the wheels, you will not survive.

In 1976 the Kinks were well enough placed for a breakthrough. In Britain they were the group that had had all those nice, wistful sixties hits, but in America they were known as a good, fun rock 'n' roll band. Indeed, on stage there Ray Davies's ambivalences about his family are resolved: a Kinks concert in the US was and is the opportunity for him and the group to create a family of three thousand people under one roof, a family that will be concerned with the present, not the past, and will respond gracefully and without embarrassment to the Kinks' own emotional needs.

If the sound of the original Kinks was being vindicated by punk rock, then the next few years were to see their influence being openly acknowledged in a series of covers that cemented their reputation with a new generation that had only just been born when 'You

● **Ray Davies, 1978**

Really Got Me' was a hit: 'David Watts' by the Jam, 'Stop Your Sobbing' by the Pretenders, and, most important, in the USA, 'You Really Got Me' by Van Halen. The Kinks were returning to first base: from the gaudiness of 1966 through the theatrical delusions of the 1970s, they began to rework the crunching hard rock of their first two years – albeit played by men twelve years older. This often workmanlike music reflected both the Kinks' own artisan approach to their music – with their emphasis just as much on perspiration as on inspiration – and the class make-up of their audience. The Kinks had long moved out of the smart metropolitan centres and were attacking the great hinterland that lay in between.

In 1975-6 Ray Davies and the Kinks turned to their adolescence in an implicit recognition that that is the state most accurately encompassed by pop music. This second adolescence suited them well and chimed with both the demands and the emotional sympathies of the American market, where pop, or rather rock, describes a permanent adolescence. Yet, as ever, the Kinks stick out at awkward angles: their album titles from the period provide glimpses of their psychic state in the constant half-light of touring – *Sleepwalker, Misfits* and *Low Budget*. However much energy they still had, the Kinks were no longer spring chickens, and their music from this period describes a knowledge that no adolescent could have – knowledge that is sometimes optimistic, sometimes cynical – together with an attitude that is at odds with the requirements necessary to make it to the American top five, as opposed to the American top twenty.

For the Kinks 1976 was a year of recuperation and realignment. Apart from the RCA compilation, no records were released that year; most of the group's time was taken up with touring, changing record companies and recording *Sleepwalker*. Dave Davies: 'Just prior to *Sleepwalker* there was a bit more depth to what we were doing. We were doing what we set out to do, and the energies in me were coming back, being used. I felt that maybe I had learned something, and I was more thoughtful about it. I used to practise a lot, and I'd learned the value of doing it right. I felt I had more value, and I could also see more clearly the value of the simplicity that was involved.'

This internal change matched what was required of the Kinks in the market. Ken Jones: 'Ray obviously came to the realization that perhaps he should get back to just doing rock 'n' roll, which is when he did *Sleepwalker*. People were always interested in this concept thing, but unfortunately the public out there weren't so much, so we had to get rid of the cult image. We always did reasonably good business or we sold out or whatever, but that's really all we were doing, ticking over. All the Kinks fans came, but it was time to get to all those other people who weren't Kinks fans.'

Sleepwalker was released on both sides of the Atlantic in March 1977. Ray Davies: 'It is an up-sounding album after all those concepts. It was the first album recorded in the new control room at Konk, using Roger Wake, an

engineer, who contributed a lot to that album. Fortunately, it ended up a happy album, but it came through turbulent times. We had problems with money. We didn't have any money. We went broke – almost.

'I had this song called "Brother" that Clive Davies was really hot on, and he said, "Ray, I got to call you now because I consider 'Brother' to be the most high-spot cut, the most cross-over possibility, and I really urge you – this is a creative input – I urge you to add an ending, a long fade-out using violins, as I told Artie Garfunkel and Paul Simon when they did 'Bridge Over Troubled Water', which I more or less produced. I urge you to extend the ending and I think you'll have a major hit." The song was finished, but I can't get these guys to do this sort of song too often, so we took great care to get all the sounds right and put the ending on. I hired a whole string section. And the song never even came out as a single!'

'Brother' makes it quite clear that Ray Davies was quite prepared to extend the idea of family to others – an implicit acknowledgement of how important an audience, and in particular the American audience, was to him.

Sleepwalker has America written all over it, physically and psychologically. The title track, 'Full Moon and Sleepless Nights', shows that Ray Davies has found in New York a twenty-four-hour environment that is speedy and complex enough to match his all-night brainstorms, an environment in which he can still be free to write vignettes like 'Life on the Road', which is 'Big Black Smoke' ten years on, with the obligatory homosexual tease. And American rock resounds through the album in Dave's exuberant guitar work and in the structure of songs like 'Full Moon' and 'Jukebox Music'. Some of these are reminiscent of another 'born again' album, Bob Dylan's *Planet Waves*. Both share the same cautious optimism, tempered by experience.

But 'Life Goes On' is severely reduced in scope and lacks the expansiveness of a song like 'See My Friends'; the Kinks now found themselves in a contracted culture where everybody's options were, suddenly, quite limited. America offered the Kinks room to move and to grow, but at a price: what had been effortless in the mid-sixties now had to be worked at, and this is reflected both in the group's playing and in Davies's song-writing. *Sleepwalker* shows Davies still preoccupied with his perennial concerns, but these are slightly simplified and dry cleaned for US taste – no more of those ellipses or ambiguities that can sustain a song by themselves – while the group, if technically more proficient, had lost much of the immediately identifiable sound that had been their characteristic in the 1960s. The price for a gallant survival was homogenization.

Ray Davies: '*Sleepwalker* did all right. One reviewer said it was like raising Lazarus from the dead. Our record sales went up to the 350,000 mark, which is good. Having started a couple of years earlier at 25,000 on *Village Green Preservation Society*, we were pushing it up. We had a really good agent at that time – Herb Spar. He said, "Raymond, you should come back to the United States and tour. I believe in this act. I think you're a con

● Andy Pyle, Mick Avory, John Gosling, Dave Davies, Ray Davies: Konk
  Studios, late 1977

summate artist. I really urge you to come back.'' I came back and he'd died. I wish he could be around now. I miss him.'

Sleepwalker is a good American rock album, a success at the Kinks' first attempt at the genre. Clive Davis's faith paid off: the album went to number 21 in the States, while the 'Sleepwalker' single just nudged the top fifty, the first time the Kinks had done so since 'Apeman' six years before. In Britain, however, it was a different story, and Ray Davies was forced to admonish a London audience at a February 1977 Rainbow date ('Do you realize who I am? But do you realize who I used to be?'), for *Sleepwalker* and the Kinks were lost in a tidal wave of shouted imprecations, paint-spattered Sta-prest and liberating noise. Punk rock reinvented pop politics in the generation gap, and the Kinks were on the wrong side. But, if they were not quite enemies – just scratch the roots of the early Clash and you will find chopped Who riffs (and who taught the Who to riff?) – they were worthy of being ignored. Dave Davies liked it all none the less: 'What I liked about the punk thing when it started was that it was about giving trouble. It was fun as well. I mean, you could have a go at people, but you could also have a good laugh – that's what I liked about it. I think one of Ray's outstanding qualities is the fact that he can say something very gritty, something human, and smile. It was the same kind of stirrings, the same kind of emotions.'

Ray Davies's position on the matter was complicated by the fact that his erstwhile protégé, Tom Robinson, was receiving a good deal of critical attention in the wake of punk rock, and part of that critical attention was concerned with Tom's railings about Konk in general and Ray Davies in particular. Tom Robinson: 'I wanted to leave the label. I informed Ray of the fact, and he said, ''Well, I don't want you to leave. I think you should make a solo album, with stuff like 'Glad to be Gay', 'Martin', 'Long Hot Summer' and 'Grey Cortina'. It's quite promising. You should make a solo album.'' I've got a draft somewhere of an imaginary conversation I was going to have with Ray. I was going to say, ''Look, you know I'm going to make it, and you can either help me or hinder me, but I certainly won't make it if I stay here, so why don't you let me go?'' He turned up at a gig at the Nashville, and I sang ''Set Me Free'' – or was it ''Tired of Waiting''? – which was dedicated to him.'

Relations between Café Society and Konk had deteriorated to the extent that the group had split up while recording their second album. Tom Robinson had quickly formed a band to record his songs and, thanks to the press, a clutch of strong songs and Tom's forthright gay image, the Tom Robinson Band were quickly in a position to sign to EMI. But Tom Robinson was still contracted to Konkwest. Tom Robinson: 'They had to buy us out of the contract. I'm not prepared to say the exact amount. Ray kept the publishing on ''Glad to be Gay'', ''Martin'', ''Long Hot Summer'', ''Grey Cortina'', thirteen songs in all, and he was given the publishing on ''Motorway''. So he still has a sort of piece of me but, looked at from his point of view, I had nothing before he met me.

● **'Full Moon',** Sleepwalker **tour, 1977**

He had invested some long-term money in me.'

Davies kept silent in print but not on record. The Kinks' Christmas 1977 single contains a distinctly tart put-down of Tom Robinson in 'Prince of the Punks': 'Tried to be gay but it didn't pay/So he bought a motorbike instead...' 'Father Christmas' is equally irritated, though more ambiguous. Davies divides his sympathy between the mugged Santa and his attackers: 'Have yourself a very merry Christmas, have yourself a good time/But remember the kids who have nothing while you're drinking down your wine.' Although he was on the wrong side of punk muggings, Davies was once too a musical mugger, and he was keenly aware of his own ambivalence.

Despite the success of *Sleepwalker,* the Kinks still had to tour constantly, often second-billed to people like Alice Cooper. That pressure, and the intense work involved in recording the next album, *Misfits*, started to break up the seventies Kinks. First off was John Dalton: 'I didn't want to be away from home any more. That was the main reason. I'd been on the road for a long time, and the time had come when I thought I'd like to spend a bit of time at home with the wife and kids.'

Dalton was replaced by Andy Pyle, but during *Misfits* both he and the keyboard player, John Gosling, left. Dave Davies: 'They both left for reasons known unto themselves. I know that John Gosling had been unhappy for some time, but he'd had a fair crack of the whip with

Preservation.'

Misfits is another transition album. Ostensibly 'about' a variety of social outcasts – black prophets, transvestites, tax exiles, rock bands – it is, as usual, about nothing so much as the Kinks themselves. *Misfits* shows the group and its writers struggling to stake out their territory not only in popular music but in society at large – a perennial concern but never quite as consistently expressed. 'Where do I belong?' the album asks. It adds to that question a proud defiance and a distinct sense that the Kinks' outsider status is self-imposed. Much of this would be merely self-indulgent, except for the fact that, as usual, Ray Davies tempers his self-examinations with enough humour and emotional depth to make them relate to people other than just himself.

The best songs are those which have some direct emotional impact. Dave Davies's 'Trust Your Heart', with its aching intensity and rock 'n' roll sensibility, is as much a statement of his worldview as 'Misfits' is of Ray's; 'I bring thunder, lightning and rain/For those who administered injustice and pain/Comfort the weak, feed the poor/What on earth do we need governments for?/Truly, oh truly/Trust your heart.' Faced with the same problem, Ray will use his intellect and Dave his feelings.

Ray pulls it out of the hat on two songs, 'Misfits' and 'Rock 'n' Roll Fantasy'. Ray Davies: 'The song ''Misfits'' is about a friend, Frank Smyth. I saw him wandering down the street one night when I was walking the dog. He stayed and drank everything I had. I met him the next day and he looked remarkably fresh, like he'd just had a full night's sleep: "You'd been sleeping in a field but you look real rested/You set out to outrage but you can't get arrested/You think your image is new, but it looks well tested/You're lost without a crowd yet you go your own way." That's him. It's a lot about me as well. You always dislike things you see in other people because they remind you of you. The hardest rock 'n' roll people in America took to that song, even though it didn't have any cranky guitar sounds or anything.'

'Misfits' parallels Davies's own rootlessness with that of American culture, and by laying himself on the line he reveals an emotional solidarity with an American rock audience trying to make sense of that same displacement. The springboard song is 'Rock 'n' Roll Fantasy', which couples Davies's own relationship with his brother and his doubts about the Kinks' continuing survival and usefulness with the doubts of an audience wondering about the survival of rock music and its culture. Ray Davies: 'I went to a Peter Frampton concert, came home, Elvis had died. There's the line "The king is dead" – that is outwardly Elvis, it's got to be – then "You might be through but I'm not done." The song also comes from being thoroughly depressed at seeing Peter Frampton at Madison Square Garden. I felt sad for him because he was on tour with us and he was a really good guitarist and still is. You know, when he was on stage all the promoters and people were eating and drinking backstage. They weren't watching the show. That really annoys me – it's a circus.'

'Rock 'n' Roll Fantasy' captured the commitment to rock 'n' roll so well that when released as a single in June it made the American top thirty, the first time the group had done so for eight years. *Misfits* did not sell as well as *Sleepwalker* but still confirmed the Kinks' growing reputation. The Kinks toured *Misfits* from 26 May to 25 June 1978. For that tour they picked up two new musicians, Gordon Edwards on keyboards and Jim Rodford on bass. Jim Rodford: 'In 1964 I toured with the Kinks when I was with another band, the Mike Cotton Sound. We made good friends with the Kinks, to the extent that at the end of the 1960s all our horn section joined them. I had a call in 1978 – "What are you doing? We need a bass player for a tour in America. We're not sure if we're going to want anybody permanently, but if we know you're available, hopefully you can do it and you can sing as well. Are you interested in the tour?" Of course I was. And I've been there ever since.'

The success of 'Rock 'n' Roll Fantasy' and 'Misfits' was nudging the Kinks on to a new level of operation. It was also at this time that they acquired an American manager, Elliot Abbot, who was already managing Ry Cooder and Randy Newman – ironically, another 'cult' performer who had moved to a cross-over success. Barry Dickens, their English agent at this time, sums up the management situation in the intervening period: 'Ray was the manager and still is. Others may be called the manager, but the person who makes all the decisions is Ray, and

● Ray Davies, Gordon Edwards, Jim Rodford, Mick Avory, Dave Davies, 1978

you'll never change that. Like all those groups in the 1960s, they thought they got bad deals. Every act you ever speak to thinks they could be a better manager than their manager. Ray was fairly successful. They weren't making fortunes but they kept themselves alive, and Ken took care (he still does) of all the live gigs. He's one of the best.'

Elliot Abbot: 'Around the time of *Misfits* I went to see them in the UK and met them at Konk Studios. They didn't have a manager in the United States, and after much deliberation I decided to try one tour and took it from there. What is required with a country like America is somebody watching the store, taking care of things while the band isn't here in preparation for when they do arrive, making sure that the right things are done in their absence to give the impression that they are here.

'When I joined them, their relationship with the record company in the United States was a very good one; they got everything that they wanted. It wasn't so good in the UK. When I took over they were playing the 2,000–3,000 capacity venues, and the first time we broke out of that cult audience was on 3 June 1978, when we played to 8,000 or 9,000 people at Providence, Rhode Island. We took the gamble. We played our first big hall and did extremely well. The next tour we took more chances, and the next tour even more. I'm conservative by nature and didn't want to get things wrong.'

This new team of management and musicians gave the Kinks new confidence after the doldrums of much of the previous year. But the perennial tensions were still there, as Ira Kaplin reported in the *Soho Weekly News* on 15 June 1978: 'At the Palladium a few weeks ago, Dave took time out from "A Well Respected Man" a number of times to give Ray the finger. I asked just how much of the fighting is serious. "Very little, I'm afraid," was the reply. "It's just one of those things. We sometimes look at one another and we hate each other. I wouldn't want to destroy him or anything like that. He sees bits of me that he hates. And it just starts."'

● Ray Davies, the Pink Pop Festival, Holland, 1978

It's clear that the brotherly tensions were, and are, one of the factors that keep the group lively, and this liveliness was celebrated in a favourable *Newsweek* piece which came out soon after *Misfits* and commented on the dilemmas of growing old in a young man's medium. 'We felt the need,' Ray Davies explains, 'to get back to purely performing, playing simple songs with a tightness and discipline that was lacking before. I still think rock breaks down age and class barriers and that it's a way of communicating ideas that might not otherwise get expressed. We had to take a step back into that before we could take another step forward.'

Jim Rodford: 'When I joined, the horn section was being used about fifty-fifty during the set. It was gradually getting smaller, and about two years after I joined the horns got gradually phased out. The horns were really symbolic of the late middle period of the Kinks. It was the end of the concept thing; the band was coming back to a more rock 'n' roll set.'

The Kinks toured this new, spruce live set all throughout that autumn and spring; August/September in the United States, October in Europe, most of November in Australia, January in the UK and February/March back in the United States. They were now beginning to work in a global market.

In March 1979 a new single was released in the States, '(Wish I Could Fly Like) Superman'. Its quick success – number 41 in the charts – precipitated the next Kinks album, which was not even ready at the time.

Low Budget was made primarily by a four-piece Kinks band, since Gordon Edwards had left the group. It testifies to the effect of constant touring and the spreading influence of punk rock, which caught the Kinks on the crest of a wave. Dave Davies: 'It was the first time we'd ever recorded out of England, which injected a different type of feeling. We tried to do it quick. We did the back tracks in ten days which for us is really quick.'

The decision to record *Low Budget* in New York, away from the temptations to indulgence that Konk offered, was crucial. Ken Jones: 'I feel that we shouldn't record here. I think it's terribly wrong. It's too near, it's too easy, but, what's worse than that, we're not a band. Jim goes home. Mick goes home. In New York the environment is much better for Ray as a writer; in my opinion, his songs benefit from the general buzz.'

Jim Rodford: 'It's not strictly true that we recorded the whole album in New York. But it's true to say that it was conceived more or less in America and recorded more or less wholeheartedly there. It was the adjustments that were made over here. I feel that you get a fresher approach when you know that you are paying for time which is not your own. You have to get it done quicker.'

Ray Davies: 'A few tracks, ''Low Budget'', ''Pressure'' and ''Superman'', were done in England and the rest in New York. When ''Pressure'' was done I was shouting out the chords to the guys while we were doing it. It was done in one take. I wrote ''Low Budget'' because we wanted to do a tour in England during Christmas 1979, and the record company wouldn't give us tour support unless they had a product. So I made "Low Budget", "Pressure" and another track as an EP. "Low Budget", I think, was written in a car journey through south London. "Superman" I had to produce a little bit; I really got it to be a good dance record on the re-mix. The proof was when I was in a discothèque in Stockholm, where all they play is disco music. It came on, and it knocked the balls off everything else. That achieved what I wanted.'

Low Budget was a return to form after the halting *Misfits*. Ray Davies had regained his sense of humour and his emotional responses: both he and the rest of the group were at their best, playful, gritty, tight, with a clean, clear production. The Kinks had turned into an exclusively US rock band but with quirks. Although the surface of the album meant that it was virtually ignored in the UK, it is now clear that Ray Davies and the Kinks were playing with the form as much as submitting to it as they embrace and thrash out a variety of dominant US rock styles.

If US white rock is a musical form which most often celebrates power, then *Low Budget* undercuts these pretensions with a series of terse, pithy songs celebrating human frailties and the difficulty of overcoming them. 'National Health' pits Ray's best tracked-out British accent against the lines 'Valium helped me for a while/ But somehow Valium always seems to bring me down/ There's no pill I can recommend/The side effects are guaranteed/To send you round the bend.' 'Pressure' mushes up Chuck Berry and the Ramones just like any bad punk band, and the hit single 'Superman' harps on the old 'Life is So Complicated' theme in an admission of vulnerability in a musical form, disco, which at that time was most often punctuated by heroic poses.

Low Budget is a series not of journalistic observations but of emotional responses to American life in a recession. The stage favourite, 'Gallon of Gas', observes that the depression has hit the Americans hardest in the gas tank, and perhaps the constant drug taking that the Kinks could see at their concerts was a substitute for that old pioneer spirit – although the song was also a cue for poly-drug abuse in the Cloud-Cuckoo-Land of the stadia. The song 'Low Budget' sets those old angry Muswell Hill voices to a song that makes light both of the recession and of the Kinks' own ramshackle status in the well oiled American music business. The punch line, as often, twists the point right back home where it belongs: 'Don't think I'm tight if I don't buy a round.'

The final song, 'Moving Pictures', shows the difference between *Misfits* and *Low Budget*. Whereas 'Live Life' on the former album was stilted and querulous, 'Moving Pictures' tackles the same theme with a deft shuffle, concealing some world-weary lines ('You make the choice, so you must pay the price'), and it fades on an endless 'It's only moving moving moving pictures.' 'Misery' contains the album's springboard lines: 'You're such a misery/Why don't you learn to laugh!/Don't take yourself so seriously!' On *Low Budget* the Kinks sound as though they have rediscovered the meaning of fun.

A sure sign of their being back on form was that the Kinks were able to have their cake and eat it. However

● **Low Budget** rejects, 1979

much *Low Budget* pokes fun at and plays around with US rock, it was also their most successful album to date in that market place, reaching number 11. The Kinks had found a new market. Ken Jones: 'When *Low Budget* came along everybody wanted it to happen – every promoter, every radio station, every DJ. It was as if they had been waiting for the real Dave Davies sound, the real Kinks song, the real Ray.'

On the tour that followed *Low Budget* the Kinks were regularly playing stadia like the Spectrum Theatre, Philadelphia (which would hold over 10,000 people), whereas on the previous tour they had been stuck in the 3,000/4,000 bracket. It was a new challenge. Ray Davies: 'We hadn't really done a whole campaign before – just bits and pieces. The only real campaign we did was on *Low Budget*. They got it right, and it did well for us. We become a stadium act. I remember the guys saying, "What do we do? We got energy – what do we do when we go out there?" I said, "You know what you do? You go inside yourself, and you play less. You can't play up to that maximum size, so you play within, keep it contained and tight." I had noticed that the best bands had a little tight sound; it just sounded louder because they mixed it clean. All those high-pitched voices – in ten years' time there's going to be x heavy metal singers with hernias. You know, it's going to be awful. They'll all have to learn to play the vibes or something!'

● **The brothers just after an argument, 1978**

STATE OF CONFUSION

The eighties are here! I know cause I'm staring right at 'em . . .
Take off your headphones, hear what's going on
You can't live in a time zone
You got to move on . . .
It's all in the music
It's all in your brain
You used all the old licks
Now it's got to change . . .
Change your attitude!

Kinks, 'Attitude', quoted in the
New Musical Express, 6 October 1979

The problem with the Kinks, if you want, is between Ray and Dave. Dave, I think, started the Kinks and Ray is the one that everybody thinks is the Kinks. He's the most important – he writes the songs, he's the singer, he is an incredible performer. To me, next to Jagger, he's one of the best performers in the world.

Barry Dickens in conversation, 1982

Although the Kinks had become a successful American rock band, life, as ever, was not easy. The history of these last few years has been the now familiar catalogue of fights, career mistakes and general bad behaviour, rescued by the inner vitality of all concerned and some good records pulled out of the hat at the last moment. Success didn't bring stability to the Kinks, yet their volatile state has become a kind of stability in itself. Without this constant state of confusion, and its potential for a final, disastrous flare-up, the Kinks would have called it quits long ago.

The pivotal relationship within the group is, as it has been for most of their career, the relationship between the two brothers. Dave Davies: 'I think that we do function very differently. It's a very strange relationship. I don't think there's probably too many relationships like it, really. Sometimes we don't need to say something and other times we do; it's very complex, but really very simple in a lot of other ways.'

The Kinks had changed from being dominated by two personalities, as it had been in the 1960s, to being basically Ray Davies's vehicle. Ray writes most of the material, handles most of the decisions and produces the records. Jim Rodford explains the relationship from his point of view: 'If Ray wants a certain lick or a certain bass feel, he'll convey it to me and I'll give him what he wants. But he still lets me embellish it a bit – hopefully, I'm fairly near to what he wants anyway. I've always believed that the song writer knows what he wants and you've just got to take his direction, so that is what I do. Dave has his own slant on a tune. He'll make it different.

He'll suggest things and then we compromise between what Ray and Dave want. That's fine. The lead guitar and song writer, the lead vocalist, you're led by them. The Kinks have created a whole twenty years of history without me, and I'll do what they want.'

It was Ray Davies's determination to keep going throughout the mid to late 1970s that kept the group together. Robert Wace now says he thinks Dave Davies has been squashed and that this has been evident in the many on- and off-stage fights over the previous decade. Yet if it was as simple as that, the Kinks would have disintegrated long ago. Dave could have been a solo performer or featured guitarist in another group. Ray can, and does, act, write plays, make videos or direct films. Neither of them has pursued his own interests to the extent that the group has fragmented. Perhaps this is through loyalty, fear and an understanding of how vital that sibling conflict is. Survival in pop music is a peculiar mixture of necessity, stubbornness, continued growth and worries about whether it is all worth it. Until the Kinks do finally dissolve, that peculiar relationship will still be seen to be working.

There is just one more piece to fit into the puzzle: in order to tour in July 1979 the Kinks needed a new keyboard player. Ian Gibbons: 'Jim phoned me up, as I'd previously done session work with him. I did an audition while Ray was mixing *Low Budget*. On the first day I went up into the piano booth with Mick, Jim and Dave. Mick was playing congas, Dave was playing acoustic guitar and I played and sang backing vocals. Ray popped his head in, asked for me to be given a tape of a couple of songs, and told me to play "Celluloid Heroes". When I came back the next day, Jim gave me a tape of *Low Budget* and I started rehearsing straight away. We only did three or four days' rehearsing for the *Low Budget* tour. We went straight over to America. Mick showed me the delights of New York City. We played two nights in a club called the Palladium in Dallas as a warm-up, and then we went off for the big summer tour from July to September, with a break in the middle of ten days in Los Angeles. At the end of that tour we recorded a live video.'

Ray Davies: 'I walked into the piano booth where Ian was singing "Let It Be" and the rest of the band were joining in. I thought Ian was cheeky enough to get the gig.'

The Kinks' success in the States was paralleled by a slow rise in their status in the United Kingdom after a couple of covers by influential groups. This was fighting the UK market on its own terms, and a perceptive article in the *New Musical Express* by Charles Shaw Murray in October of that year delivers the message that they must have been dying to hear: 'The years of concept albums

● **Live, Brussels, 1980**

and fake nostalgia and retreats into alcoholic evocations of a mythical past have fallen from Ray's shoulders. Ray Davies is Born Again, and for the first time in too many years the Kinks are a group who can be loved for their latest work rather than for their greatest hits of the 1960s.'

However, the American orientation of both *Low Budget* and their next live album eluded the British public. Rock – particularly US rock – was distinctly out of favour. But this would change as the Kinks relaxed with their new success.

The Kinks toured *Low Budget* for over three months, and the decision was taken near the end of the tour to do something that Ray Davies had been trying to do ever since *Arthur* – to put out a visual package that would complement an aural one. Various concerts during the tour were recorded on video, including some more in New York City in January 1980. They were also recorded for a live album. The result was *One for the Road*, an album and a video cassette, released near enough simultaneously and a marketing first.

Live albums tend to celebrate, if possible, either conspicuous success or an *interesting* relationship with an audience. The Kinks have released three live albums during their career: *Kelvin Hall*, recorded in April 1967;

Everybody's in Showbiz, recorded during the Muswell Hillbillies tour; and *One for the Road*. Each celebrates success, but in a different market and with a different audience each time. The most instructive difference lies in the crowd. On *Kelvin Hall* the shrieks of the Scottish audience are an integral part of the music, and the group sails on their tide. In a unified culture the group and the audience are, literally, one. On *Everybody's in Showbiz* there is more of a distance, yet audience and performers are still close enough to swap some banter in a relationship that, despite the audience's greater size, is still warm and intimate. The audience on *One for the Road*, however, is a more amorphous mass. It is not possible to distinguish any individual voice; rather, the audience remains in the mix like a sombulent Behemoth. The difference between the crowd and the Kinks is huge – and alienating. Despite the musicians' brave attempts, this cold dislocation percolates throughout the live album and its accompanying video. This is the numbers game.

The album shows the group energized and stripped for a new generation of concert-goers. The horn section has disappeared and the *Low Budget* material is complemented by a selection of old songs that emphasize both the Kinks' influence on the new market and their status as hard rockers – 'You Really Got Me', 'David Watts', 'Stop

Your Sobbing', 'Till the End of the Day' and 'Twentieth-Century Man'. It is clear that this is a tightly disciplined and well planned show. What the Kinks lack in spontaneity they have gained in technical proficiency, energy and crowd command.

Dave Davies: 'I still think that's the best modern album because some of it is just so energetic. I think when we play live, seven times out of ten something really special happens. We're at our best at a live gig.'

The album also emphasizes Ray Davies's mastery of both the group and his audience. Ken Jones: 'A Kinks concert has a family feel to it because of the way the stage act works and the way Ray communicates with the audience. People like them so much because they want to feel close to the band.'

The *One for the Road* video shows the Kinks to be as humane as possible in an inhuman environment. This is all fine and good, and yet the inclusion of archive material raises some unfortunate niggles. What was once magnificence and inspiration is replaced by workmanlike, professional graft. Pop music is a cruel game, and it favours the young. The Kinks' enthusiasm and commitment on this album and video cannot be faulted, but it is their tragedy and the tragedy of a perennially adolescent medium that *One for the Road* celebrates a success not of quality but of quantity. In doing so it gained the Kinks a further new audience, but it also alienated many of the group's older followers who had lasted from the 1960s. The November 1980 *LA review* captures this reaction to the tour that followed *One for the Road*:

> The forum holds 18,000. Badly. Ray's glib on-stage *double entendre* and sly commentary – even the better jokes – bounce off the dome-like parameters and teenage ears accustomed only to rock 'n' roll assault. Most of the fans who could (and did) sing along to all the intricate lyrics and phrasings of an old semi-hit like 'A Well Respected Man' at shows a couple of years ago have fled, Ray assumes, to the sanitized comfort of their sixteen-minute *One for the Road* video tape at home. And maybe he's right.

Hell hath no fury like a fan scorned, and it is important to take this with a pinch of salt. Yet, it is a good litmus test. If *One for the Road* alienated the second generation of US fans, it was completely ignored in the UK. As Ray Davies told *Melody Maker*'s Colin Irwin in August 1980: 'I'm not bitter … but I'm confused. The audience is there, no doubt about that; what's wrong is the middle ground. Radio in particular. The only things the radio stations play are the old stuff.' Reviews of that summer's Lyceum concert were hardly favourable and, naturally, Pye chose the occasion of the live album to re-release the first four Kinks LPs in their original sleeves. For the UK press comparisons were odious. It was also noticeable that it was the sixties Kinks that had been covered by the Jam and the Pretenders. Davies's complaints are legitimate, yet this double live American album hardly fitted what an English audience expected or wanted from the Kinks. Ray Davies still had to do his homework about his home market.

It was at this time that Dave Davies's first solo album, *AFLI-3603*, was finally released, twelve years after the idea of a Dave Davies solo album had originally been mooted. 'Rather than relying on other musicians or other producers or other people, I thought, the only way I can try and get some of these songs out is just to do it all myself; at least I'll only have myself to blame. That's how I did it. I had such a lot of fun making it – playing the drums and then running into the control room and fiddling. I worked with an engineer, of course, and some of the tracks had some other musicians on them, but the bulk of it was me. I really enjoyed the actual process of doing it regardless of the way it finished. That was a great kind of exorcism.'

On this album, and the subsequent one released a year later, *Glamour*, all of Dave Davies's pent-up anger and frustration come bursting out in a series of songs that mix a flashy rock 'n' roll sound with lyrics that celebrate release. 'Don't want to surrender any more to the likes of you/Don't want a pretender to show me what to do' ran 'Move Over', a song that many interpreted as a direct attack on Ray. Not so, according to Dave: 'People get out of a song whatever they want. It's like psychiatrists showing 100,000 people a piece of blank paper full of ink blots and they all think it's something different. It's just like that. It's up to people to draw their own conclusions from it, but it wasn't intended. I don't think that I could write anything that obvious.'

It's clear that the anger directed against his brother is an important part of Dave Davies's more cosmic anger, which is diverted more often on these albums, as in real life, into more mystical preoccupations and the processes of self-examination that had started ten years before. Dave Davies: 'I really enjoyed making *Glamour*. I've met kids who liked it but I've yet to meet anybody in the business who has liked it. There are two songs that I like particularly. One's called 'Reveal Yourself', and the other is the last song, 'Eastern Eyes'. It is simply about East and West coming together. I feel like the East is a material cripple and the West is a spiritual cripple, and if they were one person, it wouldn't be so bad. That's really what 'Eastern Eyes' means. 'Glamour' is about someone who looks like Ronald Reagan, like a movie star, but everything is falling apart around him and he's a bit aloof from it all. I like that paradox. The world could be falling apart and it would still make sure that it looked nice and washed its teeth and everything like that. 'Reveal Yourself' is to do with the same thing; it's about people acting more spontaneously. But a lot of critics in America said that they thought it was a bit of a doomy sort of theme. The people who thought it was doomy were the people who think only about material things – it would be depressing if that's all you thought about. I think that's why it got a lot of criticism from people, particularly in America, but I don't think it ever really got a chance to be heard over here, to be judged.' These affirmations of faith work surprisingly well with Dave's tough rock 'n' roll instincts, and the albums, while they have their lyrical and musical *longueurs*, are better than their sales figures would suggest.

● **Dave Davies, 1980**

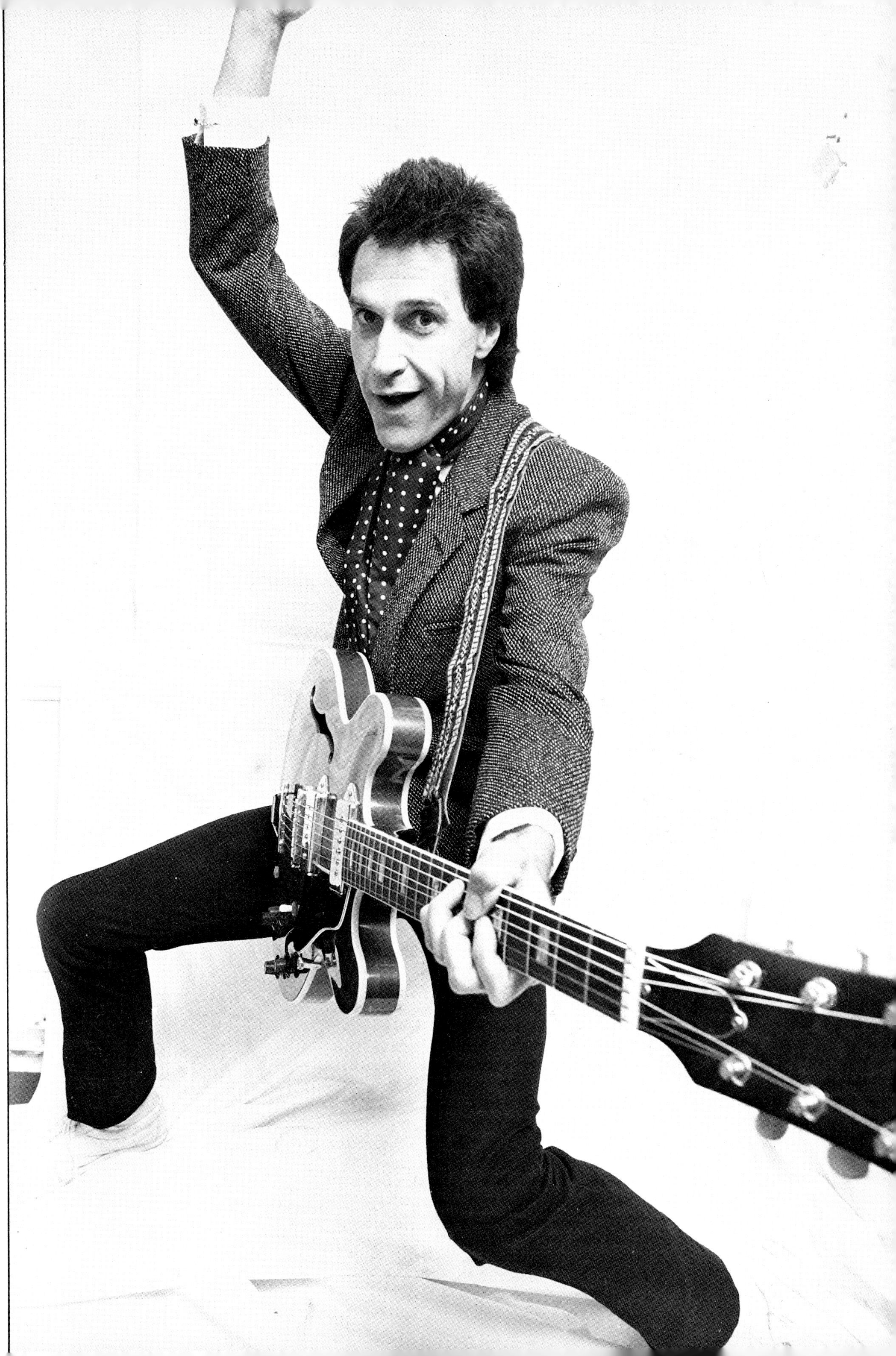

• Attitude: Ray Davies, 1981

Destroyer

Met a girl called Lola
And I took her back to my place
Feeling guilty, feeling scared
Ev'rywhere. Stop!
Hold on
Stay in control
Girl I want you here with me
But I'm really not as cool
As I'd like to be
'Cause there's a red
Under my bed
And there's a little yellow man
In my head.
And there's a true blue
Inside of me
That keeps stopping me
Touching you
Wanting you
Loving you

Paranoia the destroyer

Ray, meanwhile, had other projects of his own. During the latter part of 1980 and the early part of 1981 he had returned to the theatre, writing the songs for a Barrie Keeffe adaptation of an Aristophanes play. Davies has fond memories of 'Chorus Girls' which opened at the Theatre Royal, Stratford East on 6 April 1981: 'I thoroughly enjoyed it. It got panned because it was political. It was about Prince Charles going to open a job centre in Stratford and being kidnapped. I loved working with Barrie. It was great. We had four weeks to the opening date, so we went to a Portakabin in Stratford East and worked. I had a piano in the middle of the room – it was really my first taste of freedom as a writer. As Barrie was tapping away, I suggested lines, he suggested lines. But at the same time, Barrie was going through a terrible ordeal. His girlfriend, Verity, was dying of cancer. Verity came out of hospital for a day to get married and then went back into hospital and died a few days later. I was best man. It's weird being best man and then being almost in the same place at the funeral. Verity was a very, very strong person. Her death was a tragedy.'

Afterwards it was back to work to prepare the yearly Kinks album; this was to be their first studio album for over two years. In the meantime the Kinks' fortunes had recovered slightly in the UK: a single released to coincide with the mini-tour at the end of June, 'Better Things', made the top fifty for the first time since 'Supersonic Rocket Ship' over nine years before. 'Better Things' was a rapprochement between the flowing style of their sixties hits and the band's later American aggressiveness. Its bitter-sweet sense of optimism fitted well with the English conception of the group.

The next UK single, although not a hit, was a breakthrough for the group: after fifteen years of trying Ray Davies and the Kinks at last got a decent video. Directed by Julien Temple, *Predictable* is one of the best pop promos – certainly the best by that director and the Kinks. Stuffed full of televisual and nostalgic puns (playing on the retro cult just beginning to surface in pop promos), the *Predictable* video fleshes out what is, by itself, a humorous but slight song about depression and boredom by exploiting Ray Davies's considerable comic talents. He exhibits a variety of expressions to suit the various archetypes that he plays – a sneer from the Ted, a peace sign from a hippie or a flounce from a top mod. Best of all, it immortalizes Davies's peerless and ill-recognized klutziness. If a piece of toast is ever to land butter-side down, Ray Davies is your man. The video features a catalogue of disasters: Davies picking up cigarette butts thinking they're peanuts, dropping an entire salt cellar on to his bag of chips and suffering the rape of his loon pants by a vacuum cleaner.

The video was a smash on the then new twenty-four-hour-a-day cable music channel, MTV, and made the Kinks market leaders in this competitive field, which the murky and pedestrian *One for the Road* video had failed to do. This video obsession was sustained in the title song of the new album released in August, *Give the People What They Want*.

Ray Davies: 'It was a script for a film. It started off with television and with our show tape, and ended up with me running past the building on the album sleeve. It was about people's view of entertainment and the song 'Give the People What They Want' virtually summed up the whole show. The last song took place in the circus arena, with people fighting real lions; people in battle gear machine-gunning one another. Everything was falling apart. The more people get, the more they need, then they get harder and harder to please. It's something about the Romans. "Their agents really did something right; they put on a show to thrill and excite. But the punters got bored, so they threw the Christians to the lions and they sold out every night." The song would have had more punch if it could have had a promo, a film. It was the first feature promo I'd written.'

Give the People What They Want is a sardonic yet realistic view of the way in which the mass media operates and, as ever, it also has to do with the Kinks' own status within those operations. Of course, the Kinks give the people what they want, as the shining hard-rock surface of this album attests, yet Davies is far too sly, and the whole band far too maverick, to get trapped in a set of mutual expectations. Apart from the unfortunate opener, 'Around the Dial', which unconvincingly transplants Ray Davies's individualistic concerns into an American context, most of the album is concerned with various kinds of violence, both social and emotional – not least the violence that stems from the media's view of 'reality' imposed willy-nilly on the passive public.

For instance, the song 'Killer's Eyes', about the man who shot the Pope, is in itself simplistic but gains from its context. The implication is that Roman circuses are all very well, but the violence is not easily contained within the Colosseum. Just to show that he is not being entirely journalistic, Ray Davies lets slip a line of real outrage: 'Why did you go and do a thing like that?' Other songs handle intolerance and emotional violence with the customary Davies wit and with terse performances from the rest of the group: 'Oh excuse me, is this your tooth?' inquires Davies to lighten a heavy little song about S&M, 'A Little Bit of Abuse'.

Despite the band's endearing bashing, 'Destroyer' is a serious song. Ray Davies makes it quite clear that his creativity and determination to keep going is bought at the price of self-inflicted violence: one cannot exist without the other.

'Art Lover', a cute little song about a child ogler, also stems from his own emotional experiences: 'I did become a Sunday parent for Lou and Tor. I used to walk around Regents Park and see all the sad cases with their kids: no communication. They'd always buy them expensive gifts. I maintain that if you're in that situation, you must never let them see that it affects your lifestyle. Don't do extraordinary things. If you have to play a game of football on a Sunday morning, you play it. They'll have to come along. Once they see you pandering to them and breaking up your lifestyle, it turns them off, turns them away from you. I see it such a lot. Also 'Art Lover' is about being a little bit of a pervert because I do love looking at beautiful bodies. So there's a double edge

there.'

The album's centrepiece is 'Yo-Yo'. Ray Davies: '"Yo-Yo" is about a woman's role in a man's life. It starts off with the little wife waiting at home. She says to him, "You needed me when you were crying. Now you're laughing and your job is going well. I'm the last thing on your mind. First you love me, then you don't." That's the line that inspired the song: "First you love me, then you don't. Knock me down like a yo-yo." In the second half of the song it's the man's point of view because the woman has gone out and got a job and he's got no work. It's a reversal of roles, that's what it is. Everybody plays yo-yo games, body games and mind games. It's an important song; it's not necessarily unhealthy.'

Dave Davies: '"Yo-yo" is better live. That's a real key song in our stage act. We do it differently. There are more guitar breaks in it, and it has more dynamics. Sometimes when you do a song in the studio it sounds good, but it's only when you get on stage that you start to learn the song properly: you learn the dynamics of the song on stage.'

These songs capture the Kinks giving the people rather more than what they want. The band has just the right amount of enthusiasm and freshness, while Davies still manages to make his private concerns work in a wider context, provided they are inflected by his own emotional states. The apparent cynicism of the title, although partially correct, undersells the group's motivation and performances. Not that it mattered. *Give the People What They Want* went gold, and stayed in the top forty for four months after its release. That autumn, as usual, the Kinks toured the album around the States for a couple of months, but this time they reached a new high spot on 3 October 1981, when they played Madison Square Garden for the first time. Ray Davies: 'I had a copy of *Village Green Preservation Society* under my arm when I walked on stage, but it didn't have a record in it – just the sleeve. But the thought was there. It's a high spot for people who run the music industry, but it's not my way. We have never fitted in with all the hoopla. The only thing I love is that when you get on stage it's razzle-dazzle time, it's show time. I love all that.

'I think the tape that begins the concert is a little masterpiece. Whenever it hits a certain chord I do my Mohammed Ali taps. I love the wind-up aspect of it. It could be a gym in Knoxville, or Madison Square Garden, it doesn't really matter.'

Despite his commitment to performing, Davies is only too aware of the ultimate futility of the numbers game. After Madison Square Garden – what? Pop music is essentially a young man's game: beyond a point, experience counts for little or nothing. Pete Townshend: 'You can only do it so long. I think it's like dancing – or boxing perhaps – in the end your knees literally go. Bill Curbishley, the Who's current manager, is just like a boxing promoter: He'll say, "You can do it, boys. You can go out there and do it one more time. This time you'll make five million fucking pounds – go on, *do it!* If they knock you out, if you come back with a nervous breakdown, you can afford the best doctors!"'

● **Uncle Frank and 'Little Grannie'**

Yo-Yo
There are many diff'rent people
Living double lives
One for the office
And one that they take home to their wives
He sits in the armchair
Watches Channel Four,
But his brain's not expected home
For an hour or more
He's still driftin' to and fro
Like a yo-yo

Wife is in the kitchen
Fixing her old man's tea
She's thinking to herself
He's not the man that married me
They used to laugh together
Now he's never at home
Now she's fighting back the tears
She can't even laugh alone
She's just sitting by the telephone
Like a yo-yo

You needed me
When you were cryin'
Now you're laughin'
I'm the last thing on your mind
First you love me
Then you go
I won't come down
Like a yo-yo

You thought you knew me
Really well
With people like me
You never can tell
You can only guess
Which way I'll go
You've got me sussed

But you don't know
I'm a yo-yo
Just like a yo-yo on a string
I'm a yo-yo
Little child
Playing with a yo-yo
Yo-yo, yo-yo
I'm a yo-yo

Girl, you have me dangling
Like a yo-yo on a string
But with you at the controls
I could accomplish anything
You were just playing
I was a little boy
But when I grew into a man
You threw away your toy
Like a yo-yo

You must have thought
It won't last for long
So don't give up the danger
In case it all goes wrong

Look at your ego
Watch it go
Up and down
Like a yo-yo

You needed me
When you were cryin'
Now you're laughin'
I'm the last thing on your mind
First you love me
Then you go
I won't come down
Like a yo-yo

● **The 'Come Dancing' shoot, 30 November 1982**

● The 'Come Dancing' shoot, 30 November 1982

The Who achieved a level of success in the US that the Kinks never had: Kinks albums might go gold but not top three, nor has any of them defined an era as *Tommy* did. This is partly what has kept the Kinks going as long as they have – the fact that, in a way, they have never arrived. Ken Jones: 'When we can sell out four or five days at Madison Square Garden, that's when I think the Kinks will be near the top. It's nothing to do with money or with people wanting to come and see us. But we're not there – we're not nearly there. We're getting there, but every time we take a step forward, Ray will do a side-step and we'll drop back. Or something will go wrong. But the fact that we weren't playing a week at Madison Square Garden eight years ago may be what has kept us going. We still have something to achieve. We haven't played Florida for two and a half years. We haven't played Memphis for a year and a half. We haven't played New Orleans. You can't leave out those territories because there are eight million other bands coming in behind you. There are lots of Kinks fans, but the ones you need are the floaters. A guy hears your record on the radio, goes into a shop and asks, "You got that new Kinks album?" "No, we don't have it." Then the guy looks at Van Halen and says, "Well, I'll have that instead." Ten dollars gone. He won't save that for you next week, because next week is somebody else. Concert tickets are the same and radio play and all the activity while you're touring.'

Just to emphasize the nature of their self-allotted task, the Kinks trotted off for a winter tour of the US, Australia and Japan early in 1982. Then it was back to America, and as ever the tensions were there. As Fred Schruers reported in *Rolling Stone*, April 1982:

> The chaos that has always been part of the Kinks' repertoire seemed held in check. Each tour, though, does have its blow-up. The latest battle came at Nassau Coliseum on Long Island, when Dave accused Mick of not ending a song on the down-beat. Mick rose, kicked a drum stand over, threw his sticks at Dave, and walked off. 'I think our drummer's just had a phone call,' Ray told the audience, as he chased Mick into the dressing room. 'He said, "I'll come back and finish just for you,"' Ray recalled. 'And I said, "What about 14,000 people?" and Mick said, "Well, I'll do that as well."' Ray, an inexpert disciplinarian, threw curry at Dave backstage after the show.

After *Give the People* had been toured out, the Kinks spent the rest of the year quietly preparing their various projects. Ray began planning a film, *Return to Waterloo*, for Channel 4, tying up a lot of the themes that had concerned him throughout his career. Dave started working on his third solo album, *Chosen People*, and changed record companies, signing to Warner Brothers. The Kinks also recorded some new songs for release as a single to coincide with a twenty-day winter tour in the UK. Rasa Davies remembers the end of that tour: 'I saw Ray in concert at the Lyceum. It was unbelievable – one of his best concerts. He came on in his beautiful pink suit and he was a real showman, an artist. But when I went back-

stage he switched off. He was like the Ray that I remember when he was going through a bit of a rough time, closed up, a bit nervous. The media were about and he just wanted to get away. Yet when he was on stage, he was unbelievable. He was flamboyant and extrovert. He is a loner, but he comes alive when he's performing because he can lose himself in a sort of fantasy land. I think it is a conflict for him even now.'

The new single, 'Come Dancing', was released in Britain just before Christmas 1982. Ray Davies: 'I wrote the song in a day. We did two songs, "Don't Forget to Dance" and "Come Dancing". The initial reaction over here was to go for "Don't Forget to Dance", but I had a thing about "Come Dancing". I thought it would be a happy song, and I remade the record. I did the demo with Mick and Jim like a little reggae song. I was playing organ and bass and drums, and all the way through the demo I kept shifting rhythms. The following morning I got the tape out and started jigging around in my dressing gown in the kitchen. I wrote the song in an hour. When I got stuck for a lyric, I just wrote the shooting script at the side of it and then that became part of the lyric. It was easy. It was based on a real event: I was up at my sister's house looking at some pictures, and there was a picture of Gwen and her boyfriend dancing at the Atheneum Ballroom.'

The Kinks have always produced their best work out of conflict. Dave Davies: ' "Come Dancing" came out of a terrible argument between me and Ray. I was finishing off my *Chosen People* album and I was relaxed and excited about it. Ray and I then spent some time alone together in the country, where we worked on four or five songs for the forthcoming album, of which two were "Come Dancing" and "Don't Forget to Dance". It didn't work in the studio, though. Ray and I had a terrible row and I walked out. We came back the following morning and re-recorded the back track to "Come Dancing". I'm a bit stubborn, I suppose. I like to be convinced about an idea. If I don't see it straight away, it sometimes takes a long time convincing me. If I feel I'm doing something for the right reason and that it's right for me, then I can do it much more easily than if I'm doing it under pressure. I don't really function at my best unless I can put my whole heart and soul into what I'm doing.'

'Come Dancing' blends many of Davies's best traits – a sense of social history, a willingness to write from his own emotional experience and a knack for a strong story line – in an infectious lilt driven, as are many great Kinks songs, by a strong acoustic guitar. It brilliantly fuses fantasy and reality, the past and the present – paralleling the Kinks' own position – in a story that, as Ray Davies makes clear, was made to be filmed. 'I'm still a frustrated film-maker. I got diverted by joining this band of my brother's called the Kinks,' he told *Time Out* late in 1982. 'Come Dancing' was perfect for video. Ray Davies: 'I wanted to use Julien Temple again. He said, "You don't have to do anything more because this is a script. You've just got to find another funny character." My uncle Frankie was a real spiv. I don't think he worked in a market, but he was a flash boy, a snappy dresser. I based it on him. I think I look a bit like him with my hair back and a suit on. We cast it and did it, and it turned out to be a very good video. It's best when they happen naturally. I don't like all those artistic ones, with their fake posing – except Judas Priest, who I think are in the forefront of camp heavy metal.'

The video contributed to the song's eventual success. When first released in the UK in December 1982, it died in the pre-Christmas rush, not even making the A play list on most radio stations. But, aided by repeated exposure on MTV, it went to number 6 in the American charts five months later. A chance showing on the network BBC show *Top of the Pops* – which regularly reaches 11 million viewers – in a report by Jonathon King about the US charts, rekindled interest in the record in Britain, and it eventually became the Kinks' first major UK hit for at least eleven years.

Ray Davies: 'I wasn't able to appreciate it fully because I was doing pre-production on *Return to Waterloo*. But I was thrilled, really thrilled. It was wonderful to hear our records on the radio again. Though I just hated the word "come-back".'

'Come Dancing' set the seal on the complicated process that had begun five years earlier with those Kinks covers. Barry Dickens: 'Because of the Pretenders and Van Halen in America, who are covering Kinks songs, there's a slightly different audience. When you go and see them now, what happens is that people who grew up in the 1960s sit upstairs, and downstairs you see the young kids, the sixteen-year-olds, for whom the Kinks have become a cult band. My son's eleven, and he thinks the Kinks are the greatest thing since sliced bread.'

'Come Dancing' has made the Kinks part of the present after being part of the past for so many years. Such are the complexities of the British market that for every pop fan who buys 'Come Dancing' as a new pop record, there will be a thirteen-year-old mod walking down Carnaby Street, with a parka and Jam shoes, who thinks that 'You Really Got Me' is a classic mod track. This illusion is perpetuated by the continuing flood of Pye reissues, such as the latest, which repackages six tracks from different times as *Six Mod Anthems*. 'Depressing', says Ray, yet Pye's instincts are entirely right. Such is the rewriting of history that timescales are elided, and the Kinks' inept cover of 'Dancing in the Street' can now be as much of a mod anthem as Martha and the Vandellas' original.

The Kinks' following album, *State of Confusion*, was delayed for a couple of months while Ray changed his mind again and again, but it was eventually completed in a rush just before the Kinks' April 1983 American tour.

State of Confusion has no consistent viewpoint but, like the last two studio albums, it has the emotional coherence of a man and a group finally facing up to middle age. The album as a whole is softer than the other Kinks albums of the past four years: it is as if their success has enabled them to relax, stretch out and be playful, away from the straitjacket of the hard rock style. Many of the songs, like the singles 'Come Dancing' and 'Don't Forget to Dance' (number 29 in the States in September 1983), celebrate the weaving together of the past with

Come Dancing

They put a parking lot on the piece of land
Where the supermarket used to stand
Before that they put up a bowling alley
On the site that used to be the local Palais
That's where the big bands used to come and play
My sister went there on a Saturday, come dancing
All her boyfriends used to come and call
Why not come dancing – it's only natural

Another Saturday another date
She would be ready but she'd always make him wait
In the hallway in anticipation
He didn't know the night would end up in frustration
He'd end up blowing all his wages for the week
All for a cuddle and a peck on the cheek
Come dancing
That's how they did it when I was just a kid
And when they said come dancing
My sister always did

My sister should've come in at midnight
And my mum would always sit up and wait
It always ended up in a big row
When my sister used to get home late
Out of my window I could see him in the moonlight
Two silhouettes saying goodnight by the garden gate
The day they knocked down the Palais
My sister stood and cried
The day they knocked down the Palais
Part of my childhood died, just died

Now I'm grown up and playing in a band
And there's a car park where the Palais used to stand
My sister's married and she lives on an estate
Her daughters go out, now it's her turn to wait
She knows together we would think she never could
But if I asked her I wonder if she would
Come dancing
Come on sister have yourself a ball
Why be afraid to come dancing
It's only natural

Come dancing
Just like the Palais on a Saturday
And all your friends would
Come dancing
While the big band used to play

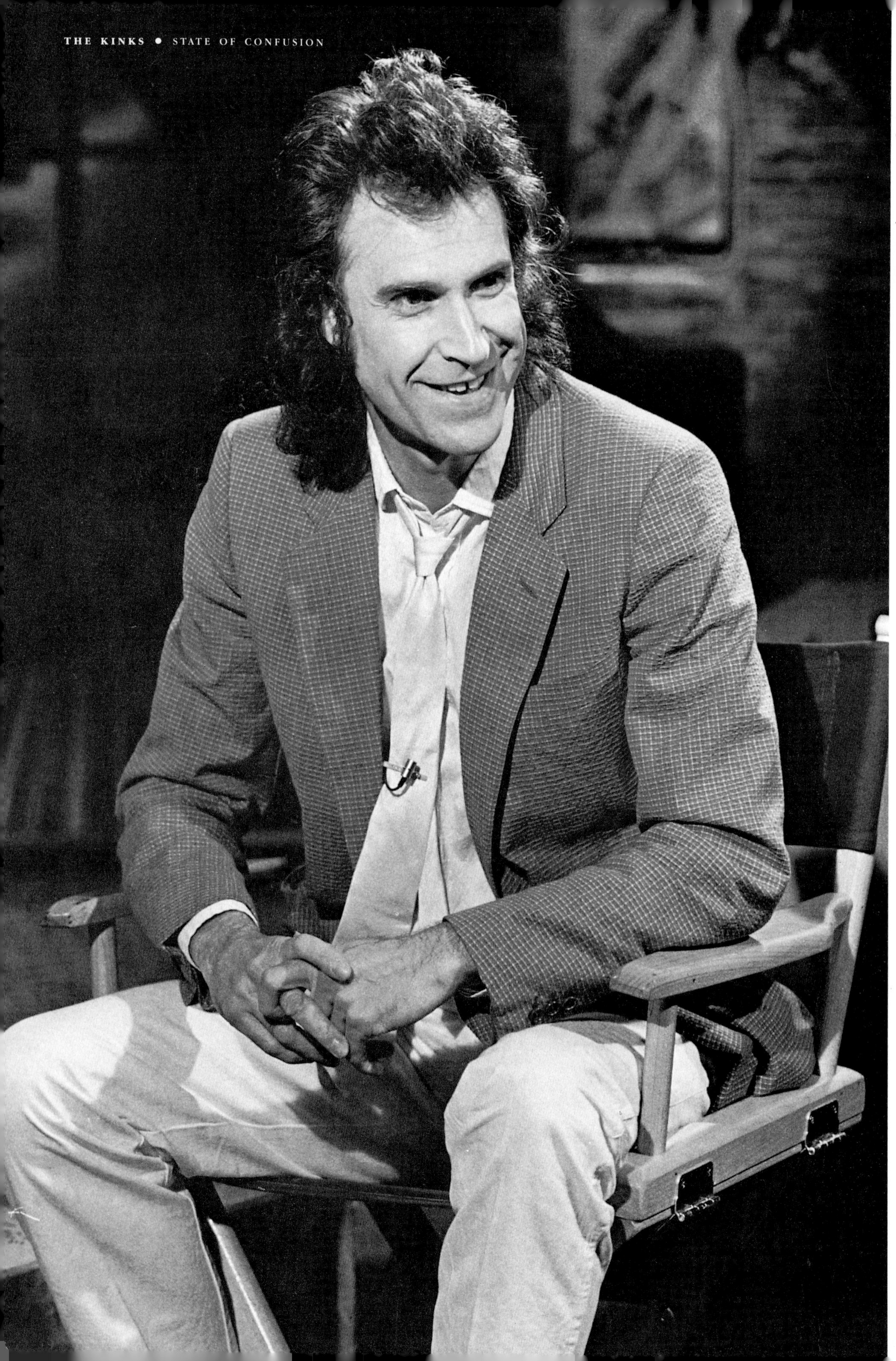

• Ray Davies on MTV, June 1983

the present. This theme is treated with economy and wit in Julien Temple's videos. In 'Don't Forget to Dance' there is some fake super-8 footage of the Kinks playing a deb dance in 1963 in between the blurred timescales of the story line. The video for 'State of Confusion' is one long celebration of Davies's stand up – or fall-down – klutz. It is this concern with the past and their ability to laugh at themselves that allows the Kinks to breathe.

If the videos for 'Come Dancing', 'Don't Forget to Dance' and 'State of Confusion' had mixed fact with fantasy, then the album's epic 'Clichés of the World (B movie)' completed the job in one of Ray's periodic bulletins about the nature of perception, this time related to his concern with the state of Britain. The hero of this threatening song is 'disillusioned by promises that they made' – a fair comment on the failure of post-war British socialism whose decline Ray Davies has charted so well. The political consequences of this decline is discussed in 'Young Conservatives', uniting Ray's art-school antinomianism with a hefty slice of class resentment, as the quotes from both 'David Watts' and 'Well Respected Man' make quite clear. 'The establishment is winning/ So the battle is nearly won/The rebels are conforming/See the father, now the son,' spits Ray Davies derisively. Finally, just to show that the Kinks really are a bunch of rock 'n' roll snots and not entirely as adult as they would like us to believe, they close with a trashy rocker about yet another sleazy girl, 'Bernadette', sung by Dave doing his best Little Richard impersonation.

Whether consciously or not, the album's title reflected the state of the Kinks during the rest of the year. The nature of the songs and the antics of the Kinks were to leave their audience and the group themselves confused. Although 'Come Dancing' was a top-ten single, *State of Confusion* did not do as well as expected. Jim Rodford: 'The album only went top twenty. "Come Dancing" was lovely, excellent, but it wasn't truly representative of probably 80 per cent of what the Kinks do on stage now, and it confused some of the audience. People who would buy "Come Dancing" probably wouldn't buy a complete Kinks album of the last five or six years.'

Despite the maturity of much of the music, the Kinks were in as much of a state of confusion as they had ever been. Barry Dickens: 'They can be their own worst enemies. They should have toured Britain with "Come Dancing". They were going to tour in December but they didn't, and then they were going to America but didn't in the end. I don't know how much longer they will be able to get away with it. At some stage I think Ray has got to learn to trust somebody. I think Dave should do other things. Even now he still lives in Ray's shadow.'

Indeed, in the autumn of 1983 the relationship between the two brothers precipitated another crisis, one that raised doubts about the Kinks' commitment to the US market place and translated into smaller record sales. The problem started with the release by Warner Brothers of Dave's third solo LP, *Chosen People*, in August 1983. Although the album was better than his first two solo LPs, it sold poorly, and its failure provoked a crisis of confidence. Dave Davies: 'This year I've been very frustrated

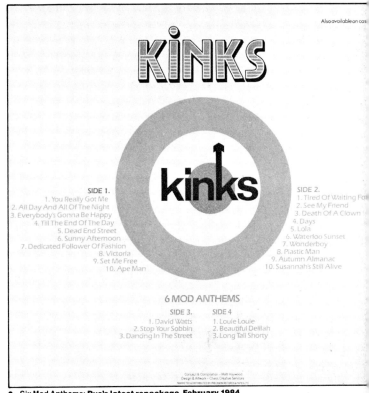

● Six Mod Anthems; **Pye's latest repackage, February 1984**

because I've had a lot of problems with my last solo album. In America if a record company decides to make a record a hit, it will be a hit whether it's great or awful. Without that investment it will sink without trace. It really irritates me to be at the mercy of a big record company. Some of the things that I was writing about were very important, and they needed to be accessible to everybody. On the last Kinks tour I was going to places and kids were saying, "I didn't even know you had an album out." In a way I still feel that I'm struggling. I feel that I've always been struggling.

'We helped to create the business in the 1960s and now the business has taken over. It dictates what we do now. Sometimes I'm really irritated by the prospect of going on another tour, lining other people's pockets – and my own, of course, making some money myself which I need to live. It seems very empty to me, doing it all over again. If I felt that everybody around me really cared about each other and what they were doing, that would be different. These things don't lead anywhere.'

Also the group felt that Ray Davies was spending too long on his *Return to Waterloo* film project. Ray Davies: 'Dave – and the band, I hear now – criticized me because they felt we should have stayed on tour longer with the other albums. But when a band's been going as long as we have, I think we should try new things. I think as a writer the film has helped me. It's my final stand. It tells a man's story, his whole life story, and he doesn't say a word. Everybody else says it for him. Anyway, I now know that I've got to be careful with the band. I've got to dedicate a couple of years to them and take it as far as we can go. You can't get any bigger than playing Madison Square Garden. I said after that date we'd go and play Roseland, and we did. Everybody else says they're going to go back and do something smaller, but they rarely do. We did, and they loved us for it.'

Dave Davies: 'Ray and I were arguing badly, worse than usual. One day we decided that if we didn't get together soon, things were going to fall apart completely. So we met and talked in my front room, and got everything off our chests. Ray was pissed off because I didn't want to do the tour, and I was pissed off at how much *Return to Waterloo* was distracting his attention from the group. In the end we decided to go over to the States at Christmas time to do a couple of gigs, just to clear the air.'

After a brief series of dates in the US over the new year, the Kinks returned to Britain in mid-January with the cracks temporarily papered over. The combination of receptive American audiences and seasonal good cheer had given the group enough momentum to get over the autumn's crisis. The next hurdle was an eleven-date tour of Britain to start at the end of March 1984.

In America the Kinks are seen as current; they have a ready-made audience and a contemporary relevance. They work. In Britain the long years of neglect have taken their toll: despite the chart success of 'Come Dancing' in August 1983, the legacy of those sixties hits are a millstone around their necks. They are still seen primarily as a sixties group, and in the fashion-obsessed pop culture of the present they are terminally unfashionable.

At London's Hammersmith Palais concert the Kinks came out as underdogs. Despite all the pressures, they played a set that underscored their continuing involvement with, and relevance to, a country that Ray Davies, at least, regards as depressing but to which he is bound by indissoluble emotional ties. At Roseland they had played a set drawn predominantly from the material made familiar by *Low Budget, One for the Road* and subsequent albums. At the Palais they reached farther back for a series of songs that highlighted the way in which they see Britain and their place in it, opting for social consciousness rather than rock 'n' roll: 'Oklahoma USA', 'Waterloo Sunset', 'David Watts', a rousing version of the first depression pop song, 'Dead End Street', and an infinitely sad version of 'Don't Forget to Dance', in which the Kinks confront their past and present.

It has been a long road from 'You Really Got Me' to *State of Confusion*, one that has taken the Davies brothers from Muswell Hill on an unceasing journey around the world. Their travels have cut them adrift from family and class through the weight of experience and have cast them into a fickle, hostile environment where one must ever be on guard, always adapting. It is a tribute to their force of character and their talent that they continue to face the search for another identity and a new sense of family with energy, courage and humour.

● **Ray Davies, 1983**

● 'Come Dancing' 1983

BETTER THINGS...?

Where I'm going no one knows
Only know I gotta go
Gotta move
Gotta move
Gotta move . . .

Kinks, 'I Gotta Move', 1964

The Kinks on themselves in 1984:

Ian Gibbons: 'After this tour we'll probably start working on new songs. Ray Davies is an inexhaustible source of new material; he's one of the most prolific writers I know. We'll do a new LP or some festivals. We'll be doing another tour later on in the year. There's talk of going to Europe: we've only done festivals there since the end of 1981. I think the Kinks are something that could probably go on for a long time. Ray will always want to work and to write – that's one of the things that makes it last. The Kinks are the most exciting band I've played in. It's completely unpredictable – you never know what's going to happen, and that keeps you on your toes. I think the Kinks have got a few more years.'

Jim Rodford: 'There's still a long way to go. This is the great thing about the band: it's had different surges; it's always been popular; it's always bubbled just below the level at which it could be as big as any band in the world and in many ways it is. I think that when history is written in a hundred years' time, it will be among the top ten bands of the whole period.

'The future is still going to be very unpredictable, very up-and-down. I don't know exactly what I'll be doing after these next British gigs, though we all know roughly what we should do. We must do an album, and then we must cover as much of the world as we can in our twentieth year. But we'll only do whatever we have time for. We've neglected Europe for two years. We've got to go back to Japan, and we've got to go back to Australia. Whether we'll do it all in the next two years, I don't know. There's a knife-edge, precipice feel to this group which I've never felt before. I've never experienced anything as unpredictable as the situation I'm in now. There is far more love, loyalty, resilience between Dave and Ray than anybody knows, and it reflects on all of us. But you need to work hard at the relationships, because we're all quite hard-headed people. But then nothing that does any good is easy. It's not easy in the Kinks, but it's great.'

Mick Avory: 'I know what we should do this year; whether it'll turn out that way is another matter. We should do another album – Ray's working on some songs at the moment – and make it better than the last one. We should celebrate our twentieth year with a new album and a worldwide tour, but after that it's really crossroads

THE KINKS ● BETTER THINGS..?

time. Whether we will all sign another deal, that's a question that we've got to sit down and decide on between ourselves. We could go on, and I think we will in some form or another. We've been established so long that it's a business, quite apart from the family connections as well; so I think it'll all go on in its own merry way – in leaps and bounds. Unless we stop it for no good reason, we might even end up like Count Basie.'

Dave Davies: 'I think this is an important year for the Kinks and I want to try and make it go as well as we can. I think that in a way we've always struggled, and we've always tried to do something different. With our recent success, we're doing reasonably well. Now I find I'm struggling with my own material, trying to get it accepted and making it more accessible. It's always been like that. It makes your brain work, your juices keep working. I don't think that I could ever sit down and think, "Ah, that's it. I'm just going to have a great time and rest a bit."

'I've probably learned more about myself and about people than I would have if I'd done anything else. I was a kid brought up in a working-class family in north London with no prospects. The mere fact that I've travelled so much has changed my perspective of people completely. I feel that I've condensed a lot of experience into a short space of time. I feel rich, I feel very strong inside because of it, and I think that's the only thing to me that is of true value. Also I always think that there is something else, something more, to do. I can't really explain it any other way.'

Ray Davies: 'The nature of pop music in Britain is to titillate itself and justify its weekly existence. I despair when I think about the pop music industry. Pretty soon there's going to be a big backlash; there's so much fraud in the music business now. There are a few real people out there who justify their place in the charts: the Jam, the Sex Pistols, who when they first started were as exciting as the Rolling Stones – more exciting. I still think there's such a thing as a "legitimate hit". I'll tell you what they're doing now – they're dividing up the territory: "Let us have a go this week. Your turn next week." Then they can ship their 300,000 records but say it sold a million. England is like a candy store. America's a bit the other way. It takes a lot for music to establish itself there. I wish that countries like Germany and Holland could have an upsurge in their music because they've got great talent in those countries. But there's the language problem.

'It's not a new business – the music business hasn't changed since Larry Page – but it's harder for new bands. It's taken a lot of fun out of the music. There isn't a DJ or a promotion man who gets a hook into a record and says, "I like this. It's a hit. I'll break this record because I believe in it." You can't do things like that alone any more.

'Going into a pub and hearing a new little group playing on a drum machine – that gives me a thrill. There's music happening and people are still fighting and looking for recognition – I think that's what it's all about. I don't think rock music should be organized, I really don't. Otherwise you are organizing the music and making it computerized.

'Success is nothing to do with time. It's to do with going on stage and hitting a snare drum, hitting a bass drum, hitting a bass and a guitar. I went to a pub gig the other night to see Jim Rodford playing. It reminded me of when I was playing at the Richmond Jazz Club – this was before the Stones – with the Hamilton King/Dave Hunt Band, and David Graham walked on stage like a god, picked up my guitar and played the most amazing solo blues set I've ever heard. I stood there in complete awe. That was my guitar, which I used on "You Really Got Me". It was as though I'd been touched with a bit of luck.'

DISCOGRAPHY

UK Singles

5611	**Long Tall Sally/I Took my Baby Home** *Feb 1964*
5639	**You Still Want Me / You Do Something to Me** *Apr 1964*
5673	**You Really Got Me / It's Alright** *Aug 1964*
5714	**All Day and All of the Night / I Gotta Move** *Oct 1964*
5759	**Tired of Waiting for You / Come on Now** *Jan 1965*
5813	**Ev'rybody's Gonna be Happy / Who'll be the Next in Line** *Mar 1965*
15854	**Set Me Free / I Need You** *May 1965*
15919	**See My Friends / Never Met a Girl like You Before** *Jul 1965*
15981	**Till the End of the Day / Where Have All the Good Times Gone** *Nov 1965*
17064	**Dedicated Follower of Fashion / Sittin' on my Sofa** *Feb 1966*
17100	**A Well Respected Man / Milk Cow Blues (Export only)** *Apr 1966*
17125	**Sunny Afternoon / I'm not Like Everybody Else** *Jun 1966*
17222	**Dead End Street / Big Black Smoke** *Nov 1966*
17314	**Mr Pleasant / This is Where I Belong (Export only)** *Apr 1967*
17321	**Waterloo Sunset / Act Nice and Gentle** *May 1967*
17356	**Death of a Clown / Love Me till the Sun Shines (Dave Davies)** *Jul 1967*
17400	**Autumn Almanac / Mr Pleasant** *Oct 1967*
17405	**Autumn Almanac / David Watts (Export only)** *Oct 1967*
17429	**Susannah's Still Alive / Funny Face (Dave Davies)** *Nov 1967*
17468	**Wonderboy / Pretty Polly** *Apr 1968*
17514	**Lincoln County / There is no Life Without Love (Dave Davies)** *Aug 1968*
17573	**Days / She's Got Everything** *Jun 1968*
17678	**Hold My Hand / Creeping Jean (Dave Davies)** *Jan 1969*
17724	**Plastic Man / King Kong** *Mar 1969*
17776	**Drivin'/Mindless Child of Motherhood** *Jun 1969*
17812	**Shangri-La / This Man He Weeps Tonight** *Sep 1969*
17865	**Victoria / Mr Churchill Says** *Dec 1969*
17961	**Lola / Berkeley Mews** *Jun 1970*
45016	**Apeman / Rats** *Nov 1970*
45313	**Where Have all the Good Times Gone / Lola** *Nov 1973*
46102	**Dedicated Follower of Fashion / Waterloo Sunset** *Oct 1974*
45482	**Sunny Afternoon / Sittin' on my Sofa** *Jun 1975*

7N 17961	**Lola / Berkeley Mews** *Mar 1980*
7N 45482	**Sunny Afternoon / Sittin' on my Sofa** *1980*
7N 17961	**Lola / Berkeley Mews** *1981*
7N 45482	**Sunny Afternoon / Sittin' on my Sofa** *1981*
FBS 1	**You Really Got Me / All Day and All of the Night** *Apr 1979*

PRT

RK 1027	**You Really Got Me / All Day and All of the Night** *Feb 1980*
FBS 1	**You Really Got Me / All Day and All of the Night** *Dec 1980*
FBS 15	**Sunny Afternoon / Tired of Waiting** *Feb 1983*

Old Gold (Lightning)

OG 9128	**Death of a Clown / Susannah's Still Alive (Dave Davies)** *Nov 1981*
OG 9140	**Dedicated Follower of Fashion / Waterloo Sunset** *Jan 1982*

RCA (Victor)

RCA 2211	**Supersonic Rocket Ship / You Don't Know My Name** *May 1972*
RCA 2299	**Celluloid Heroes / Hot Potatoes** *Nov 1972*
RCA 2387	**Sitting in the Midday Sun / One of the Survivors** *Jun 1973*
RCA 2418	**Sweet Lady Genevieve / Sitting in my Hotel** *Sep 1973*
LPBO 5015	**Mirror of Love / Cricket (French import)** *Apr 1974*
LPBO 5042	**Mirror of Love / He's Evil** *July 1974*
RCA 2478	**Holiday Romance / Shepherds of the Nation** *Oct 1974*
RCA 2546	**Ducks on the Wall / Rush Hour Blues** *Apr 1975*
RCA 2567	**You Can't Stop the Music / Have another Drink** *May 1975*
RCM 1	**No More Looking Back / Jack, the Idiot / The Hard Way** *Jan 1976*
PB 9620	**Doing the Best for You / Wild Man (Dave Davies)** *Dec 1980*

Arista

ARISTA 97	**Sleepwalker/Full Moon** *Mar 1977*
ARISTA 114	**Juke Box Music / Sleepless Night** *Jun 1977*
ARISTA 153	**Father Christmas / Prince of the Punks** *Dec 1977*
ARIST 189	**Rock 'n' Roll Fantasy / Artificial Light** *May 1978*
ARIST 199	**Live Life / In a Foreign Land** *Jul 1978*
ARIST 210	**Black Messiah / Misfits** *Sep 1978*
ARIST 240	**(Wish I Could Fly Like) Superman/Low Budget** *Jan 1979*
ARIST 12240	**(Wish I Could Fly Like) Superman / Low Budget (12")** *Jan 1979*
ARIST 12240	**(Wish I Could Fly Like) Superman / Low Budget (12") (remix)** *Jan 1979*

ARIST 300	**Moving Pictures / In a Space** *Sep 1979*
ARIST 321	**Pressure / National Health** *Nov 1979*
ARIST 415	**Better Things / Massive Reductions (with KINKS 1)** *June 1981*
KINKS 1	**Lola / David Watts** *Jun 1981*
ARIST 415	**Better Things / Massive Reductions** *Jul 1981*

Konk (Arista)

ARIST 426	**Predictable / Back to Front** *Oct 1981*
ARIPD 426	**Predictable / Back to Front** *Oct 1981*
ARIST 502	**Come Dancing / Noise** *Nov 1982*
ARIST 12502	**Come Dancing / Noise (12")** *Nov 1982*
ARIST 524	**Don't Forget to Dance / Bernadette** *Jun 1983*
ARIST 524	**Don't Forget to Dance / Bernadette** *Sep 1983*
ARIST 560	**State of Confusion / Heart of Gold / Lola / 20th Century Man** *Mar 1984*
ARIST 12560	**State of Confusion / Heart of Gold / Lola / 20th Century Man (12")** *Mar 1984*

US Singles

Cameo

C 308	**Long Tall Sally / I Took My Baby Home (promo copy only)** *Apr 1964*
C 345	**Long Tall Sally / I Took My Baby Home (reissued)** *Dec 1964*

Reprise (all issued as white label promos and stock copies)

REPRISE 0306	**You Really Got Me / It's Alright** *Aug 1964*
0334	**All Day and All of the Night / I Gotta Move** *Oct 1964*
0347	**Tired of Waiting for You / Come on Now** *Feb 1965*
0366	**Everybody's Gonna be Happy / Who'll be the Next in Line** *Apr 1965*
0379	**Set Me Free/I Need You** *May 1965*
0366	**Who'll be the Next in Line / Everybody's Gonna be Happy (repromoted, flip as A side)** *Jul 1965*
0409	**See My Friends / Never Met a Girl Like You Before** *Sep 1965*
0420	**A Well Respected Man / Such a Shame** *Nov 1965*
0454	**Till the End of the Day / Where Have All the Good Times Gone** *Mar 1966*
0471	**Dedicated Follower of Fashion / Sittin' on my Sofa** *May 1966*
0497	**Sunny Afternoon / I'm not Like Everybody Else** *Jul 1966*
0540	**Dead End Street / Big Black Smoke** *Dec 1966*

0587	**Mr Pleasant / Harry Rag** *Jun 1967*	
0612	**Waterloo Sunset / Two Sisters** *Aug 1967*	
0614	**Death of a Clown/Love Me till the Sun Shines (Dave Davies)** *Aug 1967*	
0647	**Autumn Almanac / David Watts** *Nov 1967*	
0660	**Susannah's Still Alive / Funny Face (Dave Davies)** *Feb 1968*	
0691	**Wonderboy/Polly** *Jun 1968*	
0762	**Days / She's Got Everything** *Aug 1968*	
0806	**Starstruck / Picture Book** *Feb 1969*	
0847	**Village Green Preservation Society / Do You Remember Walter?** *Aug 1969*	
0863	**Victoria / Brainwashed** *Dec 1969*	
0930	**Lola / Mindless Child of Motherhood** *Jul 1970*	
0979	**Apeman / Rats** *Dec 1970*	
1017	**God's Children / The Way Love Used to Be** *Jul 1971*	
1094	**King Kong / Waterloo Sunset** *May 1972*	

Reprise Back to Back Hits (reissues)

1708	**Sunny Afternoon / Dead End Street** *May 1968*
0712	**Dedicated Follower of Fashion / Who'll Be the Next in Line** *May 1968*
0715	**Set Me Free / A Well Respected Man** *May 1968*
0719	**All Day and All of the Night / Tired of Waiting** *May 1968*
0722	**You Really Got Me / It's Alright** *May 1968*
0743	**Lola / Apeman** *Feb 1972*

Eric (Oldies label, licensed use)

242	**All Day and All of the Night / Tired of Waiting** *Feb 1980*
243	**You Really Got Me / A Well Respected Man** *Feb 1980*

Warner Brothers

7-29509	**Love Gets You / One Night with You (Dave Davies)** *Sep 1983*
7-29425	**Mean Disposition/Cold Winter (Dave Davies)** *Nov 1983*

RCA (Victor)

All issued in promotional and stock formats. For the sake of simplicity the promotional copy will be listed only where the song is a different edition from the stock copy. Many promo copies have a mono side; these are not listed here, as there is little discernible listening difference, and they were intended for the convenience of mono stations.

74-0620	**20th Century Man / Skin and Bone** *Dec 1971*
74-0807	**Supersonic Rocketship / You Don't Know My Name** *Jul 1972*
74-0852	**Celluloid Heroes / Hot Potatoes** *Oct 1972*
74-0940	**One of the Survivors / Scrapheap City** *May 1973*
LPBO 5001	**Sitting in the Midday Sun / Sweet Lady Genevieve** *Aug 1973*
APBO 0275	**Money Talks / Here Comes Flash** *May 1974*
PB 10019	**Mirror of Love / He's Evil** *Aug 1974*
PB 10121	**Preservation / Salvation Road** *Dec 1974*
PB 10251	**Starmaker / Ordinary People** *May 1975*
PB 10551	**I'm in Disgrace / The Hard Way** *Dec 1975*
PB 12089	**Imagination's Real / Wild Man (Dave Davies)** *Sep 1980*
PB 12147	**Doing the Best for You / Nothing More to Lose (Dave Davies)** *Nov 1980*

Arista *(Same criteria for listing as above)*

AS 0240	**Sleepwalker / Full Moon** *Mar 1977*
AS 0247	**Jukebox Music / Life Goes On** *May 1977*
AS 0290	**Father Christmas / Prince of the Punks** *Dec 1977*
AS 0342	**A Rock 'n' Roll Fantasy / Live Life** *Jun 1978*
AS 0342	**A Rock 'n' Roll Fantasy / Get Up** *Oct 1978*
AS 0372	**Live Life / Black Messiah** *Oct 1978*
AS 0409	**Superman / Low Budget** *Mar 1979*
CP 700	**Superman / Low Budget** *Mar 1979*
AS 0448	**A Gallon of Gas / Low Budget** *Aug 1979*
AS 0458	**Catch Me Now I'm Falling / Low Budget** *Sep 1979*
AS 0541	**Celluloid Heroes / Lola** *Aug 1980*
AS 0577	**You Really Got Me / Attitude** *Nov 1980*
AS 0619	**Destroyer/Back to Front** *Oct 1981*
AS 0649	**Better Things / Yo-Yo** *Nov 1981*
AS 1054	**Come Dancing / Noise** *Apr 1983*
AS1-9016	**(Above renumbered after RCA takeover of distrib.)** *Jun 1983*
AS1-9075	**Don't Forget to Dance/Young Conservatives** *Aug 1983*

Flashback (Arista Oldies label)

FLB 106	**Father Christmas / Superman** *Feb 1980*
FLB 115	**Lola / You Really Got Me** *May 1981*
AFS-9127	**Father Christmas / Superman** *Dec 1983*
AFS-9131	**Lola / You Really Got Me** *Dec 1983*

UK EPs

Pye

NEP 24200	***Kinksize Session:*** **I've Gotta Go Now / I've Got that Feeling / Things are Getting Better / Louie Louie** *Nov 1964*
NEP 24203	***Kinksize Hits:*** **You Really Got Me / It's Alright / All Day and All of the Night / I Gotta Move** *Jan 1965*
NEP 24214	***The Hitmakers*** **(various): You Really Got Me** *Jun 1965*
NEP 24221	***Kwyet Kinks:*** **Wait Till the Summer / Such a Shame / A Well Respected Man / Don't You Fret** *Sep 1965*
NEP 24242	***The Hitmakers*** **(various): Tired of Waiting** *Feb 1966*
NEP 24243	***The Hitmakers*** **(various): All Day and All of the Night** *Feb 1966*
NEP 24258	***Dedicated Kinks:*** **Dedicated Follower of Fashion / Till the End of the Day / See My Friends / Set Me Free** *Jul 1966*
NEP 24289	***Dave Davies Hits:*** **Death of Clown / Love Me till the Sun Shines / Susannah's Still Aliv Funny Face** *Apr 1968*
NEP 24296	***The Kinks:*** **David Watts / Tw Sisters / Lazy Old Sun / Situa Vacant** *Apr 1968*
7NX 8001	**God's Children / The Way Lo Used to Be / Moments / Drea (stereo)** *Apr 1971*
PMM 100	***Mini Monster:*** **You Really G Me / Set Me Free / Wonder Boy / Long Tall Shorty** *Aug*
BD 105	***Pye Big Deal:*** **Lola / Sunny Afternoon / Waterloo Sunse Dedicated Follower of Fashi (12")** *May 1977*
AMEP 1001	***Yesteryear:*** **Long Tall Sally / Took my Baby Home / You St Want Me / You Do Something Me** *Nov 1978*
FBEP 104	***Kinks:*** **Waterloo Sunset / Da Watts / A Well Respected Mar Stop Your Sobbing** *Jun 198*

PRT

PMM 100	***Mini Monster:*** **You Really G Me / Set Me Free / Wonder Boy / Long Tall Shorty** *1981*
BD 105	***Pye Big Deal*** **(2nd issue) (12** *1983*
KDL 1	**You Really Got Me / All Day a All of the Night / Misty Water** *Sep 1983*
KD 1	**You Really Got Me / All Day a All of the Night / Misty Water** *Sep 1983*
KPD 1	**(Pic. Disc) You Really Got Me Day and All of the Night / Mis Water (7")** *Sep 1983*

UK LPs

Pye

NPL 18096	**The Kinks** *Sep 1964*
NPL 18108	**Hitmakers (various)** *Dec 196*
NPL 18112	**Kinda Kinks** *Mar 1965*
NPL 18115	**Hitmakers Vol. 2 (various)** *Mar 1965*
NPL 18127	**Hitmakers Vol. 3 (various)** *Nov 1965*
NPL 18131	**The Kinks Kontroversy** *Dec 1965*
NPL 18144	**Hitmakers Vol. 4 (various)** *Mar 1966*
MAL(S) 612	**Well Respected Kinks** *Jun 1*
NSPL 18149	**Face to Face** *Oct 1966*
NSPL 18193	**Something Else by the Kinks** *Sep 1967*
MAL 716	**Sunny Afternoon** *Sep 1967*
NSPL 18191	**Live at the Kelvin Hall** *Jan 1*
NSPL 18233	**Village Green Preservation Society** *Nov 1968*
MAL(S) 1100	**Kinda Kinks** *Nov 1968*
NSPL 18317	**Arthur** *Oct 1969*
NPL 18326	**The Kinks (2LP)** *Feb 1970*
NSPL 18359	**Lola vs Powerman and the Moneygoround: part one** *Nov 1970*
NSPL 18365	**Percy** *Mar 1971*
HMA 201	**Lola** *Sept 1971*
GH 501	**Golden Hour of the Kinks** *Oct 1971*
HMA 244	**The Kinks** *Dec 1972*
GH 558	**Golden Hour of the Kinks Vol.** *Sept 1973*
11PP 100	**All the Good Times (4LP Box)** *Jan 1974*
GH 50	**Golden Hour: Lola, Percy and**

	Apeman come face to face with the Village Green Preservation Society *Oct 1974*
)001	**The Kinks (2LP)** *Oct 1977*
)006	**The 60s File (2LP)** *Oct 1977*
2031	**20 Golden Greats** *Oct 1978*
18112	**Kinda Kinks** *Nov 1979*
18131	**The Kinks Kontroversy** *Nov 1979*
18149	**Face to Face** *Nov 1979*
18096	**The Kinks** *Apr 1980*
L 18191	**Live at the Kelvin Hall** *Aug 1980*
L 18233	**Village Green Preservation Society** *Aug 1980*
L 18193	**Something Else by the Kinks** *Oct 1980*
L 18317	**Arthur** *Oct 1980*
L 18359	**Part One** *Oct 1980*
L 18365	**Percy** *Oct 1980*
L 18615	**You Really Got Me** *Apr 1980*

A

243	**Muswell Hillbillies** *Nov 1971*
2035	**Everybody's in Showbiz** *Sep 1972*
392	**Preservation** *Nov 1973*
2 5040	**Preservation Act 2** *Aug 1974*
411	**Soap Opera** *May 1975*
028	**Schoolboys in Disgrace** *Jan 1976*
059	**Celluloid Heroes** *Jun 1976*
3603	**Dave Davies** *Sep 1980*
LP 6005	**Glamour (Dave Davies)** *Oct 1981*

sta

RTY 1002	**Sleepwalker** *Mar 1977*
RT 1055	**Misfits** *May 1978*
RT 1099	**Low Budget** *Sep 1979*
RTY 6	**One for the Road (2LP)** *Jul 1980*
RT 1171	**Give the People What They Want** *Jan 1982*
IX 4	**5-track sampler for Give the People What They Want** *Feb 1982*
ALER 1	**Dealer's sampler (various)** *Feb 1982*

ne (MFP-EMI)

5048	**Sleepwalker (reissue)** *Jan 1982*

to (Pickwick International)

010018	**The Kinks (double cassette in box) (import from Germany)** *Jan 1983*

deo

JSV 1136	**One for the Road Video** *Nov 1983*

RT

OW 4	**The Shape of Things to Come** *Apr 1983*
OW 12b	**Candy from Mr Dandy (10" LP)** *Jul 1983*
NK 1	**The Kinks Greatest Hits (withdrawn January 1984)** *Dec 1983*
NK 2	**The Kinks Greatest Hits** *Feb 1984*

S LPs

prise

6143	**You Really Got Me** *Nov 1964*
6158	**Kinks-Size** *Mar 1965*
6173	**Kinda Kinks** *Aug 1965*
6184	**Kinkdom** *Nov 1965*

RS 6197	**The Kinks Kontroversy** *Mar 1966*	
RS 6217	**The Kinks Greatest Hits** *Aug 1966*	
RS 6228	**Face to Face** *Dec 1966*	
RS 6260	**The Live Kinks** *Aug 1967*	
RS 6279	**Something Else by the Kinks** *Jan 1968*	
RS 6327	**Village Green Preservation Society** *Jan 1969*	
RS 6366	**Arthur** *Oct 1969*	
RS 6423	**Lola vs Powerman and the Moneygoround: Part One** *Dec 1970*	
2XS 6454	**The Kink Kronikles (2LP)** *Mar 1972*	
MS 2127	**The Great Lost Kinks Album** *Jan 1973*	

RCA

LSP 4644	**Muswell Hillbillies** *Nov 1971*
VSP 6065	**Everybody's in Showbiz (2LP)** *Aug 1972*
LPL1-5002	**Preservation** *Nov 1973*
CPL2-5040	**Preservation Act II (2LP)** *May 1974*
LPL1-5081	**Soap Opera** *Apr 1975*
LPL1-5102	**Schoolboys in Disgrace** *Nov 1975*
APL1-1743	**Greatest – Celluloid Heroes** *May 1976*
AFL1-3520	**Second Time Around** *Aug 1980*

Arista

AL 4106	**Sleepwalker** *Feb 1977*
AL 4167	**Misfits** *May 1978*
AB 4240	**Low Budget** *Jul 1979*
A2L-8401	**One for the Road (2LP)** *Jun 1980*
A2L-8609	**One for the Road (2LP)** *Mar 1982*
AL 9567	**Give the People What They Want** *Aug 1981*
AL 9617	**State of Confusion** *May 1983*

Warner Brothers

23917-1	**Chosen People (Dave Davies)** *Aug 1983*

RCA

AFL1-3603	**Dave Davies** *Jul 1980*
AFL1-4036	**Glamour (Dave Davies)** *Jul 1981*

Compleat

CPL2-2001	**The Kinks – A Compleat Collection (2LP)** *Feb 1984*

Pye

505	**The Kinks** *Nov 1975*
509	**The Kinks Vol. 2** *Feb 1976*

Cover Versions: Singles

(mostly of material not recorded by the Kinks);
wr. = written by; pr. = produced by; pl. = played by

Decca

F 11856	**Shel Naylor: One Fine Day / It's Gonna Happen Soon** (A Side wr. D. Davies) *Mar 1964*
F 11861	**Orchids: I've got that Feeling / Larry** (A side wr. R. Davies) (US: London 45-9669) *Mar 1964*
F 12188	**Dave Berry: This Strange Effect / Now** (A side wr. R. Davies) (US: London 45-9781) *Jul 1965*
F 12216	**Applejacks: I Go to Sleep / Make up or . . .** (A side wr. R. Davies) *Aug 1965*

F 12271	**Majority: A Little Bit of Sunlight / Shut 'em Down** (A side wr. R. Davies) *Oct 1965*
F 12369	**Leapy Lee: King of the Whole Wide World/Shake Hands** (A side wr. and pr. R. Davies; B side pr. R. Davies) *Mar 1966*

Capitol

CL 15413	**Peggy Lee: I Go to Sleep/Stop Living in the Past** (A side wr. R. Davies) (US: Capitol 5488) *Sep 1965*

Liberty

55822	**Cascades: I Bet You Won't Stay / She'll Love Again** (A side wr. R. Davies) (US: Liberty 55822) *Sep 1965*

Fontana

TF 707	**Barry Fantoni: Little Man in a Little Box/Fat Man** (A side wr. R. Davies) *May 1966*

Planet

PLF 118	**Thoughts: All Night Stand/Memory of Your Love** (A side wr. R. Davies) (US: Planet 45-118) *Sep 1966*

Columbia

DB 8534	**Wild Silk: Vision in a Plaster Sky / Toymaker** (B side wr. R. Davies) (US: GRT 3) *Jan 1969*

Kapp (US ONLY)

974	**Wild Silk: Monday, Tuesday, Wednesday/Jessie** (A side wr. R. Davies) *May 1969*

Cover Versions: LPs

Pye

NPL 18132	**Honeycombs: All Systems Go** (Emptiness wr. R. Davies) *Dec 1965*

White Whale (US)

WWS 7124	**Turtles: Turtle Soup** (pr. R. Davies) *Sep 1969*

Konk (ABC US)

KONK 101	**Claire Hamill: Stage Door Johnnies** (pr. R. Davies; pl. R. Davies and M. Avory) *Oct 1974*

Konk (Anchor US)

KONK 101	**Claire Hamill: Stage Door Johnnies** (pr. R. Davies; pl. R. Davies and M. Avory) *Jan 1975*
KONK 102	**Café Society: Café Society** (pr. R. Davies, D. Davies and J. Gosling; pl. J. Gosling and M. Avory) *1975*
KONK 103	**Andy Desmond: Living on a Shoestring** (pr. D. Davies and J. Gosling; pl. D. Davies and J. Gosling) *1975*
KONK 104	**Claire Hamill: Abracadabra** *1975*

Chrysalis

CHR 1295	**Trevor Rabin: Wolf** (Associate pr. R. Davies) *1981*

RCA (US)

LSP 4298	**This is Leon Bibb** (Ballad of the Virgin Soldier) *1970*

BIBLIOGRAPHY

Pye

7N 17095	**The Truth: I go to Sleep/Baby You've Got it (A side wr. R. Davies)** *Apr 1966*
7N 17175	**Mo and Steve: Oh, What a Day it's Gonna Be / Reach Out (A side wr. R. Davies)** *Sep 1966*
7N 17862	**John Schroeder: Virgin Soldier March (A side wr. R. Davies)** *Nov 1969*
7N 45142	**Cold Turkey: Nobody's Fool / Sesame Street (A side wr. R. Davies)** *May 1972*

Decca

F 13008	**Mapleoak: Son of a Gun / Hurt Me So Much (pl. Bass Pete Quaife)** *Apr 1970*

White Whales (US)

WW 306	**Turtles: House on the Hill / Come Over (Both sides pr. R. Davies)** *May 1969*
WW 308	**Turtles: You Don't Have to Walk in the Rain / Come Over** *May 1969* **(Both sides pr. R. Davies) (UK: London HLU 10279)** *Jun 1969*
WW 326	**Turtles: Love in the City / Bachelor Mother** *Sep 1969* **(Both sides pr. R. Davies) (UK: London HLU 10291)** *Oct 1969*
WW 334	**Turtles: Lady-O / Somewhere Friday Night (B side pr. R. Davies)** *Dec 1969*

Argo

AFW 108	**Gothic Horizon: Girl with Guitar / Can't Bear to Think (A side pr. R. Davies / K. Daly; B side pr. J. Gosling)** *Oct 1972*

Konk (ABC US)

KNK 90001	**Claire Hamill: We Gotta Get Out of this Place / Luck of the Draw (Both sides pr. R. Davies)** *Dec 1974*

Konk (Anchor US)

KOS 1	**Claire Hamill: Geronimo's Cadillac / Luck of the Draw (pr. R. Davies)** *Jan 1975*
KOS 2	**Andy Desmond: So It Goes / She Can Move Mountains (pr. D. Davies and J. Gosling)** *Mar 1975*
KOS 3	**Claire Hamill: Rory / One Sunday Morning** *Sep 1975*
KOS 4	**Andy Desmond: Beware / Only Child (pr. D. Davies and J. Gosling)** *Sep 1975*
KOS 5	**Café Society: (The) Whitby Two-Step / Maybe It's me (pr. R. Davies, D. Davies and J. Gosling)** *Sep 1975*

Real

ARE 6	**Pretenders: Stop Your Sobbing / The Wait (A side wr. R. Davies)** *Jan 1979*
ARE 16	**Moondogs: Imposter / Baby Snatcher (pr. R. Davies)** *Apr 1981*
ARE 18	**Pretenders: I go to Sleep / English Roses** *Nov 1981*

RCA (US)

74-03 22	**Leon Bibb: Ballad of the Virgin Soldier / Smile Away the Rain (A side pr. Kusik, Snyder, Davies)**

As yet no other books about the Kinks have been published. My sources for this book were primarily the group themselves, the music press and various overviews of both popular music and social history. The bulk of the quotations in this book are taken from interviews conducted throughout January, February and March 1984 with the Kinks and with some of the people who have been involved with their story.

To mention every article that has been printed about the Kinks would be redundant, but a careful study of the files of **Melody Maker** and the **New Musical Express** has been both fascinating and informative. Two articles in particular have been vital in providing basic background information: 'Bam Balam 3', published in Edinburgh in December 1975 by Brian Hogg, which is devoted entirely to the Kinks, and Phil McNeill's comprehensive two-part Ray Davies interview and Kinks retrospective in the **New Musical Express**, 16–23 April 1977. Both made my task much easier. Mention must also be made of the sympathetic Jonathan Cott interview with Ray Davies in the 10 November 1969 issue of **Rolling Stone** (UK edition), and profuse thanks are due to Kinks scholar Doug Hinman, without whose day-to-day listings from 1964 to 1971 this book would have taken much longer to write.

The following books have been most useful:

Christopher Booker, **The Neophiliacs**, London, Collins, 1969 (perhaps the fullest and the most idiosyncratic account of British social life during the 1950s and 1960s)

Robert Christgau, **Christgau's Record Guide**, New Haven, Conn., Ticknor & Fields, 1983

Nik Cohn, **Pop from the Beginning**, London, Weidenfeld & Nicolson, 1969

Nik Cohn, **Today There are No Gentlemen**, London, Weidenfeld & Nicolson, 1971

Simon Frith and Howard Jones, **Sound and Vision**, forthcoming (an account of the influence of the art schools on British life in the 1950s and 1960s)

Charlie Gillett, **Sound of the City**, rev. edn, London, Souvenir Press, 1983 (a comprehensive account of the music industry and of musical styles since 1945)

Charles Hamblett and Jane Deverson, **Generation X**, London, Tandem, 1964

Phil Hardy and Dave Laing, **Encyclopedia of Rock 2**, St Albans, Panther, 1976

Harry Hopkins, **The New Look**, London, Secker & Warburg, 1964 (another excellent social history covering the period from 1944 to the beginning of the 1960s)

Richard Mabey, **The Pop Process**, London, Hutchinson, 1969

Greil Marcus, **Mystery Train**, London, Omnibus, 1977

Dave Marsh, **Before I Get Old**, Medford, NJ, Plexus, 1983

George Melly, **Revolt into Style**, Harmondsworth, Penguin, 1972

Jo and Tim Rice, Paul Gambaccini and Mike Read, **The Guinness Book of Hit Singles 4**, Enfield, Guinness Superlatives, 1983

Mandy Rice-Davies, **The Mandy Report**, London, Confidential Publications, 1963

Lillian Roxon, **Rock Encyclopedia**, New York, Grosset & Dunlap, 1969

Michael Wale, **Vox Pop: Profiles of the Pop Process**, London, Hutchinson, 1969

Paul Williams, **Outlaw Blues**, London, Pocket Books, 1970

Peter York, **Style Wars**, London, Sidgwick & Jackson, 1980